Cynthia M. Westover

Bushy

A Romance Founded on Fact

Cynthia M. Westover

Bushy
A Romance Founded on Fact

ISBN/EAN: 9783744770910

Printed in Europe, USA, Canada, Australia, Japan

Cover: Foto ©Andreas Hilbeck / pixelio.de

More available books at **www.hansebooks.com**

"OH, LISTEN TO ME, JIP; YOU ARE SO IMPOLITE!"

—*Page 140.*

BUSHY

A ROMANCE FOUNDED ON FACT

BY

CYNTHIA M. WESTOVER

ILLUSTRATED BY

J. A. WALKER

'Tis strange—but true;
For truth is always strange,
Stranger than fiction.
—BYRON, *Don Juan*

NEW YORK
THE MORSE COMPANY
1896

INTRODUCTION

Bushy is real, but she is no longer a little girl. In her memory the scenes and incidents of that strange child-life in the Rockies mingle to form a single pleasant dream. Their hardness is all gone. They have become impersonal, so that it would often be difficult for Bushy herself to determine where the line runs that separates individual experience from environment. But no matter ! The whole picture is a truthful one, as those who knew Bushy in the mines could testify.

The resolution of the equation of existence to its simplest form, amid the most rugged surroundings, makes a singular school for the development of womanhood. A child situated as Bushy was, finds little encouragement for that element of innate poetry which ranges from " Jack the Giant Killer " to " The Tempest," and from " Grimm's Fairy Tales " to Tennyson's " Round Table." The habit of self-dependence, the perpetual exaltation of the practical, the continuous nearness to nature, bring their compensation, nevertheless, in the forced growth of character; character worth having and worth studying.

In the hope that the value of such character may be illustrated here, this story is dedicated to an indulgent public.

THE AUTHOR.

LIST OF ILLUSTRATIONS

BUSHY

CHAPTER I

Until Bushy Sukolt was four years old she had lived with her father and mother in the town of Afton, Iowa. Mr. Sukolt was of the firm of Sukolt & Block, the largest iron foundry of the State. Mr. Block dipped into politics, just enough to bring in big contracts to enrich the firm, and Mr. Sukolt was satisfied to fill all orders that Block's business methods secured. The office of Mr. Block was in the town and Mr. Sukolt's headquarters were at the foundry, and in this way the partners saw very little of each other.

The death of Mr. Block, which happened when Bushy was about four years old, caused an examination of the accounts, and it was discovered that he had, unknown to Bushy's father, issued a large amount of paper in the firm's name. This was fast approaching maturity and was enough to make an assignment necessary.

Bushy's mother, a frail, delicate woman, could

not survive the trouble, and in three months after the failure she was buried in the little churchyard of Afton.

Mr. Sukolt, feeling he could no longer remain in a place where he had known so much sorrow, gladly became one of a geological party, bound for the Rocky Mountains. His intention had been to leave Bushy for three or four years in the care of a Mrs. Golden, a dear friend of the family. But on the day before his departure, as Tom Cole, who was going with Mr. Sukolt as a driver, was loading the wagon with the necessary articles for such a journey, Bushy was found rolled up in some blankets that were to be put into the wagon.

As Tom pulled her out she pushed her bushy hair back from her eyes and said:

" Don't oo touch me ! Don't oo touch me; I's doin' wiv my papa's tachel."

Tom eyed her a second, as if debating within himself whether it would be safe to approach such a fiery little piece of humanity; then, gathering her up in his arms, he carried her out to the wagon where Mr. Sukolt was superintending the loading.

" Mr. Sukolt, Bushy says she is going with your satchel. I found her almost melted, hidden in them blankets. It beats me how she got there. I brought 'em down only a few minutes ago myself, and I know she wasn't in 'em then."

"I twawled in when you was eatin' bwead and milk in de tichen," sobbed Bushy.

Mr. Sukolt, taking her from Tom, kissed her chubby hands a dozen times. She cuddled down in his arms and tried to hide her face in his bosom.

"Does Bushy love papa so much?" He hugged her closer to him. "But never mind, dear; when I come back I will bring you the biggest dolly you ever saw—one that will cry 'wah, wah!' just like a real baby. Won't that be fine?"

Her only reply was to snuggle yet closer, thus feeling that he could not possibly put her away from him.

He looked at Bushy, at the wagon, at the house, and again at Bushy; then he seemed to gaze off into the unexplored regions of the Rockies. He was so long quiet, and the expression of his face so sad that Tom, growing uneasy, turned to the wagon and pretended to adjust some of the luggage, his one object being to hide the tears that would trickle down his wrinkled face.

The long silence caused Bushy to raise her head and with childish curiosity peep into her father's face. At that moment it became resolute. Calling to Tom he said: "Pack no more just now; pile everything here by the wheel, and then go to Warren's for that box of provisions; I wish to speak to Mrs. Golden about Bushy."

"Oh, I's all weddy, papa!" cried Bushy. Wriggling out of his arms and running to the blankets, she pulled from under them a little roll. "See, papa; see! I've dot my ove'shoes. I've dot my sun bonny. I've dot my nightie." And here one of the sobs that had been coming up her little throat, to her surprise found its way out and cut her words short. She stood before him with a shoe in one hand and a nightgown in the other, her tear-stained but now happy face looking up into his for the sign of approbation her little heart felt she would receive for her thoughtfulness.

"My baby! my baby!" he cried, snatching her up and tossing her on his shoulder. "Go with papa's satchel? Of course you will! How could I for a moment think of leaving you—you, the only joy in the wide, wide world now left to me?" and they started for the house.

"I's doin'! I's doin'! I's doin'!" came from the child's sweet lips, as she waved the nightgown to express her happiness and patted her father's head rather roughly with her shoe, which she still clung to, her little heels digging vigorously into his big, broad chest.

"'Oorah! 'oorah! 'oorah!"

"Mrs. Golden—where are you, Mrs. Golden? Come here; we want you—Bushy and I. Yes, it is Bushy and I from henceforth, for where I go Bushy

"OH, I'S ALL WEDDY, PAPA!"

shall go, and where Bushy can't go I won't go!" he exclaimed, as he handed her over to good, old Mrs. Golden. Her startled face showed she was thinking: "The man's gone clean mad! Poor fellow!"

"Call on some of your friends to help you. Buy a roll of gray flannel and make it up into pinafores for Bushy. I have decided to take her with me. Put into that small trunk of mine all the things you think she will most "——

"But, man alive!" gasped the old lady, "she is only four—a mere baby. What will you do with her?"

"I can keep her warm and feed her," sternly replied the father. "If you will not do this for me I must get some one else, for Bushy goes with me or I don't go. Bushy and I are going to begin a new life in a new country. We start Wednesday morning at 5.30. Can I depend on you, Mrs. Golden?"

She nodded assent and wiped her eyes on a corner of Bushy's apron.

"I'll do it. But you are taking her to her death, poor, dear heart!" she cried, as she disappeared in the house.

That night in putting Bushy to bed old Mrs. Golden hovered about her longer than usual.

"Come, dear, say your prayers," said the old lady as she secured the last button on the "nightie."

"You won't forget to kneel down and say your little verse every evening, while away from auntie, will you, darling?"

"Des I won't, tause I tant s'eep when I fordet," was the lisped reply. Then dropping on her dimpled knees she placed her head in Mrs. Golden's lap, clasped her little hands and began the prayer:

"Now I lay me down to s'eep—but I ain't a layin' down to s'eep, auntie!"

She lifted her head and peeped inquiringly into Mrs. Golden's face.

"It means that you will go to sleep in just a minute, dear."

"Oh," said Bushy, and down her head rested again on the old lady's knee.

"Now I lay me down to s'eep—auntie, tan I say sumpin' else?" A second time the head was raised and the little one looked into the auntie's eyes.

"Certainly, dear, if you want to."

Snuggling so close was the little face now in the folds of Mrs. Golden's dress that it was with some difficulty the old lady heard the quaint prayer offered by her tiny charge.

"Now I lay me down to s'eep, tause I must dit up awful early, tause I'm doin' away wiv my papa.

"I pray the Lord my soul to teep away from all the bad sings what Tommy Tiddles said would eat me up—the bears, and—and—sings like dat."

There was a pause; then the wee voice inquired:

" What tums next, auntie ? "

" If I should die "——

" If I should die before I wake," broke in the child's voice; " but I'm not doin' to die, tause I must dit up awful early. I'll tell Tommy Tiddles he don't know nuffin 'bout where I'm doin', and if I say my prayers no bears 'll eat me up.

" I pray the Lord my soul to take me wiv my papa's tachel, Amen.

" Now, auntie, lay me down to s'eep," she cried, jumping to her feet and pulling up her nightgown she examined her knees to see how the red spots looked. The red spots that came through her kneeling always amused Bushy and she examined them as regularly as she said her prayers.

Mrs. Golden tucked Bushy safely into her little cot, knowing well that the child was thinking much more about naughty Tommy Tiddles and his bear story than about her prayers.

" She's very dear to me ! " sighed the old lady as she left the door ajar and went into the next room to plan for Bushy's flannel clothes. " I don't blame her father for taking her along; but what will I do without her ? " A tear fell on the wrinkled hand, and a sigh and a sob died away together.

Mr. Sukolt found, as he anticipated, that the company at first objected to his taking Bushy, but he refused to go without her, and as he was the best practical geologist in the party, they could not afford to lose him. Satisfactory arrangements were made and Bushy rode off as her baby head had planned, " wiv her papa's tachel."

CHAPTER II

Bushy took her cat with her. It was a Maltese, with the softest fur, and large eyes that Bushy said looked like stars in the night. Bushy loved Pete, for that was his name, more than she did anything else in the world, except her father.

Mr. Sukolt had no idea that Pete would stay with the wagon, but he thought if it made Bushy any happier she could try and take him along.

So they put a collar of bright red leather around Pete's neck and fastened to that a leader, just as if he were a dog. Bushy was told to keep a tight hold on it, or her Pete would be making tracks for home. She was very much frightened, of course, and to make him more secure she had her father tie the leader to her bracelet, and thus the two were ever seen together. The bracelet was a small circle of gold that had been slipped over her fat hand a few days before her mamma died, and when Bushy started out West it was still on her arm. Old Mrs. Golden had tried several times to get it off, but the hand was too fat to let it slip over without hurting her.

You can imagine how funny Bushy and Pete looked, always together, and sometimes, if Pete wanted to go anywhere very much, he would start on a keen run and pull Bushy after him. Once he smelled a mouse that had been brought along in the feed wagon. Bushy was watching Tom as he gave Ned, who was known as her pony, and the other horses their breakfast, and all at once Pete made a bound for the sack. He jumped and ran and pulled and mewed to get away, and Bushy's little feet had to trot very fast to keep her from falling. Pete was a very big cat, and when Bushy tried to carry him, her arms would just meet around his fat body.

They were six weeks on the way to the Rocky Mountains and Pete got so accustomed to following his little mistress about, that all she had to do to make him obey was to say, " Pete, tum on," and he would trot along by her side without being pulled by the string, as she had to do at first. He would play " dead " and lie in her lap for five minutes at a time without moving even his tail, but when she cried, " Oo is well, now, Pete," he would jump down and race around and around her till the leader would wind them into a tangled ball; they would play hours this way. Pete seldom scratched her, but he was very cross if the men touched him. Every time her father washed her face she thought it necessary to wash Pete's too. He did not seem to like it, yet he knew he could not get away, so he let her wet his face till she thought it quite clean. Once she tried to wash his paws, but he showed his claws and growled so that Bushy thought it not necessary to keep his feet clean. Pete disliked to get his paws wet, and Bushy would pick him up and carry him whenever she was out where it was wet and muddy.

Like all travellers in immigrant trains that started west in those days, the motto adopted by these geologists was " Pike's Peak or bust; " when in fact their destination was far north of Pike's Peak, a place known as the Great Pine Mine district, and where eventually Mr. Sukolt severed himself from the surveying party and remained for years as overseer and part owner of Great Pine Mine.

Outside of prickly pears, cactus, " old man weed " and Pete, Bushy recalls very little of that first trip across the plains, but that day the wagons drove up to the one good shanty at Great Pine she will never forget.

" Here we are, by Jove ! " shouted Tom as he leaped from the wagon and reached for Bushy and Pete.

It is needless to say that the curiosity shown by the miners over the surveying party was nothing when compared with that they displayed over the child and her cat.

An old fellow, named Walt, said he couldn't stand it. "It reminds me too strongly of home, by thunder!" he remarked as he walked away. Two hours later he was found dead drunk under a tree near his cabin. The bottle had been his consolation.

Shanks, a big strapping Englishman, possessor of one of the best hearts in the world, a jolly, easy-go-lucky chap, a good scholar and surgeon, had gone early to the mining fields because his health had failed him, and since 1849 he had been haunting all new gold strikes, had had no particular good luck, but had managed to pay his way, and at this time boasted a constitution that seemed made of wrought iron.

It was not long before Shanks became the fourth one in this family—not counting Pete, the cat, Rover, the dog, and Ned, the pony, every one of which Bushy considered quite as important as herself.

Of all the wonderful Rocky Mountain scenery Great Pine Mine was the centre of the most picturesque spot to be found. No pencil or brush could ever reveal the weird and awful grandeur of those wild gorges, the walls of which in places rose perpendicularly from the foaming streams to a height of 3,000 feet. The canyon leading from the mine in a southerly direction widened into a valley through which a rather good road had been made, but as it ascended the cliffs it narrowed into what the civilized world would have called a dangerous, rocky path.

Some estimate of the difficulty in reaching these mines can be gained from the fact that it took the surveying party six hours to make the last mile and a half.

To the north there was a chasm ten miles in length, hemmed in by walls two hundred to four hundred feet in height; while on the west rose cliffs eight hundred to two thousand feet in altitude.

At the place where the mine was situated the sun never shone more than three hours a day, but those three hours turned the pinnacles, buttresses, and opalized walls into all kinds of awe-inspiring forms, brightened with all the colors of the rainbow.

Mr. Sukolt always declared that Aladdin's wonderful garden (to which Tom generally confined his bed-time stories) paled into insignificance when the sun shone on Great Pine Mine.

The story must be told by and by how Bushy's love for Pete made her disobey her father. It was the only time in her life that she was ever quite so naughty. Bushy always had a cat even after she lost Pete. The miners would ask everywhere they went if there was a cat in camp, and if gold could buy it, the cat was sure to go to Bushy. You see, she loved cats so she squeezed them hard when she hugged them, and then she would pick them up sometimes by the tail, sometimes by the head, and often by the back, and carry them as far as they would let her. Her tiny hands were often covered with scratches, because she found none so gentle as Pete had been, and she would forget that they were not all Petes. It kept the miners busy furnishing Bushy with cats, as the life of one, after Bushy became its mistress, was of short duration. One of the miners fenced off a piece of ground and called it the cat graveyard, and there Bushy buried all her pets in a row, with pine headboards, on which were burned with a hot poker the names of her lamented darlings.

Now for the story about Pete. They had been at Great Pine Mine just a year when the Indian trouble began. The miners had built a small fort by digging a hole in the ground and covering it with stone and sod, leaving portholes a foot apart all around just under the roof's edge. Anybody inside could see all over the country and pick off any Indian who was brave enough to come within rifle range, while the Indians had no show whatever. They might shoot all day at the fort without there being the slightest danger of hurting any one inside. The fort was deep and half-filled with ammunition, food, bedding, and a keg or two of water. This precaution had been taken, although it was thought the Indians would not come so far north as the Great Pine Mine until warmer weather.

It was eight o'clock at night, and several miners were playing cards—California Jack, they called the game. Mr. Sukolt was busy at a table near sorting specimens and Bushy and Pete were curled up asleep on a buffalo robe in front of the big fire-place. The only light in the shanty came from the bright blaze of the pine-knots.

" Hist ! " cried Mr. Sukolt, looking up from the rocks and listening. The card-players checked their laughter and turned their faces toward the door. Pete stretched himself and Bushy sat up and rubbed her eyes.

" It's a horseman riding like mad," exclaimed one of the men, rising and going to the door. Mr. Sukolt reached for his belt and buckled it with two revolvers about him; and the miners, who had taken off theirs, did the same. As if by instinct they all scented danger and mechanically prepared for it. Mr. Sukolt selected a warm blanket from the bunk near at hand and threw it down by Bushy, then joined the others, who had by this time stepped outside, and awaited the rider.

" It is some one who knows the way," cried Tom; " there must be something after him. It is pitch dark, and I defy anything to keep close to a horse running like that."

The words were no sooner said than Shanks dashed up to the door. The horse was trembling in every limb and Shanks's face was as white as a sheet.

" To the fort, boys ! The Indians attacked us in Stone Gulch, and I am the only one who escaped. I saw five of the boys scalped; then fled, for I was one against twenty, and I hoped to save you. Sh ! They are closer than I thought."

A distant thud, thud, thud, signified the approach of mounted Indians; then everything was still.

" They are dismounting," cried Mr. Sukolt. " They mean to shoot from ambush. To the fort, boys, to the fort ! "

Shanks slipped off the bridle and turned his horse loose.

" There, old fellow, if the redskins get after you, you are free to save yourself if you can." He gave him a smart stroke that sent him running down the path toward the mine.

" Tan I take Pete ? " lisped Bushy, who had not stirred from the robe, but had heard every word.

" No, dear," said her father, " one mew might forfeit our lives." He turned to get a strap, saying: " Bushy, roll into the blanket; I am going to strap you to my back." Bushy knew what that meant, for she had often been strapped to him when he had climbed the high mountains.

"Play dead," said Bushy to Pete, giving him a soft tap on the nose. He immediately stretched himself out, and she wrapped him in her shawl, then rolled herself and Pete head and ears in the blanket.

Mr. Sukolt, who had been arranging the strap, had not noticed Bushy. Shanks was waiting at the door and keeping a lookout. Then Bushy's father picked her up and strapped her in a kind of sling, leaving his arms and hands free to use his rifle.

"Play dead," cried Bushy, for Pete objected a little to the treatment he was getting.

"What is it, Bushy?" asked her father.

She was silent. It was the first time in her life she had been unable to answer her father. "Are you strapped too tight? What is it, Bushy?" he inquired again, as he hurried out and joined Shanks.

"Nuffin'," she said, and snuggled down in the sling. She was afraid to say "play dead" any more to Pete, so when he squirmed again she grasped his nose firmly with her fingers and held on like grim death. The more he squirmed the tighter she clinched with her fingers. It was a very serious affair with Bushy. The idea of leaving Pete to be killed by the Indians made her desperate. All the danger that her father saw in Pete's going was that

he might mew, and she intended that he should
not. So, though after a half-hour he quit wriggling
about, she still kept the death-grip on his nose. He
could not scratch, because of being bound up in the
shawl. They were over an hour getting into the
fort—some of the Indians got between them and it.
The savages knew nothing of the stronghold and
were trying to reach the shanty of the chief, as they
called Mr. Sukolt's place. But by good manœuvr-
ing on the part of the miners and the sound of the
riderless horse's hoofs near the mine the Indians
were misled and turned to the left, leaving the
ravine clear for the men to go through.

"Are we all here?" asked Mr. Sukolt as soon as
he got inside the fort.

"All but Pete," answered Tom, who now allowed his humor to show itself, for they were safe
at last from the Indians.

"No, I dot 'im," called the cheerful voice of
Bushy from the blanket-sling.

"What! You have? I don't see how you darst
try it," cried Tom, half-vexed with Mr. Sukolt for
displaying so little judgment.

Mr. Sukolt said nothing, but showed his ignorance of Pete's ride by hastily undoing Bushy and
shaking her a little as he lifted her out.

Bushy held Pete still by the nose, and when the
shaking was over she looked up sweetly in her

papa's face, saying: "He's all wight, Padre; he never kied one mew, 'cause I choked his nose when he wouldn't play dead." She dropped him from the shawl and he fell with a dull thud to the stone floor.

"He's dead!" exclaimed the miners in one voice, and Tom knelt down and poked him with his revolver.

"No, he plays dead," said Bushy, dancing about in high glee. "He plays dead! Now see how he can jump." She threw herself flat on her stomach by Pete and clapped her hands, crying, "Oo is well now, Pete."

But Pete did not move. "Oo is well now, Pete," she repeated, rising on her hands and knees and looking at the limp cat that lay so still before her.

The miners stepped back, and in their pity for Bushy almost forgot that the Indians were still lurking about. Bushy's lips began to tremble, and at last, realizing that Pete would never play with her any more, she got up, and slipping her hand in her father's, looked up with tears streaming from her eyes and said: "What's the weason, Padre; what's the weason?"

"I think it has all come about because my little girl disobeyed her papa," replied her father, seriously. That was too much for Bushy. She clasped his knees, and crying as if her heart would break, promised to be " a dood dirl all her life " if he would bring Pete back again.　But poor Pete was dead.

" He was about ready to die anyway," Tom said to the Padre afterward, for Bushy had hugged him to a mere skeleton.　But Bushy never quite got over thinking his death came about through her naughtiness; and whenever she was inclined not to mind her father the picture of poor Pete would come up before her and she would hesitate no longer.

CHAPTER III

It was only natural that the miners should think a great deal of Bushy. She was the only little girl in camp—the only child, in fact—and, of course, they petted her and thought everything she did was just right. I suppose she often did naughty things, like any other little girl, yet she saved their lives one day, and after that the miners could not do enough for her.

On this particular morning Mr. Sukolt had ordered the men to do an extra day's work, because a certain amount of ore was to be sent down the mountain that night.

"Tom, I want you to stop long enough to get a hot dinner for the boys; you and Bushy can bring it over, and save the time that would be spent in going to the shanty," he said, as he left early and joined the miners at the Great Pine Mine.

Bushy busied herself, as she always did, in what she called "helping Tom do up." Then she took her slate and wrote her letters—she had to get her lesson every day and say it to her father or Tom before she went to bed. After that she had a romp with Rover, and finally went to sleep with her head pillowed on his shaggy coat. Rover was of a breed half Newfoundland and half St. Bernard. He was immense in size and of a most affectionate nature, his whole object in life being his care for Bushy. She must have slept for a long, long time, because when she awoke Tom was ready to take the dinner to the boys.

"Get on your hood, Bushy, and hurry up, you little toad; I thought you were going to sleep all day," cried Tom, giving her a gentle shake. "You must help me carry these things. How can I ever get them over alone ? "

"Why, you touldn't," replied Bushy, scrambling to her feet, and looking very cross at Rover. "You bad doggy, you made me fordet all about it ! "

Poor Rover, who had been so careful not to move even his toes for fear of disturbing his little mistress, took the rebuke good-naturedly and wagged his tail hard to show that he meant nothing wrong.

"We have but one horse to-day, and you must ride in front of me and carry the bread and meat while I carry these two tin pails," said Tom, as he hurried about getting things ready.

"What you dot two for ? " questioned Bushy.

"One has coffee and the other soup. It's a surprise for the boys. They don't get soup every day, do they ? I killed a rabbit just behind the shanty.

I guess he didn't know we lived here or he would have kept out of the way."

" Where is his tail, Tom ? I want his tail," said Bushy, dropping her hood and running to the table where Tom had skinned the rabbit.

" Here it is, you little stupid," laughed Tom, picking up her hood and showing her how he had fastened the tail on so it stuck up like a feather on the very top.

Bushy clapped her hands and waited for Tom to tie the hood on her head. Her hair stuck out every way, for no one had taken time to comb it, and romping with Rover had not improved her looks. She took great delight in " fixing up " with rabbit tails and bird feathers. Sometimes she seemed more like a little Indian than a white child. One must not forget that she had no playthings to amuse her, as have children who live in the city.

In a very little while they got to the mine. Bushy was so anxious to exhibit her rabbit's tail to her papa that she begged hard to go down into the mine with Tom.

" Please let me do," she pleaded.

Tom at first was not inclined to let her descend, because there is always more or less danger of falling rocks in the mine, and if some one did not stop work and go about with her, Mr. Sukolt always felt uneasy until she was taken out. She was ever in motion, and flew hither and thither, filling the mine with her jolly little laugh or whistling like the birds she heard in the pine-trees, and loading her pockets with every bright piece of ore she could pick up with her brown fingers. Sometimes she would perch herself on the ledges or shelves near where a miner was working with his pick and watch him. A smile of peculiar softness would steal over the hard faces of the rough miners as they passed and stretched out their hard and dirty hands to pat her head and say: " Hello, Bushy ! how many tons are you going to get out to-day ? "

Miners, when following a vein, at first pick out no more of the rock than is necessary to secure the richest ore. This often leaves the sections with walls that are dug into in such a way as to appear filled with great shelves. After the rich ore has been sent up in the bucket and everything cleared away other miners follow and cut down the uneven parts into smooth surfaces, which are " planked up," and sometimes made yet more secure by having great wooden pillars built in for support.

It was on one of these shelves that Bushy was perched this day when she saved the miners' lives. Walt had been at work near Bushy clearing up, but was called away by Tom to eat his dinner.

" Stay where you are, Bushy," cried Tom, " until I dole out the victuals, then I'll take you up again."

There were several rooms or sections in the mine, and as they meant to blast after dinner all the tools and breakable things had been carried into the far end of one of the divisions, and a small keg of powder was opened and ready for use just below the ledge on which Bushy was sitting.

To be able to reach the vein Walt had built a temporary scaffold that lifted him about three feet from the bottom, and this was still standing when one of the miners, remembering that the powder was uncovered, got up quickly to put something over it.

He bumped his head against one of the wooden beams put up to support the sides of the mine, and his lamp was knocked from his hat and went bounding in a zigzag direction toward the powder, thirty feet away.

The miners were panic-stricken. The wick had burnt low, and as it turned over and over, instead of going out, the whole thing got ablaze and rolled on and on like one ball or fire, impishly bent on doing all the mischief possible.

" My child, my child ! The powder ! " screamed Mr. Sukolt, as he made a dash around a bucket of ore in his attempt to reach Bushy. Every man who had seen the candle fall knew he could never get to her side before an almost certain explosion; with the woodwork and the great coil of fuse, death would be inevitable to all those in that division.

The candle reached the scaffolding and went zigzagging on, the broad boards making its fatal arrival in the keg of powder right under Bushy seem inevitable. They saw, too, that Bushy had seen the tin holder when it fell from the hat. At the first cry made by her father she started like a frightened doe, and when he exclaimed " the powder !" her eye fell on the open keg.

Bushy had been taught all about the dangers attached to the use of powder, and she had seen the men too often wounded in the blasting not to understand that the light must not reach the keg.

One faint cry of " Padre !" reached the miners' ears, as she threw herself from the ledge on to the scaffolding, crushing out the light of the lamp with her tiny body as she fell. The boards, loosely arranged, gave way and tumbled with Bushy to the bottom of the mine, and she was quite buried out of sight with them when her father and the miners reached her.

" Thank God, she's alive !" exclaimed Mr. Sukolt, as he pulled her out and took her in his arms. " Papa's brave girl. Where does it hurt, dear ?"

There was not a dry eye to be seen as the miners

crowded around. Shanks did not wait to get her
out of the mine, but pulled off her little dress and
examined by the candle light the arm that he
thought was broken.

" I dess I bumped it here," said Bushy, putting
her hand on her shoulder. On further examination
it was seen that her collar-bone was broken.

She will always carry a reminder of that timely
fall in the mine, for there was quite an ugly bump
formed on the bone in its mending.

CHAPTER IV

Just think of Bushy as she grew older as a very little girl with fluffy hair that stood on end all the time. Her father kept it cut pretty short because there was no one to comb it for her but himself, and often he had to leave her asleep in the morning, and he would not see her until he came home at night and found her in bed again.

Mr. Sukolt knew there was danger in allowing Bushy to handle her little revolver like a plaything, but then, too, he knew there was a greater danger in her not knowing how to use it.

" Never point the weapon at anything you would not care to kill," was his daily instruction, and it grew to be a second nature to handle it carefully and skilfully. She would play all day at shooting marks, cutting off leaves of trees, hitting nail-heads and picking flies off the log walls, and although Mr. Sukolt sometimes came home expecting to hear she was hurt, he would say that such an anxiety was nothing to compare with what he would feel if he did not know that she had made the use of the revolver as natural to her as it is for a boy to whistle.

It was a bright, beautiful summer morning when Mr. Sukolt called Bushy to him and said: "It is my turn to take the tools to be sharpened. There are so many of them that I shall be obliged to wait several hours, and will not be back until late. I would take you with me, but I must carry the tools on Ned, and then, who would be housekeeper if you went along; Tom is away, and I would have no supper if the housekeeper went, would I?"

"All right," said Bushy, perfectly delighted when her father made it look as if she were a necessity. Her little heart swelled with great pride to think she could hold up her "end of the line," as Tom expressed it.

"If anything should happen that you are called upon to protect yourself, will you be afraid, dear?"

Bushy, not quite understanding her father's anxiety, filled the hut with her merry peal of laughter, then, climbing on his knee, she wound her arm about his neck, and taking her revolver from the table where it lay said: "See that knot in the log, Padre?" Her father nodded. Without a word more she raised the revolver and fired, hitting the knot in the centre. Few men could handle a weapon with deadlier aim than this little girl who knew nothing but what she had learned in camp life.

"I wish," said Mr. Sukolt to Shanks an hour

later, " that you would go back to the shanty and bring Bushy over, I have a foolish foreboding of evil to-day. Let her play about the mine, and if I don't get back before dark you take her home and stay with her until I come."

Mr. Sukolt rode off with the tools, and Shanks soon had Bushy at the mine. One of Bushy's great pleasures was to ride up and down in the bucket, but it was not often she was allowed to do it. This day one of the miners named Mac took her with him every time he made the trip. Mac was a Southerner, who did not believe in the slaves being made free, and on more occasions than one Mr. Sukolt had cautioned him to keep his opinions to himself.

" You know that you are the only Southern man in camp," he said, " and not a favorite at that. I will not be responsible for the actions of the miners if you air your rash ideas, especially when I am not here and the men have had anything to drink."

The only soft spot in Mac's heart was for Bushy, and this day the two were inseparable.

" I like you," said Bushy, as Mac carefully lifted her out of the bucket for the twentieth time. " Why does Padre say he's afraid something will happen to you when he's away ? "

" Oh, because I'm hot-headed and quick-tempered," replied Mac, as he took her hand and they went to the tool-house for a load of stuff to be lowered into the mine.

It was nearly five o'clock when a great helloing and cheering brought out all the workers from below to greet the freight wagons just arrived from the States. They carried food, ammunition, tools, clothing, etc., that had been sent for by Mr. Sukolt. All the letters to the miners were brought in this way, too. The mail was directed to the nearest town, and these freight-men would stop and bring it to the camp. It was a rule made by Mr. Sukolt that the mine should shut down for an hour whenever the wagons arrived, that the men might read all their letters without interruption, and on this day it was so late that Shanks ordered work stopped for the night.

It was still light, and the miners, between indulging in drink that one of the drivers had brought along to treat the boys with, and the good news from home, had become hilarious and noisy. Shanks had told Bushy to sit on a box by one of the wagons and stay there until he could get his coat and take her home.

How the mob started Shanks could not explain any more than could any of the others, for, like all mobs, it seemed to be a creature of very mysterious evolution.

"Lynch him!" cried one of the miners.

About thirty infuriated men, some in dust-covered mining clothes, others from the trains still with their whips in hand, circled about a man who was talking loudly and excitedly.

This troubled movement and shouting filled Bushy's heart with fear. She stood on the box and looked over the heads of the crowd of men that would first advance, then retreat, push, yell, and shout at intervals, " Hang him ! hang him ! lynch him ! "

" I tell you again I am glad of it; it serves him right ! " cried the voice of Mac in hot angry tones.

Then a wave passed over that crowd something like the movement and swirl of a cyclone, after which came a lull that showed Mac, erect against a great pine-tree, held so by a lariat that had been passed twice around the trunk, crossing him over chest and arms holding him helpless.

" Say that again if you dare ! " called out one of the leaders. There was a growl from the crowd and the men drew closer.

" No, I was thoughtless," exclaimed Mac, now realizing his danger.

" Bah ! hang the coward ! Anybody who is glad Lincoln is dead, should be dead too," yelled out the driver who had brought up the news of Lincoln's assassination, and at the same time he threw over one of the branches of the tree another lariat. The crowd grew more excited, even those who had not been so active before now falling in with the largest party, which was for lynching Mac.

When Bushy saw the rope go over the branch she knew what that meant, for six months before she and her father had come across a man near the blacksmith's who had been lynched for stealing horses. Over his head on a pine board was written in big letters, " Bill, the horse thief—to be cut down at nine o'clock to-morrow." Bushy had not been able to sleep well for a month afterward—that man's face seemed to haunt her. That was the first time she had heard the word " lynch," and when the miners cried " Lynch him ! " the picture of this other man came again before her.

" We don't know how it came about," explained Shanks to Mr. Sukolt afterward; " but when Walt turned to untie Mac, and the crowd pressed forward to help at the lynching, there sat Bushy on Mac's shoulder. She had climbed up like a cat, and, with her feet slipped behind the ropes that crossed Mac's chest, she braced herself, and, throwing her left arm about his head clinched her hand on his blue shirt; then, with eyes like sparks of fire, she faced us, with revolver raised and ready to fire.

" Well it was a shock to the crowd greater than if we had all been struck by lightning—we knew Bushy's shot was sure go. Then, who would hurt a hair of her head! 'I like Mac,' was all she said, 'and I'll sit here till the Padre comes.' The men swore and laughed and whistled, and finally went back to the wagons, sobered and thoughtful. 'Come, Bushy, get down, and we will let Mac go this time, eh, boys?' I said, and they replied in a body, 'Yes, Bushy, you have saved us from doing a foolish thing.' But Bushy, to my surprise, never changed her attitude and checked my approach with 'Go 'way, Shanks; you talked loud, too.' That was a blow I did not expect. She did not trust me any more than the others, and there she sat until you came, keeping her eye on everybody who went near the tree."

When Mr. Sukolt arrived he understood the situation at once, and, jumping from his horse, ran to the tree, took Bushy in his arms, and, turning to the men, cried in an angry voice, " Bushy, point out the leader of this mob!" But Bushy lay still, white and limp, and her revolver had dropped at last to the ground. She had fainted.

For three weeks she was quite ill—brain fever, Shanks said. When she went to the mine next time Mac was not there, and to her frightened question, " Did they kill him?" Tom replied:

" The Padre was so angry when you fainted and he thought you might die, that he ordered Mac set at liberty at once; then, pointing to his horse, said, ' Take him and all your belongings and leave the camp.' He is prospecting now, and he says if he ever strikes a rich mine he will give you every bit of gold that comes out of it."

CHAPTER V.

One night, several years later, the child was awakened with, " Bushy, Bushy ! oh, Bushy ! wake up, dear ! that's a good girl."

Bushy sleepily turned over in her little bed, which was just then shared with Rover, to see Tom, with an anxious face, bending over her.

" Why, what's the matter, Tom ? " said she, sleepily, sitting up in bed, striving with all her might to keep her eyes wide open by rubbing her brown knuckles into them. Tom had been very ill with the mountain fever, the sickness most dreaded by all the miners. Bushy had been deputized as his nurse, and most faithfully indeed had she performed her duties.

" The Padre hasn't come home from the mine yet, and neither has Shanks," exclaimed Tom. " I am afraid something is wrong. It is nearly ten o'clock and I want you to go up the trail with me."

" All right," said Bushy, jumping down from the bunk; " I'll be ready in a jiffy." She was wide awake now, for anything that touched upon her father's

"'GO 'WAY, SHANKS; YOU TALKED LOUD, TOO.'"

safety made her little heart thump like a trip-hammer.

"Don't you worry, Tom," she said, swinging her arm back to reach the other sleeve of her tiny buffalo coat; "Padre's all right. I expect he and Shanks had to stay awhile and help the men out. You know they said this morning at breakfast that they would have to timber that new drift where they struck that rich vein, or they would be having a cave-in."

"That's just it," replied Tom. "I'm afraid there has been a cave-in."

"Oh, no," answered Bushy, assuringly; "but I'll go over and see. I'll bet my head that your fever's worse, 'cause you have worried," she added, rising from the floor, where she had been sitting wrapping her feet in some pieces of gunny sack and tying them about with short ropes. Then she noticed that Tom was trying to put on his coat.

"Why, Tom, you can't go! You can't walk yet. I am not afraid, and it is colder than Greenland."

Tom had been sick for two weeks, and had been out of bed just one day. To all his urging that he had better go with her, Bushy scornfully replied that she wasn't a "Tenderfoot," and that he must stay and be ready to help in the shanty if anything had really happened.

She went out and saddled Ned. She threw on a blanket and strapped it tight, then bridled him and away they ran.

Tom stood in the doorway looking after her till the light of the lantern gleamed like a tiny fire-fly. It finally disappeared with its brave little bearer, behind a clump of snarled and twisted cedars which grew along the side of the trail up the steep mountain side.

"Too bad," thought Tom, as he staggered once more to the fire-place and sat down. "I'm no good. I could not have gone ten yards without falling. Perhaps after all the men are staying extra late to finish that propping."

Bushy galloped on, swinging the lantern high, then low, calling out, then waiting for some reply. In spite of the warm mittens her fingers were beginning to tingle. She was used to having her father stay over supper-time, yet she always bore in mind his danger; how he was constantly taking his life in his own hands, going down deep shafts in a bucket, working in long dark tunnels with only the light of a candle to guide him. Bushy at this time was nine years old, and she had been over the trail so often that she thought, if obliged to do it she could go the way blindfolded. But soon came a great surprise for her. Turning one of the sharp corners in the path everything was odd and strange.

She rubbed her eyes to see if she were really awake. Where was the mine? She looked back to see if she had come the right way. Yes, she would know the great pine from which the mine received its name, anywhere. Only last week she had climbed to its very top. What on earth was the matter? Where was the mine? Where was the tool-shed? She saw nothing but one great mass of snow, with here and there the top of some tall pine showing itself. While thus peering through the darkness and trying to stop the beating of her heart she thought she heard a voice call. Ned snorted and pawed the snow until she had to scold to make him keep quiet.

"Listen, Ned, listen!" She slipped from his back and led him near the tree. Yes, there it was again, more distinct, yet far away and faint.

She shouted: "Padre! Padre! what's the matter, and where is the mine?"

A voice answered, sounding as if it came from a deep well. Again she shouted, and hallooed at the top of her voice: "Padre! Padre! Are you dead, Padre, and up in the heaven?"

This time the answer seemed to come out of the snow, yet muffled and indistinct as before. She stumbled against some broken timbers, sticking up out of the drift, and then she realized the awful truth. There had been a snow-slide and the men, with her father, were buried beneath it.

The mass of snow on the mountain just above them had loosened, although the weather did not seem warm enough to warrant such a thing, and had come in one great avalanche, crushing everything in its pathway. She hurried on some distance and then shouted again, and this time the voice was directly under her feet.

"Padre, is that you?" she called, placing her mouth near the snow, and then throwing herself flat on the bank, she put her ear down to listen.

"Yes; is that you, Bushy?"

"Yes, yes, I'll dig you out," she cried, beginning to dig with all her might; her little hands soon making a large hole in the soft snow beneath her.

"I am not very far under," called her father, so faint she could scarcely hear, "but I am pinned down with a beam of the tool-house. I don't think I'm hurt much. Dig with anything you can find until I can make you hear and understand all I say."

Bushy got a piece of broken plank and worked for fifteen minutes as she never worked before. Ned stood by and neighed every time Bushy spoke to her father.

"Now," said Mr. Sukolt, when she had dug a deep hole down to him, "try and get me out, so I can help the boys. None of them were up but me

" YES, YES, I'LL DIG YOU OUT," SHE CRIED.

when the slide covered us. All depends on you, Bushy."

But Bushy was too little to make much headway, and her strength was not half enough to lift the great beam that was right across her father's body. "This will never do, Bushy. There is nothing left but for you to ride to the blacksmith's. No, there is a camp of miners down the gulch, only a mile from here. Ride there as fast as Ned can take you; have the miners bring shovels and picks to dig us out; the boys may be smothered even by this time."

Bushy did not tell her father that she thought the slide had cut off the way there, but she rode Ned as far as she could, then tied him to a tree and started on the half run and half jump to the camp.

Bushy had never been known to say " I can't." She carried the lantern, floundered through the snow out to the trail which would lead her to the camp. On, on she went, sometimes missing the path, then she had to go back and, by the aid of the lantern, hunt the blazed trees by which the miners had marked the way on either side of the trail.

For awhile she got along very well. It was all down grade, and she had gone so fast that she was not a bit cold. Soon came a change, for the path led over a kind of hill, and the wind swept down upon her with wicked force.   Her little legs grew so tired that it was hard to draw them along.   Once she sat down to rest a minute, and had it not been for the awful state the men were in she would have given up and cried.   Her hands, with all her swinging back and forth, would not keep warm, and her feet were now so cold they pained her every time she moved them.   At last in the distance she saw a faint outline of the camp, for the moon was looking out through the heavy clouds and gave a dim light.   Next appeared the glimmer of the camp-fire.   Oh, how far away it seemed to Bushy, now crying in earnest !   Her feet had grown numb and her eyes so heavy that she thought she would never get there.

She was about to sit down again when she thought she heard her father's voice close beside her say, in tones of reproach: " All depends on you, Bushy."   She started on again, but how she made the last few yards she never knew.

Next day Mr. Robinson, whose camp she had gone to, told her father all about it.

" You see I was waked up by hearing a kind of thump against the cabin.   I thought it was our old dog Spot.   It was such a tarnation cold night that I hadn't the heart to keep him out.   I got up to call him, and there lay your Bushy in a heap in the snow at my feet.

SHE THOUGHT SHE HEARD HER FATHER SAY, "ALL DEPENDS ON
YOU, BUSHY."

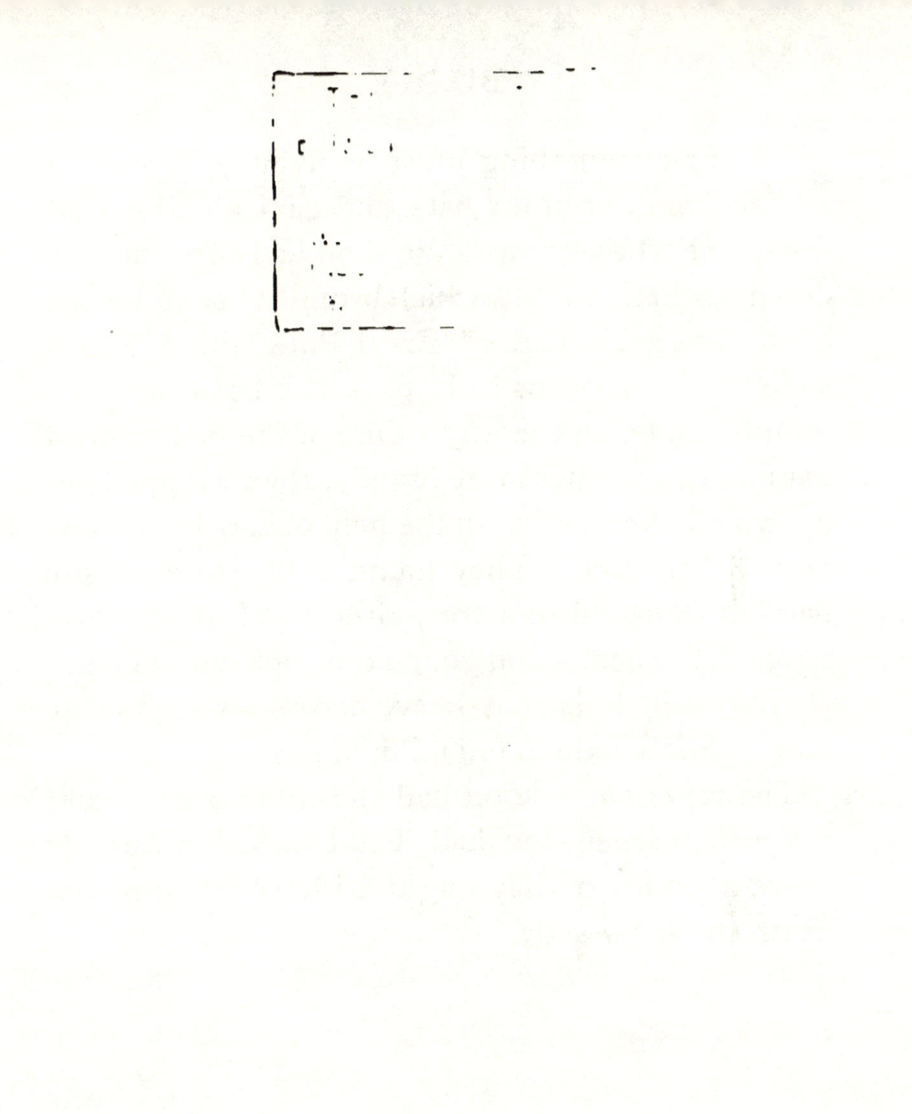

"I knew something must be awfully wrong. I was skeared out of my wits, and gave a halloo that raised the whole camp. We soon had some brandy down her little throat, which brought her to herself a bit. She said 'Padre! Great Pine Mine! Snow-slide!' Great guns! It took the boys just two minutes to be on the way. One of the men rubbed her hands, gave her more brandy, then wrapped her up in a blanket, and with the help of another fellow, carried her back. They found Ned where Bushy had left him tied to a tree, after which it was easy to reach the camp, and your Tom took care of her."

He brushed his coat-sleeve across his eyes as he said: "She's a kid in ten million, she is!"

The relief party soon had the mine opened and the men rescued, but had it not been for Bushy's brave little heart they might all have perished beneath the snow-slide.

CHAPTER VI

Some time after Bushy had helped save the men from the snow-slide she had an adventure with Rover which was very funny, though Bushy's heart was almost broken because it ended in the ruin of her one good dress.

This was a pink calico with white moons dotted all over it, and the only dress she had, in fact, for everything else she wore was made of the sacks that the horse-feed and the corn-meal came in. Flour was $100 a sack, so there were very few flour sacks to be used up in clothes for Bushy. It took all they could get to make the undergarments, so dresses generally had to be gunny sacks made over.

This pink calico dress one of the miners had brought from the States when it was his turn to bring the freight, and Bushy only wore it when some special affair was going on. This day she was left all alone in the cabin. Nobody was expected until supper-time. Rover was enjoying the sunshine so much that he could not be induced to enter into a romp—he seemed to like nothing better than to stretch himself full length across the front doorstep and make Bushy go around him or step over him every time she had occasion to go in or out.

"You are a stupid old fellow!" cried Bushy, giving him a soft tap with her bare foot. Rover only winked at her and wagged his shaggy tail.

"You are no company at all," she added, but Rover did not mind, and this time he was too lazy to wink, but closed his eyes and went sound asleep.

Time hung heavily on her hands; she had written her lesson until both sides of the slate were full; she had swept the cabin and made a roaring fire in the fire-place, that kept the pot of deer-meat boiling away like fun. It was an exceptionally warm day for that time of the year, and her father had told her not to go up the mountains hunting, because he was afraid of another snow-slide. The water was running down in streams until quite a little lake was formed in a low spot not far away.

Bushy watched the water running down on all sides and began to wonder how deep the lake was. "I wonder what kind of weather it was last year," she said to herself—she always talked out loud because she never had any little boys or girls to play with.

Then she hunted up the almanac where her father jotted down all the snow-storms, snow-slides, and everything that he particularly wanted to remember.

"Why, Rover! Rover!" she screamed, running out and shaking him until he was obliged to pay some attention to her, "it is the 17th of June. Padre didn't know it, I guess. We must have a good time, Rover. Wake up, you sleepy dog!"

Bushy rushed back to the wooden box where she kept her pink dress, and while she sang a merry tune, slipped the pink calico over her head, shook down the little ruffles, buttoned the row of pearl buttons in the back—those buttons to Bushy were more precious than diamonds—then snatching her hat, that was a great, soft, felt sombrero, she called to Rover and they ran a race down a well-trodden path to the very edge of the water.

"Oh, look, Rover, the lake is growing wider and wider; it will soon reach the divide and then run down the other side in a great river. Come on, Rover, let's wade in just a little way."

Bushy slipped off her moccasins that had been put on in honor of the day—Bushy always insisted on going barefooted the minute the snow left the ground—and began to dip her toes cautiously into the water. Rover whined and acted very disagreeably, dashing in and out and wagging his wet tail so as to throw the water over her.

"Rover! if you can't behave yourself you will have to keep out!" she cried, venturing in a little farther. "Stay out, sir! Don't you dare sprinkle me again!"

"OH, LOOK, ROVER, THE LAKE IS GROWING WIDER AND WIDER."

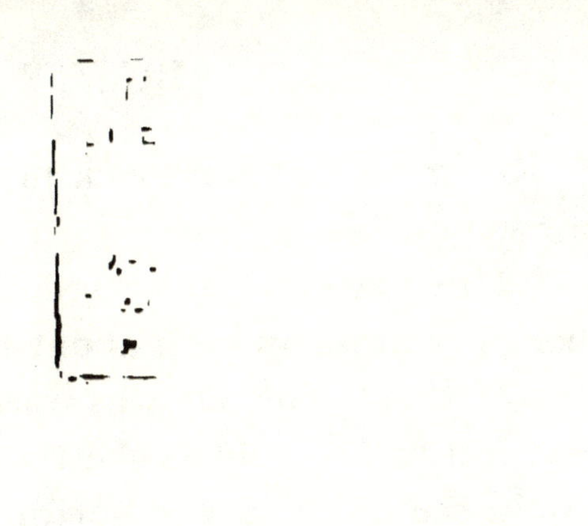

Rover howled and stuck his nose as high in the air as possible.

"Howl away!" answered Bushy, as she tucked her pink dress up high about her waist and waded still farther. The day was warm and the water did not feel half so cold as she thought it would. She could see quite to the bottom as she waded, but when her toes dug vigorously in the mud great clouds of it would circle in queer forms about her fat legs. To insure the pink dress from getting damp she threw the skirt from the back over her head, thus preventing her from seeing Rover.

Howl after howl issued from his throat. He knew that Bushy was doing a very foolish thing.

"Her father told her this very morning," said Rover to himself, "that she should be careful. She will step in a hole in a minute and then she will be drowned." He ran first up the bank then down to the very water's edge, then back toward the house, looking to see if he could not call some one to make Bushy mind; then he would squat on his hind legs and howl and yelp at every step she made.

"Hush up!" cried Bushy, who thought he was crying only because she had forbidden him coming in. "Hush up! people don't cry on Bunker Hill Day. When the parade comes home we will—oh, oh, oh!" she screamed stooping down to try and pull out something that had stuck into her foot.

Her back was to Rover. He saw her stoop and heard her scream with pain. That was enough for him. With one bound he landed in the water close beside her and with another he had clinched his teeth in the back of her dress and then commenced a backward movement that threw Bushy quite off her feet and down flat in the black muddy water.

The skirt worked down from her head. Rover pulled and pulled, her head ploughing a furrow in the mud as he dragged her along. The water almost choked her. She could not cry out, and did not realize what had happened to her until she f and herself high and safe on the bank, with Rover -ing as if he were crazy about her.

She was dripping wet; her hair was plastered down over her face by the mud; her dress, once so pink and beautiful, was black with dirt. As soon as she could get her breath she threw herself down on the ground and cried with all her might.

"Oh, Rover, Rover ! You have broken my heart. You stupid dog ! It isn't deep. I was only wading in just for fun, and now you have spoilt my "——

" Great heavens ! Bushy, what has happened ? " cried Shanks, who had been sent to the cabin for a chisel. " How did you fall in, and how did you get out ? " he cried, quite out of breath from running.

He wiped the mud from her face, and again

"GREAT HEAVENS! BUSHY, WHAT HAS HAPPENED?" CRIED SHANKS.

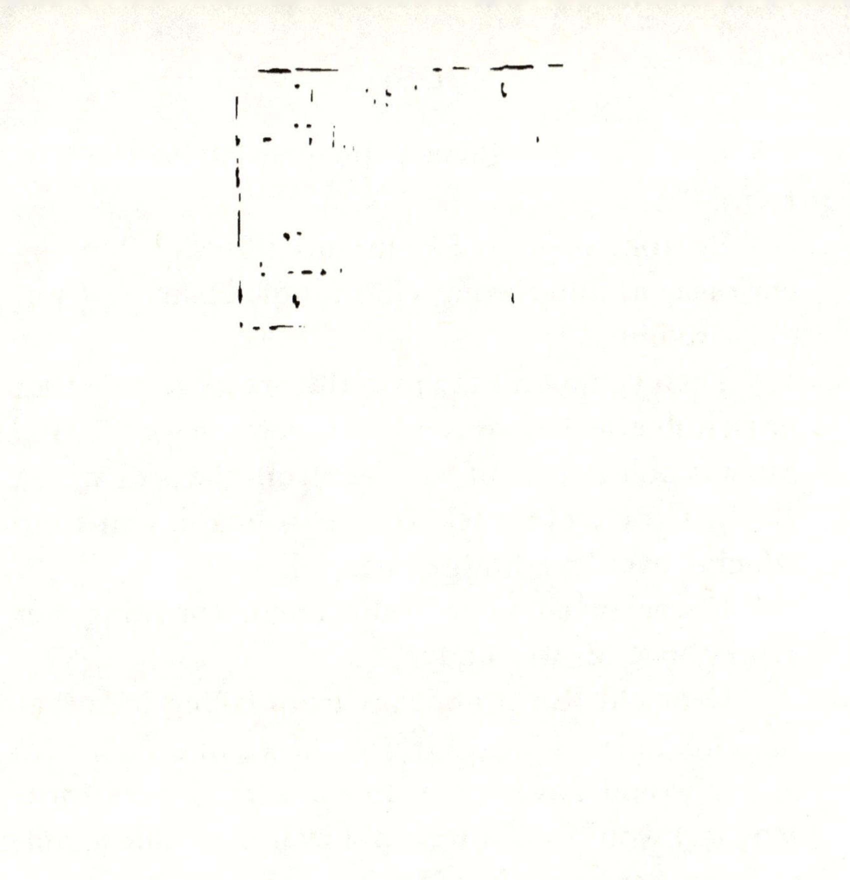

asked: " Tell me, Bushy, did you fall to the bottom ? "

" Bottom of what ? " inquired Bushy, looking curiously at him through her tangled hair. " I was only wading."

" Then you didn't fall into the prospect hole that has twelve feet of water in it, just there ? " and Shanks pointed about two feet from the spot where Bushy's toe had struck against a board, and from which Rover had dragged her.

" Rover saved me ! " she cried, throwing her arms about his wet body.

" Dear old Rover kept me from falling into that dreadful hole. I forgot it was there; one step more and I would have gone down. Oh, Rover, dear Rover, I won't call you stupid ever in my life again; and who cares for the pink dress now ! "

Rover wagged his tail with joy until Bushy stood up; then she presented such a funny appearance that he began to howl louder than ever. This made Shanks and Bushy laugh heartily.

Shanks took them to the cabin and gave them both a bath, but Bushy's hair had to be shingled; her father could not get the snarls out any other way. The pink dress was spoiled, but Bushy had it put carefully away in a box, where she found it years and years afterward, when it brought back the story of faithful old Rover and how he saved her life.

CHAPTER VII

" Padre, now my hair is short, I'm going to play boy," said Bushy a month after Rover had pulled her from the pond. " Do all the boys feel light-headed like I do ? "

" That is a puzzler," answered her father, as he turned her buckskin jacket right side out and helped her put it on. " I think you will have to wait until you know some boys and ask them."

It was morning and Bushy had been awakened to accompany Mr. Sukolt and three men, way up the mountains, over the divide and into a section where the pine-trees grew tall and without many branches. These trees Mr. Sukolt used for timbering the mine. They were cut into lengths to support places where there was danger of the walls caving in.

" No, no. I don't want my dress. I want to wear pants like you. Tom must make me a pair," cried Bushy. " I'm a little boy. Don't you want a little boy, Padre ? "

" Why, I rather think I do if he has this little wildcat's face," replied the father, again trying to help Bushy dress.

"No, no," she again protested. "Tom, can't you make me a pair of pants?"

"Of course, I can," he replied, laughing at the idea of Bushy being a boy. "Just watch me. Mr. Sukolt, you go and attend to the horses. Bless my heart! The child ought to have a summer outfit, and it shall be pants if she wants them, sure as my name's Tom Cole."

"Oh, Tom, make me into a little cow-boy. Can I have a whip and—oh, I'll wear my nightgown for a white waist, and put the buckskin jacket over it, and—what can we make pants out of, Tom?"

"Why, this skirt will do. I'll just turn it into two little skirts instead of one. Ha, ha! look at that! They are almost done already," cried Tom,. as he sewed away with twine and harness needle.

Tom soon turned the coffee-sack dress into a beautiful pair of pants. He handed them over to Bushy with the greatest pride.

"Oh, they are scrumptious!" she cried, disappearing, and in a minute came bounding back with a boy's suit on complete.

"Something is wrong with the waist; guess we can scrape up a sash," said Tom, eying her critically. He went to the clothes-box and pulled out a roll of red flannel cut in strips for bandages. "Look here," he said, unrolling it. "How is this for a sash?"

Bushy screamed with joy. "Oh, Tom, I'll be so careful of it if you let me wear it just this one day." Without waiting for an answer she wound the strip three times around her tiny waist, then tied it in a big flowing bow. Next her quick fingers twisted it like a ribbon about the crown of her wide felt hat. "Now, Tom, I am sure enough a little boy!" Then, taking up the rawhide whip, which she called a "quirt," she began to dance a hornpipe, cracking her whip in time.

"Hello!" called her father. "What have we here? Some gypsy strayed from the camp? I'll help you out." He picked up an old guitar that stood in one corner, and then to a real jig tune, Bushy danced all the steps the miners had taught her.

So they started for the woods. Walt drove the team. Tom and Shanks, mounted on ponies, started ahead, and Bushy and her father brought up the rear, Mr. Sukolt on an Indian pony, and Bushy, as usual, on Ned.

They descended through caverns where icicles still dripped, and where there was danger of some avalanche sliding down to bury itself in the black gorge below. Soon they came to a place where the melted snow and ice was plunging madly through the rocks and black dirt.

"Ah, we can use that torrent," said Mr. Sukolt,

"NOW, TOM, I AM SURE ENOUGH A LITTLE BOY!"

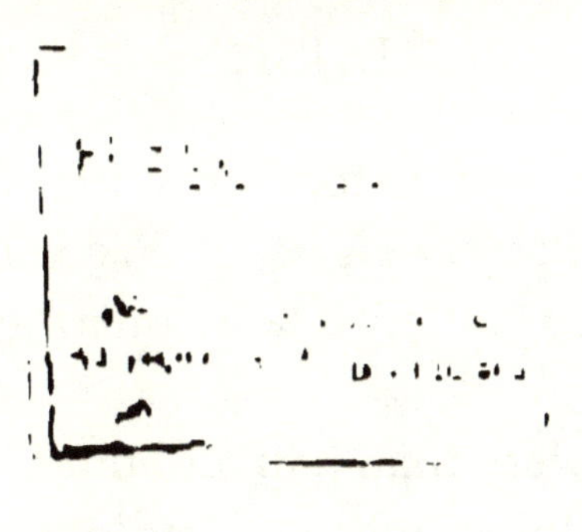

calling a halt just before entering the road that would lead off to the right. " We will cut logs and get them down the hillside by putting them in that stream."

The men in less than half an hour were chopping, hallooing, calling, singing, laughing, and working with all their might.

" I fear the creek is rising," exclaimed Mr. Sukolt all at once. " There must have been a cloud-burst along its course somewhere. To your saddles, boys; we must run no risk; there is every indication of a freshet."

Bushy heard the anxious voice and there was no need to tell her what to do. She was on Ned in a second, and with the long lariat coiled she rode up to her father's side and said: " I am ready, Padre, shall we make for the valley or go up the mountain."

" To the valley, every one to the valley ! There is no hope of escaping it. Ah ! how it roars; we must get ready to swim."

Tom unhitched the mules from the wagon and fixed their harness; then, mounting his pony, called to the men to follow. Shanks and Walt were coming down as fast as they could.

" If the water strikes you, Bushy, hold on fast to Ned. I would tie you to me, but if I go under I don't want you to be tied to me, and if I get out safe I can help you."

"Is that thunder, Padre?" asked Bushy, looking up into her father's pale face. He only urged his horse and Ned to go faster. "Make for the flat," he called to the men, "then turn the horses' heads toward Bald Mountain."

He had no more than finished speaking when the "thunder" broke into one great report and water came down the gulch seven feet high. The men were not afraid of the water, it was the timber that they had spent all day in cutting that they thought would perhaps dash down and kill them and the horses.

Bushy and her father were on the outer edge of the freshet, and when it struck, both horses lost their feet and went under.

"Lie close and cling tight," cried Mr. Sukolt, just as he, too, went out of sight. A great log that Tom had taken such pride in cutting down followed end over end, and as Mr. Sukolt and the pony came up and were straightening out for a swim, the log struck on the pony's head, stunning him so that he sank like lead.

Bushy and Ned were making for the dry land, only the current was so strong it swept Ned sideways. Bushy was dripping wet, for she had gone under, too.

"Padre," she screamed, when she saw him sinking, "swim to Ned. Oh, Ned, we must help Padre."

Ned seemed to understand, because he neighed when he looked back and saw Mr. Sukolt trying to swim toward them. Then he turned his head to Bushy, making a funny sound, as if he were waiting for her to do something.

"Oh, I see," cried Bushy, "the lariat! Oh, Ned, I have no head like you." Whether Ned did mean that or not, Bushy always insists he did. She threw the rope so her father got hold, and when Bushy was once on dry land she pulled him out, too. Then he threw it to the other men, who were floundering about like fish. The pony was drowned and Walt got his leg broken. Rover was not in the water at all. He seemed to have the instinct to run in the right direction. The wagon was swept down stream a short distance and landed unharmed on a slight elevation in the valley.

Bushy gave Ned an extra big supper that night because he was the lucky one to help pull them all out. Walt was the only one who had a hard time in getting home.

"I think much depended upon Bushy's pants," said her father that night, after they reached the camp again. "I don't believe any little girl could have accomplished what our little boy did to-day."

Bushy's greatest sorrow seemed to be that the red flannel that she so faithfully promised Tom she would be careful of was all shrivelled up.

CHAPTER VIII

"Padre, I am going out to try and catch a prairie-dog to-day!" called out Bushy to her father one bright Fall morning just after he had started for the mine. "Billy is lonesome, and I want to find another to play with him."

Billy was a prairie-dog that Bushy had drowned out of his home over six months before. He had become so tame that she could let him loose and he would never go far from the shanty. He had red-brown hair on his back, and his little feet and under parts were white. Although he was a tiny baby prairie-dog when she drowned him out, he had grown almost a foot long, and his cheek pouches were half an inch thick, and his body round and clumsy. Perhaps you don't know how they live. They burrow in the ground and at the entrance to their holes throw up a mound that looks very much like an ant-hill. The hole in the centre, or door, I suppose the dogs call it, slopes down and finally divides into long passages and hallways. The main hall is sometimes very long, and off from it run these short burrows that end in a soft bed of dry grass and leaves.

One day Bushy coaxed Tom to help her carry water to Dogtown, as the village of dogs was called, and she poured bucketful after bucketful into one of the dog-houses, until finally a great sniffing and snorting was heard. Soon the mother dog rushed out, and Bushy was so surprised she failed to catch her, but she did get the baby that was most dead when he got to the surface. Billy was that baby.

He always barked and waggled his tail every time Bushy looked at him, and the miners thought she could understand what Billy said to her, because she talked just as if she did. They would play for hours together, and Rover would look sullenly on. It took Rover some time before he would give up teasing Billy, and more than once he boxed the creature's head so hard with his paw that Billy tumbled over and over and howled. But he was a happy-go-lucky little fellow and did not mind much.

This lovely, sunny morning Bushy went way down the mountains into a kind of low place between two peaks where a few dogs had built their houses. They don't often come up so high, but these always slept during the winter and only came out when the sun shone in summer.

"Look out for the snakes," called her father as he swung his tools on his shoulder. "A snake is

ever liable to be where a prairie-dog is. You had
better take Rover along and Tom, too."

"Oh, Rover and Tom are going out after pitch-
pine stumps in Stone Gulch, and there is no way for
me to ride with them. I won't try to drown the
dog out, but take my net and throw it over him
when he comes out to say good-morning."

"All right," cried her father; "but be careful and
don't go too far."

When the dogs hear anybody walking about
their town they all come out to see who it is, and
then they stand on their hind legs and talk about it.
They spend much of their time gossiping. Their
little heads popped out when Bushy arrived, and
each one stood up and barked a " how de do " as
best he could.

"How de do," cried Bushy, throwing her net
at one of the nearest ones. But he immediately
dived into his hole and sent an owl to inquire what
was wanted.

The prairie-dog is named dog only on account of
his bark. He looks more like a big, rough-haired
rat than a dog. Prairie-dogs seldom grow longer
than thirteen inches. Burrowing owls and rattle-
snakes always live with them. The owls are small,
not over a foot high, and have stout legs and mus-
cular claws, so that if they can find no prairie-dog
to give them a home, they can dig one for themselves.

"HOW DE DO," CRIED BUSHY, THROWING HER NET AT ONE OF THE
NEAREST ONES.

The owls sometimes devour the little prairie-dogs, but members of the rival families seem, on the whole, to be on good terms.

The snakes seldom bother the prairie-dogs until fall. Then they take up their quarters in the homes of the dogs, and live there. One must not think that the dog and owl select the snake as a companion, for that is not the case. He is an intruder and too powerful an adversary to be expelled.

The little owl that came out to inquire what Bushy wanted, stood up very straight and nodded his head three times and said, " quok, quok, quok," which Bushy always interpreted as " What you want ? "

There is nothing prettier in the world than to watch these little owls nod. They do it just as anybody would. Their little heads nod and nod until they are answered or frightened away.

" I want your master or one of his children to come and live with my Billy," cried Bushy, making a long sweep with her net, that covered the owl and caused a great fluttering and floundering that only entangled him more and more in the net that made him Bushy's prisoner.

" I've got you," cried Bushy with a laugh that died on her lips, for a rattling sound that she recognized only too well greeted her ear.

It was the warning of a rattlesnake, and Bushy

turned her head to see an extra long one coiled up, with his tail rising perpendicularly out of the centre and shaking with such rapidity that the rattles looked like a fan; his head was elevated ready to strike.

Understanding so well the movements of the snake, Bushy knew that it was quite ready to spring, and would, should she change her position or make a move in either direction. Although the rattle-snake is not quick to take offence, this one had evidently considered the attack on the owl a personal affair. There was no terror in her face nor was there despair, but the sense of danger made her intensely excited.

Throwing her head backward and dropping her hand on the hilt of the bowie-knife in her belt, she fixed her bright eyes on the snake and watched. The seconds seemed to her hours.

" Why don't it strike, why don't it strike ? "

Her heart seemed pumping fire instead of blood through her veins. A peculiar rustling sound was heard, then the slimy thing darted through the air. With a lightning-like movement, Bushy threw out her arm and caught the snake just below the head and held it with her slender, wiry fingers. The other hand, meanwhile not idle, drew from her belt the bowie-knife and severed the head of the reptile, yet not before it had buried its poisonous fangs in the end of her forefinger.

Though the body of the snake still coiled itself about her arm and the cold tail flapped against her cheek, she so quickly cut the flesh from the end of her finger that the poison had no chance to circulate with the blood through her body. Then, taking hold of the wriggling thing, she stripped it from her arm and threw it writhing, twisting, and twirling down to the rocky bottom of the canyon.

"That's the end of you," soliloquized Bushy, tying a piece of string that she found in her pocket around the first joint of her finger, then binding it with a strip of her cotton handkerchief. "Tom says a black devil is in every rattler," she said, as she pressed her heel on the lifeless head and sank it deep in the earth. "I wonder if I have cut off his head as I did yours?"

She had some difficulty in tying the strip, took her sharp teeth to it, and then continued her soliloquy: "I wonder what life is, and I wonder what death is? I'll ask the Padre, he knows."

Setting her cap with a jerk always characteristic of Bushy when ready to depart, she started down the mountain with a swinging motion, neither a walk nor a run. As her feet merely touched the stones, sticks, and stumps in her progress downward, she would have appeared to you more as if she were flying than walking. She would spring with an energetic movement to a distant log or

bowlder and hugging it momentarily with her moc-
casined toes attain the proper impetus for the next
spring, a feat requiring the nicest precision.   In
this way, with the greatest ease and without the
slightest appearance of fatigue, she reached the
camp below—a style of descent which seemed as
natural to her as to the mountain sheep.

"I didn't get the dog, Padre," she remarked to
her father as he stood watching her coming in that
flying, skimming style, "but here's the owl that
made the snake fight me," and she landed plump in
her father's arms.

"It is more a mystery to me," said Mr. Sukolt,
"how you came down the mountain side without
being killed than that you found a snake there."
He dressed her finger and gave her whiskey.   Then
he put her to bed, where she slept soundly all night.
She lost the nail on that finger, but a new one grew,
and there was only a scar left to show where she had
injured the bone a little when she so bravely clipped
off the end of her finger to prevent the poison
spreading all over her body and killing her.

Next day after Bushy had been bitten by the snake, Mr. Sukolt had to go with a load of ore to the nearest smelting works, which were miles away, quite at the foot of the mountains, and as he was anxious about Bushy he thought he would feel easier if he took her along.

" You don't think I will turn all black and blue, do you, Padre ? " she asked as she jumped on Ned and rode on ahead of the load of ore.

" There is no telling; but I think cutting off your finger end as you did, saved not only your hand but your life. How did you come to think of doing that ? "

" Why, Tom told me one day that I must, because if the poison got into my blood I would swell up as the mare did when she got her foot bitten."

" Tom was right, but still I doubt that I would have done it myself," answered her father, as he gazed lovingly at his wild little girl.

" What are you up to now ? " he asked, as she rose in her saddle and took aim at something in the air.

"Do you think I can kill that bird at long range?"

"I don't think I would try," replied the father, "unless there is a greater reason for killing it. It is a cruel sport to take the life of anything unless you see a need of it."

"But I like to hunt, Padre," murmured Bushy thoughtfully; "is it wrong to hunt?"

"Not if you want food; I don't believe in hunting for sport alone. I enjoy hunting, too, and we will leave the wagon with Tom and try to kill a buffalo to-day if we see any sign of a herd in this neighborhood. A few old fellows, they say, have been driven up the valley. We will ride out ten miles and see what we can do. It would be a great thing for us to take home a wagonful of buffalo."

They travelled all one day and part of the next, but saw no signs of securing buffalo meat. But when they reached the mills where the ore was to be crushed they were told that the mail-boy, who had just arrived in his buck-board, had said that a big herd was not more than five miles to the east.

"Ah, there they are," exclaimed Mr. Sukolt an hour later, when the two horseback riders came in sight of a large herd of bison. The animals were grazing quietly by a stream, where they had gone to drink.

"There must be five hundred," said Mr. Sukolt.

" It would be a serious thing if they should stampede.

" Why, what can be the matter ! " he cried, catching hold of Ned's bridle and guiding him close to his own horse. " What has got into the animals, they are all coming this way ? We are penned in by the hills ! Look, Bushy, your eyes are sharper than mine; can you tell what has frightened them ? "

Bushy peered for a second into the distance beyond, then cried excitedly: " There are four men driving them. Ah, there's a shot; they must be hunters after meat. What shall we do, Padre ? Can't we get to one side ? "

" They have stampeded, sure as we sit here ! " said Mr. Sukolt half to himself. " We must try for the hills on the left. Keep close to me; now for the race ! If you are cut off shoot, of course, but don't stop for anything if there is hope of your getting out of their way."

They had been on the keen jump meanwhile and had made some headway, but finally the buffalo came pell-mell, dashing down almost upon them. Mr. Sukolt raised his rifle and tried to kill the leader at long range, but he missed him. " We can't get out of their way unless we kill one for the rest to stumble over," said Mr. Sukolt catching up with Bushy.

Without saying a word Bushy raised her rifle and when the leader came in range fired. She wounded him, for he fell, and immediately there was a temporary halt, caused by the followers tumbling over him. The excitement was something terrible. One big buffalo bull rolled over and over, and one or two rolled over him, until there was quite a pile of enraged animals bellowing in the centre of the stampede. Bushy and her father took this opportunity to circle about and join the hunters who had unwittingly almost caused their death.

"Had no idea a living soul but ourselves was in the vicinity," said one old trapper as he rode up to Mr. Sukolt. "It's a magnificent hunt; we've killed three, that's all we can pack away. Do you want to kill a buffalo, little girl? he called to Bushy who was following the herd.

"Yes, sir!" she screamed back. "I never killed one in my life."

"Then get on my pony; he is a regular buffalo pony. Can you ride?"

"Oh, yes, sir. I am not afraid."

"All right. Shall I let her try?" asked the man of Mr. Sukolt.

"Yes, I'd like to have her try," was the reply; so Bushy was lifted quickly from Ned and seated on the back of the buffalo pony; then the hunter jumped on Ned without as much as touching a foot to the ground, and left Bushy alone on the trained pony.

" Just let him go his own way. Don't fire until you ride directly upon the flank of the buffalo ! " called out the hunter, and Bushy was soon on the keen jump after the herd.

Mr. Sukolt kept as close as he could, but the trained pony knew just what to do. He managed to get a few buffalo circling round and round, one after the other. Every animal had his nose down close to the ground, and did not know that he was going round and round. Buffalo are very short-sighted.

" Now shoot," the pony seemed to say, because he sidled up to one of the buffalo and half halted. Bushy took the hint and fired. The buffalo ran as if nothing had happened. You can shoot all day at a buffalo and unless you hit him in the right spot he doesn't mind it; his hide is so tough it even protects him from bullets. Without any warning the pony dashed ahead, and when he got up directly on the flank of the great buffalo calf, Bushy fired again, and this time down he came.*

The other animals then broke ring and followed the main herd, but Bushy was the proudest hunter

* This buffalo was, in 1876, displayed with other animals in the Maxwell collection, in the Colorado building, at the time of the Centennial Exposition held at Philadelphia.

in camp that night over the fact that she had killed
one of the finest specimens of buffalo that had been
secured for many a day. The head was so beautiful
that Mr. Sukolt would not consent to its being
thrown away, but had the skin as well as the head
saved and sent to Denver, where a taxidermist
fixed it up as if it were alive again.

BUSHY FIRED AGAIN, AND THIS TIME DOWN HE CAME.

Picture to yourself a girl of eleven summers as she came one day out of one of the shanties at Great Pine Mine; a little girl still, dressed in coffee sacks, two making the skirt and one the blouse, which was gathered at the waist with a yellow strap. Snatching up a rope bridle that lay on a broken bench under the window, she ran to a horse " picketed " twenty feet away, sprang on his back and went dashing at breakneck speed up and down the rough road that led to the mines. An old man approaching the camp was startled by the loud clatter of the horse's hoofs, and his wrinkled face turned a shade more saffron-like when he recognized the rider. He dropped his pick and shovel, and with long strides soon reached a bend, where, out of sight, he waited for the horse and child.

" Fly, Ned, fly ! " cried the little girl, and the horse stretched his long limbs to cover more ground. They turned the bend and on seeing the old man, the little girl reined up the horse so sharply that she was nearly thrown over his head.

" Great goodness ! I most went off that time,

didn't I ? " she panted. " What are you standing in the middle of the road for, anyway, Tom ? And why do you look so queer ? Oh, dear, are you sick ? Here, can you hold the bridle ? I'll get you a drink from the brook in a jiffy."

Before he could reply she was beside him winding the rope round his hand, saying: " Hold him tight, he is skittish, you know." She snatched off her buckskin cap and in less than a minute brought it back full of clear, cold water.

" Wall, I'll swaller it since you've gone and got it; but I don't want water; nothin's the matter with me." He drank from the cap while Bushy looked on approvingly. " I jes' thought Ned was runnin' away, and I'd try and stop him as he turned this corner," said Tom, striking her cap on his knee, three or four times after he had taken the drink from it.

" Oh, fiddlesticks ! " and her sun-burnt face clouded with a frown.

" Wall, you've no business ridin' like that, anyway; I'm sure as sartin we'll never raise you, never ! And, golly, 'tain't cause there ain't enough of us to look after you, but you are so tomfoolery foolish."

" Then, you were not sick, after all," said Bushy, " and I've lost my bet and ducked my cap, and—give it to me, you wicked old man. You will get no more drink from me—so there ! " She snatched her cap and sent such a ripple of laughter from her cherry-red lips that the mountains on all sides lovingly echoed it.

"What was your bet, Bushy?"

"Oh, that I could run from the camp to the mines in five minutes if the Indians were after me." She sprinkled him well with what water she could shake from the cap; and then with a jerk drew it down tight on her tangled head.

With a jolly little laugh, she sang "hitchity, hatchet, my little red jacket, and up I go," and, mounting the pony with one leap, turned her quaint, oldish face toward Tom and motioned for him to hand her the rope bridle.

"Who'd you bet with?" he asked, tying an extra knot in the old rope before handing it to her.

"Why, with myself, of course, you funny old fellow! I couldn't bet with the rats, could I? And what else is there in the shanty when everybody is at the mine? even Rover is off hunting with padre."

"You don't say, Bushy, that the Padre is still out? That's bad. Shanks brought news from the blacksmith's that the Indians in the reservation are ugly!"

Bushy's face seemed to grow older; the smile disappeared, the lips became compressed, and her hands grasped more tightly the rope that made Ned her prisoner.

"And Padre went up Eureka Gulch, didn't he, Tom?"

"That's so, but then, chick, don't fret; he is good enough for a dozen redskins any day. You might, though, as long as you are on Ned, go to the mine and talk with Shanks about it. I'll bet you that mountain sheep's head I brought in last week that you will find the Padre with me when you get back." She was already on her way and had time only to call out, "All right!" as she disappeared in the ravine.

"I've lost the sheep's head, sure as sartin," mumbled the old man, stooping for his tools. "The padre has heard about the Indians and is layin' low to come in under cover of dark. He won't run a risk—for the chick's sake. Poor chicken without any mother!"

He swung the heavy pick and shovel on his shoulder, tucked a chunk of tobacco in his left cheek, then shambled off, shaking his head and grumbling.

"Halloa!" shouted Shanks, as Bushy approached the mine. "You always come in the nick of time. Here is Rover with a note from the Padre pinned on his shaggy coat, saying"——

"Oh, please, Shanks, let me read it!" and not

waiting for him to hand her the paper, she leaned over, deftly slipped it out of his fingers, and read:

Stone Gulch.—Spott has hurt her foot and limps dreadfully. Got a bear; trying to bring it home for Thanksgiving dinner. I walk. Send Bushy on Ned up Stone Path to meet me.

PADRE.

" All right, I'll go. Show it to Tom," said Bushy, returning the note. " Could you strap your tool-bag on Ned for me ? " She dismounted and they both tried to make a saddle out of the bag. " What's the matter ? Won't it go round ? "

Shanks was looking in despair at his strap, which lacked a foot of encircling Ned's plump body. " Here's my belt; that will just fix it. Good, good ! Now I'd just like to see a red-skin catch me ! "

" But, Bushy, I really think that you had better let me go. I heard something to-day about "——

" Oh, yes; I know. The Indians. Tom told me. But don't you see if there should be any trouble, father and I could both ride Ned, and if you go, both being so big, one of you would be left, sure."

" That's all true, little wise-head. Off with you then. Wait ! Let me fix you up with my belt and revolver. I don't suppose there's an Indian within fifteen miles of here, but if you see one, and he even looks cross-eyed at you, pop him over."

Lightly jumping on Ned, riding astride—as she always did when on a dangerous mission—and pulling down her cap, she called: " Rover ! here, Rover; I want you. Good-by, Shanks. We are off for the Padre !" Rover set up a barking loud and joyous. Ned stood on his hind legs for a moment; then the three went flying up Stone Path to render greater assistance than any of them thought.

Bushy had gone about three miles and had arrived at the point where the path she had been following led into the main road at right angles, when she noticed that Rover began to show great uneasiness, and Ned snorted and tossed his head as he always did when he scented danger. She drew her rein, slipped quickly down, threw herself at full length on the ground, and, placing her ear close to the sod, listened.

" By jiminy !" she exclaimed, " some one is coming in both directions." Again she listened. " Ah ! one horse limps; that must be Spott. Now who can be coming from the other direction ? A redskin, I'll bet my head !" She jumped up quickly; and quietly led Ned behind a huge bowlder and wound the bridle around a snag that grew in a crevice. " Poor Ned," she said, " how you do tremble ! You are just as scared of the Indians as I am." She snapped her fingers at Rover, who

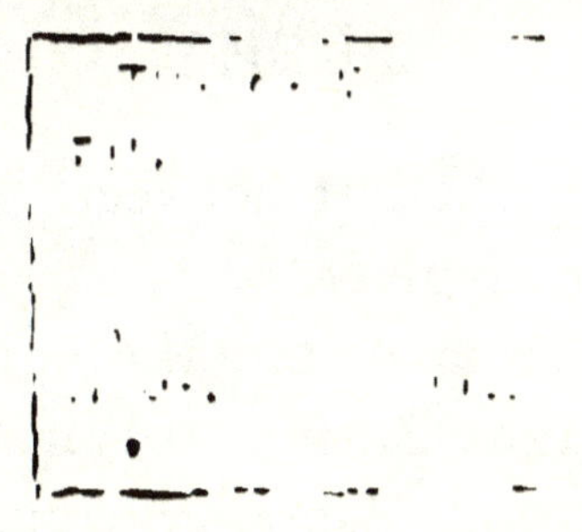

whined and crouched at her feet. Then she drew and cocked her revolver.

" I wonder if I have done the right thing in hiding here," thought Bushy. " Will they meet near here or pass beyond. Good gracious, how fast that horse is coming ! Will father never get here ! It is an Indian ! Whizeration !" she exclaimed, as she ducked behind the bowlder. A Navajo rode into sight, bristling all over with weapons. He had two sets of bows and arrows, one revolver, two bowie-knives, and a tomahawk. He bent over and looked anxiously ahead, as if expecting to meet some one.

" Oh, if he looks behind we are dead, that's sure ! " thought Bushy.

Just then Spott limped into sight. Bushy saw at a glance that her father was not prepared for the Indian. She reeled, and you would have felt certain she was going to fall; but, clutching her revolver, her face taking on that same queer, old expression, she glided out, where she could take good aim at the Indian.

Mr. Sukolt, expecting Bushy, and knowing nothing of the Indian trouble had not thought it strange to hear a horse coming. At the sight of the Indian he jerked Spott sideways, just in time to escape an arrow. At the same moment came a report from Bushy's revolver. The Indian reeled and fell head

first off the pony, but, like a rubber ball, was up with
a bound, and, giving a blood-curdling yell, raised
his tomahawk and sprang at Bushy. She fired
again, but missed him—the shot taking effect in
the breast of poor Spott, who had wheeled herself
in direct line of the firing.

Bushy saw Spott fall, and, fearing that her father
was hurt, she screamed, " Padre, Padre ! what have
I done ? " Then she was thrown flat on the ground,
face downward, by Rover, who, till then, had not
left her heels. At her cry, he sprang upon her back,
over her head, and clinched his big white teeth in
the throat of the Indian, just as the savage was
about to strike Bushy's head with his tomahawk.
The struggle between man and beast lasted only a
second, for the butt of Mr. Sukolt's revolver, which
he brought down with all his force on the skull of
the redskin, would have knocked the latter sense-
less had not the bullet fired by Bushy already done
its work. The fellow fell dead with Rover still
clinging to his throat.

" Off with you, Rover, you noble fellow," called
Mr. Sukolt. " He is dead—dead as a door-nail."
Then, turning to Bushy, who had scrambled to her
feet, he took her in his arms, saying: " Brave little
girl, this isn't the first time you have saved me with
that revolver of yours."

" Not mine this time, but Shanks's, and it was so

heavy, and I was so afraid of shooting you that I missed my second fire. Oh, come away! Oh, come back! Shanks told me of the Indians around the blacksmith's and there may be more with this one." She trembled like a leaf, and her face was ashen white.

"Look, Padre, the Indian pony's lariat is entangled about Spott's body. If you can catch him we can yet take home the bear."

"I will catch him, for the boys at camp are famishing for fresh meat," said Mr. Sukolt, "though we run a little risk by the delay."

"We will both ride Ned and I will lead this pony with his load of meat," remarked Mr. Sukolt, as he came up with the frightened animal.

"Yes, let's hurry; I'm so frightened. Ugh! The horrid Indian, don't touch him, Padre!" she screamed. But Mr. Sukolt thought best to drag the body behind the bowlder and away from the main road. With one regretful look at Spott, lying dead in the path, they rode away—Bushy and her father on Ned; Bushy guiding the horse, while the Indian pony, with the bear, was led by Mr. Sukolt.

They reached camp in time for Tom to cook some of the bear for the Thanksgiving dinner. Six miners, Tom, and Shanks, the father and Bushy, all sat around the wooden table and ate none the less merrily for the day's strange adventures.

CHAPTER XI

Bushy continued as little housekeeper for her father at Great Pine Mine until December of the next year. Mr. Sukolt was then called south to Cross Roads, a settlement composed of miners only. He went there to judge a " lead " that was up for sale and draw maps of the mining district. Bushy went with him, as she explained to Tom, to " watch out for his papers and cook his victuals."

It was Christmas morning and Bushy had got up bright and early to prepare the breakfast.

" Pickle and herring ! but this is a dish fit for a king with a crown on. Stir, dip, taste," she sang, swallowing a big spoonful of the savory soup. It seems odd to have soup for breakfast, but that is what they did have that Christmas morning.

" Very much taste, it seems to me," interrupted a voice from the corner of the tumble-down shanty in which Mr. Sukolt and his daughter had passed the night. " Within the last twenty minutes you have sampled that soup just twenty-one and a half times."

" Padre mio ! " exclaimed Bushy, striking a

most tragic attitude before him. " I do not object to twenty-one, but the half. How could I sample anything half a time ? "

" That's so. How could you," replied the father, his face beaming with love. " I had forgotten that you never do things by halves, even to loving the Padre; eh, little girl ? "

" I don't know about that," she laughed. " I'm afraid you are not so awfully good in arithmetic, Padre; " then she turned her attention to the soup again. " Golly, but it's hot ! Just try some, won't you ? " she cried, extending the spoon toward him.

" No, thank you, I will take your word for it; only tell me how much there is left when you get through sampling," replied the father.

Bushy and her father had been more than once without anything to eat, and at this time of the year, way down where they were, so far from anybody, they had again found themselves almost out of everything in the line of food.

" Oh, I guess there will be enough, but perhaps I had better put in a little more water," remarked Bushy, and with a mischievous twinkle in her eyes she darted for the water-can.

" Don't you dare do that ! " exclaimed her father, jumping up from the roll of buffalo skins on which he had been sitting writing. With a little chasing and some lively scuffling, he pinioned her arms behind her and in the midst of her hearty laughter said:

"If you don't mind, Miss Cook, I prefer my drinks not mixed; I will take first the soup and then the water."

"But do you think you can tell one from the other?" inquired Bushy, saucily.

They both took a peep into the kettle, Bushy ready to enjoy the surprise she had in store for her father.

"By my faith, but it does look like soup and smells accordingly! Why, what do you call it and how did you make such a raise?"

"Oh, Padre, don't bother your head over the name. The name wont count if you like it. This morning when you were snoozing I crawled out to look for game, for, you know, we had nothing for breakfast but crackers and bacon. As good luck would have it, I spied this squirrel. I popped him over with this," she lovingly patted her gun as it hung on the shanty wall; "and here he is, chopped in tiny bits with the crackers and bacon."

They both laughed merrily, Bushy filled the two tin cups with soup and took out fresh crackers from the provision box, while her father put away his books and papers in a very much worn carpet-bag. Then he stretched out a buffalo skin for Bushy to sit on and made two of the others into a roll to serve as a seat for himself. He took a cup of soup, seated himself, and said:

" Now for the lesson; what is it to-day, Bushy ? "

" It commences with the word ' There.' The sentence is, ' There are many Spaniards in America;' but how do you like the soup; it's good, isn't it ? "

" Excellent ! " murmured Mr. Sukolt. " A New York chef couldn't have treated me better than you have this morning." He held the cup in hand, opened the well-fingered grammar, put it beside him on the skins, and then, before taking another swallow of soup, said:

" All right now, go ahead with your grammar."

" There are many [she swallowed soup] Spaniards [more soup] in America, and I suppose there are many Americans in Spain, too. Let me see," again she stopped for soup, " where did you tell me Spain is ? " She raised her bright face to her father.

" In Europe," he replied.

" I wish I had a geography, Padre; I am so hungry for one that I just guess I'll kill the first person I find with one; that is if he don't want to give it to me," said Bushy, much to her father's astonishment.

" Bushy, you are an odd child, but you are happy, are you not ? " Mr. Sukolt waited rather anxiously for her reply.

" Guess so," she said, musingly; " but sometimes

I think my feelings don't depend so much on what you think is the best thing for me, as they depend on what I think is the best thing for me.

"Now, I'd be awfully happy if you would give me a geography that tells about the fairylands where you and my mother used to live, instead of giving me meat for supper," added Bushy, thoughtfully.

"You will note one thing as you grow older, my little girl; that when you get the geography it will call for an atlas, and the atlas for a trip round the world, and so on, your desires always being just as strong as they are now for something you haven't got."

"You don't know me, Padre. I'll outwit your philosophy by never wishing for what I can't get. Who wants to go around the world? Why I'm twelve years old and mistress of this establishment. What do I want more! Hurrah!" With another peal of laughter she waved high the tin of soup, as if pledging the beauties of the tumble-down shanty.

"This won't do!" exclaimed Mr. Sukolt, jumping up and running his fingers through Bushy's tangled hair, "you've got out of a lesson again, you little witch! We must start right off or we will not catch Tom with the wagon at Cross Roads."

While packing up the camp articles Bushy kept up a constant chatter.

" Padre," she cried, as a new thought came to her, " you told me that on this trip I would see some children. Where are the children ? "

She threw herself down on the bundle of robes that Mr. Sukolt was trying to tie up, and her laughing eyes peeped up at him through her fluffy hair which had fallen so as to almost cover her face.

" Show me the children or I will strike for higher wages. Think of it, Padre ! I cannot remember ever seeing any children. Yes, I'll strike for higher wages or for Great Pine Mine; so there." And again the shanty was filled with her ringing laugh.

" Get up, you little rascal, and help me with these bundles. Now, what would you do if we should run against a little boy, say to-day, at Cross Roads ? "

" Kiss him, and if he is very, very sweet, eat him up. Do you think we can buy a geography there, Padre ? " she asked wistfully. " I don't know which I want to see the most, a geography or a baby—a real live baby."

" Well, we will soon find out what is there," said Mr. Sukolt, firmly tying all the bundles on to the pack-horse and mounting his own. " Are you ready to start ? "

" Almost," she answered, coiling the lariat so as

to attach it to the saddle; then with it still in her hand she sprang on Ned's back and called to Rover, who was gnawing at the squirrel's head.

Hearing a noise they both looked up. Coming down the path, about a quarter of a mile away, was a horseman, and it was obvious to Bushy and her father that the rider had lost all control of the animal he rode.

"He sits badly for a Mexican!" exclaimed Mr. Sukolt, "yet I think he will come out all right."

"He isn't a Mexican; he's a soldier," cried Bushy. Then, frightened by a second thought, she screamed:

"The ravine! the ravine! This path leads straight over the precipice! Oh, Padre, his horse can never stop after he turns the bend!"

They both started toward the soldier, neither knowing just what they were going to do.

Mr. Sukolt spied the lariat which Bushy still held in her hand.

"Lariat him! lariat him!" he commanded in a stern, hard voice, checking his pony at the same time.

"But can I?" came from her pale lips.

"Try it, child! try it! There is no time for me to take the lariat now!"

Again the queer old look settled on her face. There was only time to swing the lariat three times over her head and let go when the horse dashed past her. Ned stubbornly planted his feet and awaited the accustomed pull—it came, and with it headlong into the snowy path fell the soldier. The horse, lightened of his load, went at yet madder speed around the rocks out of sight to its death.

The man lay perfectly still. Bushy sprang from Ned and ran to him. Mr. Sukolt was already cutting the rope that had settled over the soldier's head and wound around his body, pinioning both his arms tight to his sides.

"I have killed him!" murmured Bushy, opening his shirt and feeling for his heart.

"No, I think he is only stunned. The snow was deep and saved him," replied her father.

As the blood commenced to ooze from the wounds where the rope had cut into the flesh, the soldier opened his eyes and attempted to raise himself, but with an ejaculation of pain, fell back again. He gazed at Mr. Sukolt and then at Bushy, and in a bewildered manner exclaimed:

"What has happened to me now?"

Bushy was so delighted to hear him speak that she burst into tears and cried:

"I didn't kill him; I didn't kill him!"

"You were going fast to your death, young man," said Mr. Sukolt, as he raised the man to a sitting position. "You are alive now simply because the lariat checked you. Try to stand up and see if you are very much hurt."

Assisted by Bushy and her father, the soldier struggled to his feet, shook himself, then pointed significantly to his left sleeve.

"Oh, Padre, his arm is broken," cried Bushy; " but that is not so bad as a leg, is it ? " She looked up wistfully in the soldier's face; and he laughed, quietly saying, " Quite right, little girl; quite right."

" No, nor a neck," replied Mr. Sukolt, smiling.

Once more the sun seemed to shine, and Bushy, withdrawing her support, stepped a little to one side, threw up her cap, and gave three wild hurrahs to express her joy over having saved the soldier from the ravine.

They all three went then to the edge of the precipice and looked down. There was the poor horse mangled to death on the sharp rocks below. When they returned to the shanty Bushy helped to bind up the broken arm, and the soldier rode behind the child on Ned to Cross Roads.

He was an officer in the Government Army and insisted that Bushy should have a grand Christmas dinner in the camp with the rest of the officers. So Tom drove them all in the wagon over to the camp, where Bushy was made the heroine of the day. The captain learned how she longed for a geography, so he sent to New York, and said that a geography should be included in the next wagon-load of freight sent to them. It was, and Bushy has that book to this very day. She thinks it the finest Christmas present she ever got, and that dinner with the soldiers the grandest dinner she ever ate.

CHAPTER XII

" He is a mean man and I won't ever like him any "——

" Sh ! Don't say anything you will be sorry for, Bushy," said her father, as he looked down upon his little daughter, who stood grabbing at her short hair with both brown hands. Bushy had lost her temper and was racing about the tent in a passion, stamping her feet and digging her heels into the soft dirt floor.

" But Tom teases me awfully, and just now he said I looked like a boy, rode like a boy, talked like a boy, and whistled like a boy. That wasn't all, either; he said I didn't love you, that I was just pretending, and, oh, I could "——Words were not strong enough, so she took up a hammer and gave vent to her feelings by breaking into a fine powder some specimens that the miners had brought in for her father to look at.

Mr. Sukolt stooped down and took both her hands in his. " Was Tom in earnest, do you think ? "

" Maybe he was only teasing, but it makes me so

mad," replied Bushy, and her eyes filled with angry tears.

"Little girl, if you were in danger and I was not here, whom would you run to first for protection?"

Bushy's face flushed, but she unhesitatingly answered: "Why, Tom, of course! He has helped me out lots of times."

"Then there is a lesson for you to learn on gratitude. It begins "——

"Oh, Padre, don't say any more. What a naughty girl I have been to get so mad at Tom for nothing! Dear old Tom! Why, Padre, I love him 'most as much as I do you. I'll go find him and make it all up."

She hurried away singing at the top of her voice as she disappeared behind the tent.

They had arrived at Gold Dust Hill, half way home. Bushy had not made the acquaintance of half the miners at the stopping-place, but a great amount of attention had been paid her already. The men told her to call on them early in the morning before they started to work, and each would show her over his particular cabin. She found Tom feeding the horses, and they started to make the promised morning calls.

"You are the first little girl I have seen since I left mine in the States," said a miner with a cross face and very heavy black eyebrows. His kind, gentle voice would have been a surprise to anybody but Bushy. Everybody was kind to her, and if there was the least bit of tenderness left in a miner's heart, it always expressed itself in some way when Bushy came around.

"Let me see what I can find for you," he said, taking her by the hand and going into the log cabin where he kept the wooden box containing all his treasures. "Ah ! this will do. It will make up into a bright dress for you." He took from the box a roll of red flannel and put it into Bushy's arms. "That we have kept to have handy if any of us had the fever, but it had better be used, I think, to keep the only little girl in camp from getting sick."

Every miner looked about him for something to give Bushy. It seemed to be the only way he could show how glad he was to see a little child once more. "Can you read ? " asked one old shaggy-bearded man who looked, Bushy thought, like a grizzly bear. "I will give you this if you can read," and he brought carefully to view one-half of a weekly story paper. It had part of a continued story in it. "You can imagine how it ends," said the miner. "It is 'most all there."

The story did not interest Bushy half so much as the picture. It was of a woman, who seemed to her to be shaking hands with a man. There was poetry called "Oh, take my love !" under the picture, and it provoked her very much that the lines said not a word about the good-by appropriate to such a farewell scene. " I could write better than that," she said to herself. Bushy knew nothing about love-making.

By the time Bushy had made the rounds of the cabins her arms were loaded down with treasures that for years had been carefully guarded by the men. One who was particularly pleased that Bushy could read, gave her a part of a slate to write her lessons on. " Be very careful," he said, " and break off just as little as possible when you want to write, because every time you take off the splinters to write with, the slate grows smaller, and some day you will have nothing but a splinter left."

They had no slate pencils, and the only way to write on the slate was to break a little piece off the edge.

Bushy returned to her father's tent and spent the rest of the morning examining her rich store of presents. The flannel was bright red, and oh, so soft and fine ! " I will wind it all about me and wear it so," she said. " I will never let Tom cut it." She took one end and pinned it to her blouse, then began to wind and wind and wind until when she came to the other end it had gone two or three times about her neck, and arms, and legs, and waist, making her look like a clown dressed for the circus.

She put on her hat, and, with the paper spread out on her lap, took up her slate and began to write a piece of poetry, trying to put more sense into it than there was in the lines under that strange picture.

"Hallo! What in the world is this?" called Mr. Sukolt, as he came in from his visit to the mine.

"Ha! ha! you don't know me, perhaps," replied the queer red object in the tent door. Bushy stood up and bowed low before him. Bushy was not a pretty little girl—just a common, every-day little girl that all the miners loved better than they did even the gold-dust that they dug so hard for. Tom got a glimpse of her and called to some miners near, and Shanks, always up to a jolly time, threw down his load of tools, and, picking up the banjo, called out: "Attention, gentlemen! We will now present to you Mlle. Bushy Sukolt, famous not so much for her beauty as for being the only child in camp." Bushy made a little mouth at him, and the miners seeing there was a treat in store, threw themselves comfortably on the ground and looked on with smiling faces.

"Mlle. Bushy will now give you the Great Pine Mine jig, in which performance she is the star of the world."

"Bravo!" cried the rough miners, who clapped

their hard hands until the birds stopped singing to wonder over the noise.

Bushy threw kisses to the right and left from the tips of her sunburnt fingers; then as the banjo struck up her favorite tune, " The Irish Washer-woman," she suddenly made a leap into the middle of the tent, and, oh, such dancing ! She went so fast and turned so quick she looked like a great red ball whirling in the air. There were the single shuffle, the double shuffle, then a whirl that carried her into the French style, and from that she suddenly whisked off into the English style of jigging, and just as the miners thought she must be ready to drop with fatigue, she stepped off into the Spanish dance, with its free and swaying motions, so restful after the energetic negro steps that she invariably used for the liveliest strains of music. Her hair seemed to stand on end and dance in the breeze that her rapid movements created. The red flannel began to unwind, and the ends floated out in great flaming streamers, making the dance a veritable serpentine one of modern days. Shanks's fingers fairly flew over the banjo. Faster and faster went Bushy's feet, keeping time not only to the banjo, but to the clapping of hands and boot-tapping, for the miners could no more keep still than the child herself. Some whistled the tune, others hummed it in loud bass voices. One old fellow got so enthusiastic that his " Hi ! hi ! yep !" every now and then lent vim to the whole performance. Finally, when it seemed that every head, hand, and foot could not go faster without dropping off, Bushy made a sudden bound out of the tent into the very arms of Tom, who, with a profound bow, pronounced the entertainment at an end.

" It's not stretchin' a p'int to say that the gal is amazing bright," said a toothless old man who wanted to say something complimentary of Bushy to Mr. Sukolt. " It's worth while bein' a family man," said another, " if you kin own a peach blossom like that." " She is a diamond in the rough, old fellow," spoke up another, as he patted Bushy on the head and gazed admiringly into her flushed hot face. " Better take care of her." " She is a fairy in disguise, and some morning you will wake up and find her gone back to fairyland," remarked the superintendent of the mines. " No wonder the boys have given her all their treasures." He pointed to the slate, the paper, the yards of red flannel, certain nuggets of ore, ball and bat, and a bow and arrow.

" Well, Padre," said she, after the men had disappeared over the hill and the two were alone again in the tent, " this is the loveliest place we ever camped in. The men are awful nice, and I love

every one of them. They said I was a pretty girl
and a nice girl and a jolly girl—they never said a
word about my being like a boy." She wound the
flannel about her again, and with the paper in one
hand and the slate in the other began a hornpipe,
" just to calm me down a little " she said.

"Bushy !" exclaimed her father, and she
stopped short. There was something in his voice
that sounded cold and hard after all the lovely things
she had been hearing. "Bushy, you may go and
call Tom. Tell him to pack, take down the tent,
and hitch the horses."

"Why, Padre, we were to stay here four days.
What is the matter ? I am so happy; everybody
is so good to me and says such nice things." She
sighed and lovingly smoothed down the red flannel,
hugged her slate close to her and slipped the paper
inside her blouse.

"Ah, yes, that is it !" remarked her father in a
most solemn manner, and he ran his hands through
his hair as if in great trouble. "They did say you
were an exceptionally fine girl."

"Yes," murmured Bushy, and her face lighted
with pleasure.

"And they all seem to think you the brightest
little girl in the world."

"Yes, yes," again replied Bushy, as she let
drop her treasures to fall on her knees and

throw her arms about her father. "The big, tall man said he would give everything he had in the world if he could have a little girl just like me." She kissed her father's face all over, pinched his nose and pulled his ears and ended her expressions of joy with a tight hug.

"Well, Bushy, that quite settles it! Hurry and give my orders to Tom; we must get away from here to-night." Her father assumed a sternness that quite awed Bushy.

"But why, Padre?" she half whispered.

"You see, little tomboy, when you become so popular that people believe you without faults, then, Bushy, I tell you it is time to pull up stakes and move on to the next camp."

Bushy's eyes grew wide with astonishment and wonder, and, to make his explanation perfectly plain, her father continued: "You see, child, we must leave while your reputation is good, because"—here her father held her out at arm's length, and she was puzzled more than ever over the merry twinkle in his eyes—"because, you know, they might find you out."

Bushy fell all in a heap in the middle of the tent and covered her flaming face with her hands. Then summoning up all her courage, she jumped to her feet and facing him, said: "Ah, Padre, I have had two good lessons to-day! My! I was fairly walking on air ! Their praise so puffed me up ! They made me forget I had an awful temper; they made me forget I was mad this morning. I really thought I was almost an angel; but I'll not forget this lesson. You have such a funny way of showing me that I am nothing but an every-day little girl after all."

Long years afterward, when Bushy was a woman, she wrote to her father a glowing account of her success in life, telling him how many friends she had gained, how good everybody was, and altogether the letter was full of self-pride and glory, showing she was "walking on air" again. But she was called to earth with startling suddenness when, five days later, a telegram came flashing over the wires, crossing the broad continent with lightning quickness, bearing this message:

"Bushy, dear—I advise you to pull up stakes and move on to the next camp. Padre."

Bushy was back at Great Pine Mine three weeks after Christmas and was settling down to every-day housekeeping again.

"Halloo! What are you two old fellows talking about, that you stop short the minute I come in," said Bushy as she stood in the doorway with her arms loaded down with the fresh pine-boughs she had gathered, with which to make the supper-fire.

"About you, Puss."

The wood tumbled in a heap at her feet. Something in her father's voice told her that all was not well. She put her arms, still fragrant with the perfume of the pine, about his neck, and asked: "Are you ill, Padre? Have I been so long getting the wood for the fire? Oh, I have found a new bird to-night and could not come in till I had learned to sing his song. I fooled him, too. He thought I was his mate calling, and came so close that I caught him. Here he is," she exclaimed as she drew from her breast a frightened bird that gladly escaped through the door when tossed up to amuse her father. "I know that I am a naughty little woman, but you don't mind, do you ?" Then she hugged him tight.

"Look out, chicken," cried Tom, throwing out his long arms and pulling Bushy one side; "don't touch your father's foot; it is hurt."

"Oh, Padre ! why didn't you tell me ? I did hurt you, didn't I ?"

She fell on her knees before him and began to examine the foot.

"A rock in the mine got loosened some way," said Tom, "and as we were coming out to-night it fell, grazing your father's head and mashing his foot. We ought not to complain, Mr. Sukolt, for an inch to the left and it would have been your brains instead of blood we left there."

"Who dressed it ?" inquired Bushy, noticing that it was bandaged.

"I did the best I could, but what I was suggesting was that you go for Shanks, who is at the blacksmith's. He was a surgeon before he came to the mines, and, I think, ought to see this foot; I fear the bones are broken; the flesh is so cut I can't make anything out."

By the time Tom had finished his sentence Bushy was half dressed for the journey. She was sitting on the shanty floor winding strips of coffee-sack about her feet and legs, for the night was bitterly cold. Tom got down to assist her.

" Now, you two are so quick you don't give me time to think," said her father, watching them as they hurried through the preparations. " I wish some one besides Bushy could do this. Look here, Tom, don't you think it possible to manage Ned ? "

" It's no use, Padre, to lose time that way," spoke up Bushy; " he threw Tom yesterday, and you know he acts as if Old Nick himself were in him when any one else gets on his back. It's an awful nuisance, and I'm going to break him of it if I have to break his neck, so there ! but it won't do to try now, with your foot mashed like that. Wrap your shawl about my head, Tom, please, and then tie it in a knot behind. There, that's the way; now I am ready. Do you think I can take the short cut ? "

" Oh, how the snow blows ! " exclaimed Mr. Sukolt. " I don't think it wise, Bushy; the bridge at the ravine might be snowed over. Tom, come here quick and loosen the bandage. I fear I cannot stand the pain, it "——

Mr. Sukolt bent over, tried to move his foot, and fainted.

" Don't leave him, Tom," screamed Bushy. " I can saddle Ned myself," and, giving one tearful look at her father, she took from the wall Ned's bridle and went out.

At last all was ready; buckling about her waist

the belt that carried two revolvers, and drawing on her thick mitts, she jumped on Ned and away they went.

Through the cold wind and blinding snow they ran, up one hill, down another—Ned knew the way to the blacksmith's and so did Bushy. There was no fear. On, on they sped, until they came to the point where she must take the short cut or the longer route.

" I'll do it," said Bushy aloud—she often talked to Ned as if he were a boy companion. " We'll make an hour by going this way, so on with you, old fellow, and no falls, no stumbles, for we can't afford any accidents to-night, with the Padre lying so white and still in the shanty."

Ned shortened his long strides and began to pick his way over a snow-drift, when in the quiet that fell about them a faint bark, way, way off in the distance was heard. Ned stood stock still, raised both ears straight up, turned his head toward the west, then toward the east, and listened. Bushy's heart beat so loud she could hear it go thump, thump, against her ribs.

" Padre mio ! not wolves, not wolves ! " she murmured. " Oh, Ned, Ned, you can never take me through a pack of wolves ! " Another bark, and another and another came more distinctly to their ears. Ned gave one snort and plunged forward so suddenly he almost unseated Bushy, but she grabbed the pommel, regained a firm seat, took up the reins and cried: " Go it, Ned ! we are in for a race for life or death. On with you ! but if you stumble you will never have Bushy to ride you any more."

There was no need to urge Ned; he was running as fast as he could.

" If they come in sight I'll try to shoot the head one; it always makes a break in their running, for they are a cowardly lot without a leader," thought Bushy.

Finally Ned struck a long stretch of road that circled a mountain.

" Now they will come in sight before we get around this," thought Bushy, and so they did. Nearer and nearer came the pack, with their fiendish yelling and howling that frightened poor Ned until he became almost unmanageable.

" Whoa ! whoa ! Ned. They are gaining on us. I've got to kill one or we are lost. Whoa ! there's a good fellow ! Whoa ! "

Bushy braced herself well, as Ned slackened into a steady run without the irregular strides he made in his wild dash; then, turning and taking aim, she held on to the back of the saddle with her left hand, and when the wolves gained so that they were in range of her revolver she fired.

I have told you before that Bushy was a good shot, and this time her aim was not false; the leader of the pack fell, and the others went tumbling over him. It caused a halt, as Bushy had thought it would. The greedy animals, imagining that something, perhaps Bushy herself, had tumbled off for their hungry mouths to devour, made a decided halt. Bushy fired again and killed a second, which Tom afterward told her was a very foolish thing to do. She might need her ammunition, he said, and it was only a waste to kill two at one halt, when there was no possible hope of ever killing them all.

Ned needed but one word of encouragement to stretch his legs again to their utmost. But soon came another danger in the form of a broken bridge ahead of them. You remember Mr. Sukolt mentioned the bridge over the ravine. It was not drifted over, as he feared it would be, but gone; and Ned was going at a madder speed then ever and the wolves were barking louder and were quite close.

Bushy saw that of the two evils she must select the lesser, and that was to try to make Ned jump the fissure. There was no time to check Ned if she wanted to, and if she could have done it it would be to throw the two in the teeth of the starving animals already at their heels. It seemed death, try either way, but she screamed: " Oh, Ned, Ned, Ned, jump, jump for Padre's sake, jump!" She gave him one quick stroke with her bare hand—she had lost her mittens—and Ned at the word "jump" pricked up his ears and looked about, for he knew what that meant. He had jumped many a wide place for Bushy before, but nothing like this. He saw the space and gave a wild long leap that landed him on the other side, but on the very edge, and there he balanced for a minute, as if he were going to the bottom after all.

I don't know how it happened, but Bushy swung off and pulled hard on the bridle and some way helped Ned keep his footing, and they were saved. I don't suppose it could ever be done again, and I am sure Bushy would never attempt it. The new leader of the band of wolves went headlong into the opening and down to the very bottom, where he was dashed to pieces. The others stopped on the edge and howled. Bushy, with half-frozen hands, reached the blacksmith's, and, leaving Ned there—for he was badly sprained—she took a new horse and, joined by Shanks, went the long way back to Great Pine Mine.

Bushy's mad run had made the time much shorter than it would have been otherwise, so Shanks was with Mr. Sukolt in time to prevent any very bad results from the delay in setting the foot.

"OH, NED, NED, NED, JUMP, JUMP FOR PADRE'S SAKE, JUMP!"

The miners to this day tell about Bushy's ride, and say General Putnam's break-neck plunge down the rocks with the British after him was nothing compared to Bushy's leap with the pack of howling wolves at her heels.

CHAPTER XIV

"I know what I will do, I will make biscuits for supper—biscuits like Tom makes," said Bushy one morning as she gazed at a sack of flour that had cost Mr. Sukolt just one dollar a pound.

It was a rare thing to have flour in the camp. Everything had to be brought so far in wagons that by the time freight reached these little out-of-the-way stations, flour cost more than many of the miners could pay. This sack had arrived after all the men had left for the mine.

"I'll surprise them," thought Bushy, and she clapped her hands in delight. She ran out to see how the shadows stood, and concluded that there was just time to make an ovenful of biscuits if she hurried. Mr. Sukolt had a watch, but he took that with him, and Bushy could only guess at the time by the shadows. She had taken a stick, driven it into the ground and marked the place where the shadow fell at noon, had made another mark for three o'clock, and a third to indicate the hour to get supper for the men. Generally Tom got the meals, but Bushy felt she was old enough to run the house.

"I'll take the new tin pan and mix the bread in that," murmured Bushy as she flew about, happy in planning this great treat for the men. "Now for the sack!" She took a case-knife and sawed away for some time before she could cut the cords and dip down into the beautiful soft white flour.

"Oh, how lovely!" she cried, sinking both hands to the wrists. "I wonder if this is what the ladies that the stories tell about put on their faces? I'll try it." Out came her hands and almost a dollar's worth of the flour clung to her arms and fingers. It took but a minute to spread the powdered stuff all over her face, quite covering her red checks and getting it into her hair, so that she looked like a story-book ghost.

"I suppose I ought to put some on my neck, too, or I won't be all alike. I don't want to look like crazy Indians, spotted all over. Oh! the dish-pan—the bright, new one!" she cried, and running to the table turned the pan bottom up and gazed down in admiration upon what she saw reflected there.

"I guess I must put more on my neck and arms, and make it like it is on my face." She worked hard rubbing in the flour, until her spectral appearance would have frightened the wits out of any-

body coming suddenly upon her in the dim light.
Of course, Bushy could not see how dreadfully
white she was by looking at the imperfect reflec-
tion of the dish-pan. She gave a sigh of satisfaction,
whitened her arms way above the elbows, and then
proceeded to make the biscuits.

"Let me see. I put in the flour first, and then
the water, and then the salt, and what else ?" She
could not remember, although she felt there was
another something. She stirred the water and
added the flour until it grew too stiff, and then
with water it suddenly grew too thin, and thus in
balancing it up she found her pan was quite full of
dough by the time that she could knead it.

"What a pity I made so much ! I wonder why
the water was always too much for the flour, and
when I put in the flour it was always too much for
the water. I suppose Tom manages better, for I
never saw so much dough in all my life."

But nothing could discourage Bushy. "I will
treat all the men in the camp. Padre won't mind
this once." Thus thinking, and kneading, and trying first one side of the table and then the other,
rolling first one-half of the dough and folding it
into the other, then mixing it all in and sprinkling
it with dry flour to keep it from sticking to her
fingers, she got it so she could cut out beautiful
hunks with the tin cup that had no handle. It was

SHE GAZED DOWN IN ADMIRATION UPON WHAT SHE SAW REFLECTED
THERE.

lots of fun to put the cup over the dough and then bear down with all her might and feel it cut through with a fluff and a puff, ofttimes sending the dry flour into her eyes and nose.

"My, what a lot of biscuits!" she cried, as dozens were placed side by side in a row about the table. Bushy was all excitement. Her hands grew very tired making each biscuit as round as she could, a great deal as she would roll a snowball. When her arms grew weary she rolled the balls on the rough table, not noticing that now and then the soft dough picked up a pine splinter.

What Bushy called the oven was an iron arrangement something like a skillet, but larger and with a heavy iron cover. This she placed over a great mass of red coals, and when it got hot took off the cover and put in the first twelve biscuits.

"I must have these extra fine," she said, "so I'll cover the lid with coals as Tom does and have the biscuits lovely and brown."

Her delight was quite hilarious when she took off the lid later and saw a dozen of the most beautiful looking biscuits that ever greeted her eyes. For fear of injuring them she lifted out each one with the dish towel and placed it in a deep pan to keep warm till the men should come. Her joy found vent in an occasional war-whoop or a handspring that threatened the overturning of the pan of biscuits every time; but how could she keep still when her heart was so full of the good time she had arranged for the men?

The second pan of biscuits had been placed on the table, the coffee had been made, some slices of deer meat had been broiled as daintily as the best of cooks could have done it, and supper was quite ready when Mr. Sukolt and Tom and Shanks turned the corner and entered on the scene.

"Whew! how good this smells!" cried all three together. Mr. Sukolt dumped into one corner of the tent a lot of specimens of gold-bearing quartz. Tom threw down his tools and went out to wash his face, and Shanks, seeing supper was quite ready, said he saw nothing for him to do, so he would take off his heavy miner's boots and put on moccasins to be comfortable while he ate.

"But where is Bushy?" said Mr. Sukolt, looking all about the tent. "What is the matter with you, Bushy? Are you back there?" he asked, shaking the blanket that made a partition between the dining-room and Bushy's sleeping apartment.

"Nothing is the matter with me, Padre; but when I come out I want you to treat me as I should be treated."

Mr. Sukolt did not catch what she said, for his anxiety was gone when he heard her voice, and after washing his face and hands he joined the other two men at the table and began to eat.

"Ahem! ahem!" was the slight noise that made all three turn their faces toward the blanket, and astonished men they were! With stately step Bushy sallied forth from her dressing-room. It was the white face that so startled the men. The dress, of course was queer, but those pallid features made her eyes seem far back in her head, and as black as dead coals, and her hair, standing straight on end, was filled with flour and dough. Her dress represented, as near as Bushy could make it, the dress in the picture in the weekly paper that the miner had given her. The red flannel trailed behind her in five strips, which were run through her belt and left to flow in graceful folds. Her buckskin jacket had been discarded, and an old one that Tom had declared only good enough for Indians she had cut down to represent the low silk bodice of the woman in the picture. A red blanket was pinned about her for the dress skirt, and a pistol belt, to which she had suspended a cow-boy's whip and a small chain to which she had attached an Indian beaded bag and an arrow or two, represented the Egyptian girdle worn by the same lady. Two strands of Indian beads passed as bracelets about her floury arms.

"Great Scott!" exclaimed Tom, "are you the

daughter of the man in the moon? You don't seem to like our country—you look scared."

Bushy had forgotten all about her white face, and, not knowing just how funny she looked, was inclined to be offended, when Tom burst out in roars of laughter.

"My days in heaven, Bushy!" cried Shanks stepping forward, "why, you "——

"I pray you to be seated, gentlemen. It behooves me to proclaim that you are most welcome," said Bushy, giving what she thought was a queenly bow, and motioning for them to proceed with their dinner. Then, in her natural voice, she added: "I don't see why you sat down and spoiled the whole thing before I could get in."

"Boys, you are both as stupid as Rover," cried Mr. Sukolt, rising and with great courtesy escorting the little lady to her place at the table. "We have here the Queen of the Mountains, and we are her guests. If you don't know your place, boys, you will have to get out, that's all!"

"And then you would miss the biscuits, which would serve you right," remarked Bushy, taking her seat with great difficulty.

"What! biscuits? Ah, now we understand." A smile flitted over all the faces, and the paleness of Bushy was explained. "The flour has come and we are to be entertained by the Queen of the

Mountains in regal fashion ! Ha, ha, I'll take some, if you please," said Tom, rubbing his hands in glee. " Biscuits, just think of it ! biscuits for supper ! "

" I think you should say dinner, Tom," said Bushy in her fine-lady voice. " You—ah—you—ah, have never been in the queen's palace before, have you, Tom. Poor fellow, you don't know what good things are ! "

Tom took a biscuit. So did Shanks, and then Mr. Sukolt reached his hand out for one. Bushy's face beamed as well as it could through the thick layer of flour. " I knew you boys would like a treat," said she, " and I have blistered my hands rolling the bread. It is awfully hard to do it, isn't it, Tom ? "

Tom's face wore an odd expression which no one could then understand, yet he answered: " Yes, it isn't everybody who can make bread. Biscuits especially are a scientific production. Bushy is to be congratulated."

Bushy was so excited over the rôle she was play-ing that she did not touch the biscuits herself, but in a very lady-like manner waited on table, poured the coffee, and used all the big words she could re-member that were in the unfinished story in the weekly story paper.

" I trust your family is well, Mr. Shanks. Will you have roast chicken, lamb, or deer meat ? "

"Deer meat, if you please," said Shanks, timidly. "I always was rather partial to game." He emphasized the word game and winked at Tom.

"What do you mean by that?" cried Bushy, her dignity all gone in a minute when she saw some fun afloat. She leaned back and glanced first at her father, who had eaten heartily of everything except the biscuits. Tom had three in a row in front of his plate and not one touched. Shanks reached over and was trying to load his revolver with one.

"I must say that this infinitely charms me. What concealest thou from me, Padre? Thine eyes are as merry as those of my subjects. What is passing in the thoughts of This and This?" she pointed disdainfully first at Tom and then at Shanks.

"Something is amiss, I fear, with the biscuits. Just order the servant to put aside two for me to assay to-morrow," answered Mr. Sukolt, mischievously, in the high-toned voice of the hostess.

"Ah, they were the apple of mine eye—they dazzled my senses with their brown beauty as—as "——

"Don't get stuck on a word now, Bushy, when you have done so well so far," cried Tom as he lifted a hammer and brought it down with the full strength of his mighty arm upon a brown biscuit that he had placed on the stone at the cabin door.

"Tom, Tom," she cried, "tell me something "——

" I'll tell you, Bushy, that they are excellent coffee biscuits, and I couldn't have made better. See, I have filled my cup with two and the third will follow." And Tom, in the goodness of his heart, ate the three biscuits without flinching.

"You dear old man ! " cried Bushy, rushing about the table in anything but a queenly fashion, and fairly covering him with flour from her face and arms, "you deserve to be knighted for this. I'll proclaim you Sir Tom for ever and ever. Amen ! "

Late in the night, after everybody had been in bed and asleep several hours, Mr. Sukolt was startled by a soft hand on his face, and hearing the words, " Say, Padre, I've been wondering and wondering what I left out, and it has just come to me." She leaned over, and when her mouth touched his ear she whispered low, so Tom could not hear, " It was baking powder; and I just want you to tell Tom and Shanks to-morrow that I am not so stupid as I seem."

On the promise that her father would take her part next morning Bushy went to her hammock again and slept soundly the rest of the night. Her little heart would have been much more troubled, however, had she realized that her first biscuit-making had cost her father something like $10 for flour.

CHAPTER XV

" Don't do it, Tom. I know you can't do it," said Bushy in a sharp, excited voice. Indians had suddenly appeared near the cabin and the two were alone inside. The moment was a critical one.

She tried to pull him away from the door by catching his coat and holding on with all her might, but he gently unclasped her fingers and looking at her seriously said: " Now, Bushy, you must not show the white feather just when your courage is needed most." Bushy nodded her head as much as to say she would be brave, yet she was so frightened she could not talk.

" You know where you hid from me that day we played hide and seek ? Do you remember how you frightened us all because we couldn't find you ? Well you must get into that same place, and I will try to reach the mine by the way of the ravine and bring back help. If I stay here and fight alone we shall both be killed, and there is some hope of our coming out all right if you do as I tell you."

Tom gave her a revolver and a box of ammunition, and put into her pocket a piece of bread, then opening the back door of the shanty he said: "There! Like a good, dear girl, crawl on your hands and knees until you get to the rock, then squeeze into the crevice and pull the tree-trunk over it as you did before. I will go to the front and attract the attention of the Indians by opening the door, and pick off any one of them who may try to come down the hill."

Bushy said: "Oh, Tom, I know you will never reach the mine." Then throwing herself flat on the ground she crawled through the tall weeds and grass that grew between the shanty and the huge rock where she was going to hide herself.

One day when she had been playing on the mountain-side the ground had given way and she had sunk down into a hole that was made by a big rock that had split in two. Over the opening had grown a tree, and its roots had spread quite over the hole, and no one would have ever discovered that the rock was divided had not the tree been struck by lightning and died.

Bushy had spent one whole day in cleaning out what she afterward called her cave, and on the day that Tom spoke of she had frightened all the miners by hiding there just for fun. Into this hole she now crawled and pulled the dead trunk over so that no one could see her without moving the tree.

Tom meant to try to crawl down into the ravine,

then take to his heels and run for the mine, where all the men were at work.

There had been no Indian trouble for a long time, and nobody had expected this one. It was a great surprise to Tom and Bushy to hear a shot early in the morning, and on going to the door to get an arrow so close that it went through Tom's hat.

Tom crawled down the little incline toward the ravine until he reached a place where he had to come in full sight of the Indians because there was no grass to hide him. Bushy watched him from her cave. Her heart beat and her hand shook.

"He will not get through, I know!" and her lips grew white with fear, but her eyes were ever fixed on Tom, and her revolver was raised ready to shoot.

"He is half way through," she said to herself. "Now he is almost over. Oh, dear, oh, dear, why can't he hurry? Why don't some one come? What will I do if he gets hurt?" There came a swish, swish in the air, and an arrow buried itself in Tom's side, making him fall over in a heap on the ground.

"Tom! Tom!" she screamed, and was trying to push away the tree when a big Indian bounded into sight. On reaching Tom he poked him with his foot, then turned him over, and grunted something that brought three redmen to his side.

"He is killed," sobbed Bushy in her retreat, "and I can never see him any more. He is dead, like Pete, and will never come back nights with the Padre again. Poor Tom! Poor Tom!" she wailed, and it is a wonder that the Indians did not hear her.

One of the tallest, who had his head dressed in bright feathers and his blanket trimmed with fringe, took up a sharp knife and began to scalp Tom. Bushy did not cry any more. All her sorrow was forgotten in her rage. She forgot there was danger in making her place of hiding known. The Indians were in range of her revolver, and she knew that she could kill them; this is the way she reasoned:

"There are only four. I will try and kill them all before they find out where I am. If any more come I will keep as still as a mouse and they will think me some man who has got frightened and run away, for I know they will not find this place." She peeped through the roots of the old tree and took aim. Just as the Indian lifted the hair, Bushy shot him, and he fell on his face across Tom's body.

Bushy did not hesitate an instant, and before the others had even looked up she killed the second; then the third fell, with a yell that sent the fourth on a jump up the hill out of Bushy's sight.

"Now, that's too bad," thought Bushy. "He

will bring a lot more and I can't kill them all."
Her face was very hard and drawn, and she looked
like a little old woman. She was very white but
she did not tremble any more; she only crouched
back into the crevice and watched. Now she reloaded and was prepared for more Indians. Bushy
could reload quicker than any of the men at the
camp.

Nobody came. Noontime passed and no one
visited the shanty. "Somebody will surely come
to see why we do not take over lunch to the men,"
thought Bushy, "and he may get killed, too."
Her heart ached with fright, and though it was a
very warm day she shivered and shook with the
cold. The rock was like ice, and the old tree kept
out even the light.

Ah, what was that ! Some one talking. She
peeped out and saw something moving where she
thought only a heap of dead men lay. A head was
lifted and Bushy took aim, but before she fired she
screamed: "Tom, is that you ? Tom, answer if it
is you, because if you don't I am going to fire."

"Don't shoot," he said; then fell back on the
ground and moaned.

"Can I come out, Tom ? "

Only a moan was the reply.

" I'll go to him and pull that old Indian off him,"
said Bushy, pushing aside the tree, but jumping

BUSHY SHOT HIM, AND HE FELL ON HIS FACE ACROSS TOM'S BODY.

immediately back out of sight. Another of the heap had moved.

" Yes, it's an Indian. His head is covered with feathers," said Bushy. " I'll drop him, or he will finish Tom. Ugh ! it makes me feel so queer and things get so black and "——

She aimed at the Indian, who was crawling slowly toward Tom, as he lay stretched out in the hot sun that had beaten on him for over three hours.

Her shot proved fatal, for with a yell the Indian gave a leap and fell to one side of Tom, who seemed to come to himself a little. He rose up again and tried to push the Indian's body away. " Oh, boys, give me some water ! I am dying for water !" he cried, and fell back in a faint.

Stealthily Bushy slipped out and into the shanty. With a small tin bucket filled with water and carry- ing a towel she soon appeared again and crawled through the grass, just as Tom had done, until she reached him. Then she washed his face, pulled the Indian away from him, gave him all he could drink, and, pouring water on the towel she bound it about his poor scalped head and left him to hide again in the cave. He did not know her, for once he said: " Give me water, boys; just water !" Bushy waited another hour. Then she heard a breaking in the branches on the other side of the shanty.

Feeling that something must have happened,

Mr. Sukolt and four of the men had started from the mine at one o'clock to see why Tom and Bushy had not appeared with the lunch.

The Indian who had been wounded and had fallen near the house, on seeing them come, leaped wildly around the shanty and leaned up against the very rock that Bushy was hid in. She scarcely dared to breathe for fear he would hear her. He had taken a position on the wrong side for Bushy to see him through the hole from which she had fired all the shots. In a second, however, she heard the whizzing of an arrow. She did not know at whom it was aimed. It was replied to with four rifle shots. Suddenly the Indian fell a dead weight on the log above her head.

"Padre! Padre! I am all right!" she cried, thinking he must be near. "I am in the rock."

It did not take long for four pairs of hands to throw the Indian down the ravine and unearth Bushy and her revolver.

"Where is Tom?" they asked. "Where is Tom?"

"Over there," was all she said, for her lips trembled so that she could not talk. Bushy always did well till everything was over; then she got "dizzy and shaky in her knees," as she expressed it.

"Poor fellow, you are 'most done up this time," they exclaimed. But Shanks, who was always the doctor, said he would live, and all because Bushy had had the courage to shoot at the right time, and bathe his head and give him the water. He was sick a long time. After his head got well he wore a close-fitting cap, because no hair, of course, grew to cover it up. Shanks said the Indian had been very skilful in the scalping, because he had not cut a hair's breadth deeper than was necessary to get the crown that the Indians like to hang on the belt.

"I did mind you, Tom," said Bushy one day, when he was pulling his cap down to cover his bald head. " But if you had minded me, Tom, we could have killed them from the shanty, 'cause there were only four, after all."

" Bushy," said her father, " Tom lost his scalp in trying to save you, and "——

" There, don't," pleaded Tom, taking Bushy in his arms as she burst into tears. " I wonder if any other man can say he wears his scalp in his trunk as I do." He nodded toward his clothes-box, where he had carefully put away the scalp as it had been rescued from the hands of the dead Indian.

Bushy dried her eyes and joined the laugh on Tom, who worshipped the ground little Bushy walked on. And his love was not lessened by noticing that her tears always overflowed if any one mentioned how he lost his scalp for her.

CHAPTER XVI

" I'll give you the finest set of gold jewelry I can find if you beat me killing Rocky Mountain sheep," said Tom to Bushy one day the following summer, when she was boasting that she had killed almost as many as he, and would have beaten him long ago if she had had the same opportunities.

" Oh, it's safe enough to say that," exclaimed Bushy; " for where can you find jewelry out here ? How many have you killed in your life, Tom ? "

" Ten, counting the little one that I brought down last week."

" Why, I've killed just that many, too," cried Bushy, clapping her hands. " I'm even with you. I'll wager I kill the next one. Let me see, I'll give you "——

" I'll bet you that set of jewelry if I ever live to go East again," interrupted Tom, taking hold of Bushy's hands and spinning her about like a top. " I'll bet you the whole set of pretty things—say a necklace like the lady in the picture wears, earrings and brooch, and, yes, and a pendant to show off your neck when in full dress as you were when you played Queen of the Mountains. I'll bet you all that against "——

"Make it something that I shall have to buy when I go to the big city, too, Tom," exclaimed Bushy, stopping long enough in her whirling to throw her arms about him and peep up coyly into his face. "Let it be a beautiful wig of curly black hair, with just a tiny bit of gray in it like your dear old head used to wear." There was a suspicion of a tremble in her voice and the eyes grew dangerously moist, threatening a shower of tears if she kept long on the subject.

"All right," cried Tom, and he called out to Shanks and Mr. Sukolt that they must be witnesses to the bet.

"You had better begin to save the gold-dust to-day," remarked Shanks to Bushy as he cleaned away at his rifle. "Tom said only yesterday that he knew where there were mountain sheep, and he will slip out and bring one in before you even think of cleaning your gun. There is nothing so shy as the mountain sheep or big-horn, and it's just luck on your part, Bushy, that you killed so many. Tom knows their tricks. I'll bet you a year's schooling in any place you like that Tom'll come out ahead."

Bushy called the big-horn and mountain goats all sheep. They are almost alike, have recurved horns, sheep-like noses, with a short furry under coat and the upper coat long and shaggy. They are the most difficult to get of all the animals in North America. The herds were even at that time few, and they lived high up in the mountains, taking refuge where often Rover could not follow.

"Since we need meat, suppose you and Bushy try to-day for the goat," said Mr. Sukolt, just before shouldering his tools for a trip to the mine. "Take Rover along with you and bring in anything you can find." So it was arranged. Tom and Bushy were soon climbing the peaks and looking down hundreds of feet into the chasms. They went through caverns and crossed ravines; they made bridges of tree-trunks and climbed over rocks that were so steep that they could not keep from falling except by taking off their shoes and clinging to the surface in their stocking feet. Finally they reached a place high in the cliffs where Tom said a herd of goats lived. Just below was a deep gorge, through which a torrent of water madly plunged, at last spreading out into a calm and glistening stream in the valley below.

"There they are," cried Bushy, suddenly, but Tom was looking down the deep ravine and did not hear. Bushy's eyes danced, for she thought she could climb behind one of the bowlders and while Tom was searching below, perhaps head off the herd and get a good shot. When the sheep bounded down the mountain-side, she fairly hugged herself with delight that Tom was going directly away from the herd. " They are not more than fifty feet from me," cried Bushy to herself. Softly, softly she crawled forward. Oh, how steep it was ! She must scale one of those smooth red rocks. By going around it she would surely miss getting a shot, but if she could only climb to the top of it and surprise them, her bet would be won.

Up, up she went, with her eyes watching both sides, and her rifle in hand ready to fire on short notice. When almost at the top, she grew careless and slipped. Ah, that was dangerous ! " Oh, Tom, I am falling," she cried, but Tom was out of hearing, and down she rolled over and over, bumpity bump to the very bottom, where a scraggly tree which had worked its way through a crack in the rock caught her, and with its dry branches held her fast.

" Well, I'm much obliged to you, Mr. Tree," said Bushy, as she scrambled to her feet and looked down the precipice where she would surely have fallen several hundred feet had not her buckskin blouse been clutched by the queer-looking pine-branch.

She was a little scratched but not badly hurt. She took off her stockings, as she should have done in the first place, and began the ascent again. She found the rifle half way up, where she had dropped it when trying to get a hold on the rock to check her fall. Bushy succeeded in reaching a small pine-tree near the top, and there, stretched at full length, she clung to its trunk, drew herself to the very edge and looked over.

The herd was within rifle range, and Bushy grew so excited that she almost had a second tumble. She fired before she was really in a steady position. The rifle bar struck against the edge of the rock and the bullet was sent way to the left of where she had intended it should go. She frightened the sheep, lost her hold, and went sliding way to the bottom of the steep rock again. It was very easy to slide down safely when the sliding was not unexpected, for she spread her arms out and slipped slowly to a point where she could get a good foothold, then with rifle in her right hand she crawled along the very edge of the precipice, hoping to intercept some of the sheep as they would bound by. These sheep are very queer animals. They have such great horns and the head is so well protected with thick wool, too, that they can jump from place to place and fall on their horns, folding their front feet up close to their body, quite hiding and protecting them in the thick woolly coat they wear. Bushy knew they could easily descend, even though she could not.

She passed the steep place and reached a spot

where the mountain sloped more gently. "Ah, there is where they will go by," she said, and planting her feet against the root of a tree that looked as if it had spent the greater part of its life trying to keep from sliding down hill, she reloaded, raised her rifle to her shoulder and waited. A minute later a shout from Tom and wild barking from Rover as they appeared on the grade one hundred feet below, sent the sheep dashing about in a violent flurry, and, as Bushy had anticipated, they crossed her path not fifty feet away. They were wild with fright, and seemed to fairly fly down the precipice, falling with a thump and a bump from one steep place to another. She waited until one beautiful specimen leaped from the rock above her as if to land on a kind of shelf below.

"Those are the horns for me," she said, and fired when the sheep was in mid-air. The bullet went straight, and the poor fellow fell not far from where Tom and Rover stood watching below. The fall sent his body bouncing down, until Tom and Bushy felt their hearts sink with fear that it would land in some of the gloomy dark gorges where they could never get it.

"You have won," cried Tom, and he took off his cap and waved it and hallooed with joy. He seemed to rejoice that he had lost, though he really and truly meant to win if he could.

"Not yet," answered Bushy from her high position on the great red-rock slide. "The Padre said we must have a steak, and Shanks asked for the horns."

"Come down," yelled Tom; "we will try and find him."

By sliding and jumping and rolling, Bushy finally reached Tom and Rover, and then, after she had put on her stockings and moccasins, slowly and carefully they descended.

When they were about to give up the hunt they came plump upon the sheep's soft body all in a heap where the horns had checked it by catching on to some low brush.

Tom laughed and so did Bushy. They were as happy as two little children over her success. By the aid of the lariat the sheep was lowered down the steepest places, and at other times they bound it on to two sticks and dragged it over the rough rocks without tearing the skin the least bit. It took them four hours to reach the foot of the mountains and get into the path that led directly without obstruction into the camp.

"Now, Tom, carry him," said Bushy, "and I will take the firearms and ropes." So Tom, with Bushy's help, got the body thrown across his shoulders, and grasping the fore-feet in one hand and the hind-feet in the other he bravely got over the quarter of a

"THOSE ARE THE HORNS FOR ME," SHE SAID, AND FIRED WHEN THE SHEEP WAS IN MID-AIR.

mile. He threw the sheep down before Mr. Sukolt and Shanks with the exclamation, " You are in for it, boys. Bushy has won the day. She goes to school, Shanks, at your expense for a year."

Mr. Sukolt cried, " Bravo for the Queen of the Mountains ! Tom, you must be a ninny to have let her beat you."

" I am," he said, " my back is almost broken and my head feels balder than ever. No wig, no glory, and out of pocket a lot of gold-dust for jewelry." His pretended disappointment set them all laughing, and the rest of the evening was spent in preparing the skin for mounting, eating delicious steak at supper, and listening to Bushy's account of how she allowed Tom to go directly away from the sheep while she advanced toward them. Tom didn't mind a joke at his own expense and laughed as heartily as the rest over his discomfiture.

CHAPTER XVII

" The supply-wagons are ten days late," said Mr. Sukolt, anxiously; " and I am beginning to grow uneasy, for we are getting out of everything to eat, as well as powder and fuse for the mine."

Mr. Sukolt, Shanks, and Tom were talking the matter over one night after they had returned from the mine, and had half concluded that if the wagons did not make their appearance by the next evening somebody ought to go down to the fort for news of them.

" It might be," said Shanks, " that the Indians have overtaken the freight teams, killed the teamsters and carried off the mules and supplies."

" Wal, there ain't no use waitin'; a feller can't work without he's got grub that'll stick to his ribs." spoke up Tom. Shanks suggested, however, that they hang on until the last of the week and then take a load of ore with them to the valley. It was then Monday evening.

" I guess you are right, Tom," Shanks laughingly admitted. " I feel myself as if I'd forgotten how potatoes taste, and if you don't go soon, I'll forget how they look."

"I think you had better go," said Mr. Sukolt, turning to Shanks, "because, should there be need of a doctor's service, you know what to do."

"Oh, please hurry and go," chimed in Bushy, who was helping her father clean and polish his old musket and listening to what was said with the interest she always paid to subjects pertaining to the welfare of the camp. "I'm so tired, too, eating bear and johnny-cake all the time. I wish we had some flour so Tom could give us some more of those biscuits that are so good with molasses."

The men all laughed as they gazed on Bushy's eager face, and her father declared that Shanks should go in the morning if she was as hungry as she looked at that moment.

"Oh, no, Padre, I didn't mean to be so selfish as that sounded," she cried, as she kissed his bronze cheek and gave him a bearish hug. "I can eat what the rest eat; but I was so afraid that you were going to wait till the last of the week, and there is only the tiniest bit of molasses in the keg, and you men folks won't eat johnny-cake or flapjacks without it."

The next day wore slowly away. The hours seemed very long indeed to Bushy, who was longing for the good things in the wagons that were expected. Mr. Sukolt went out a dozen times to a high point on the mountain-side that overlooked the winding road. He swept the landscape far and near with a powerful field-glass, but he could see no signs of the freight wagons. So Shanks started for the fort early the next morning. It would take him four days to make the trip and perhaps longer, for it was agreed that if he did not meet the wagons he was to get a few supplies from the fort. In that case he would have to walk and pack the things on his pony.

Work was slack at the mine, for they were entirely out of blasting powder by this time, so when Bushy suddenly broke into her game of " cat's cradle " with Tom, and cried: " Padre, Padre, let's go berrying ! " her father and Tom gladly assented. Buckets were soon ready, and Ned was saddled so that Bushy could ride. It was four miles up the gulch to where the berries grew. They were wild raspberries of a beautiful luscious red, which no tame raspberry can equal in flavor. They grow on the steepest mountains, choosing to push their hardy roots under great rocks and nestling close to fallen timbers, as if trying to hide themselves altogether.

The prickly, dwarfed bushes were bending almost to the ground beneath their load of fruit. Bushy could scarcely wait to tie Ned, she was so eager to be picking.

"Now, Bushy, you stay here by Ned and pick in this patch, and Tom and I will go farther up," said Mr. Sukolt, as he handed her two small tin pails.

"All right," said Bushy; "I'll race both of you, and let's see who gets a pailful first."

She began very well and picked hard for five minutes, but then forgot all about the race, and a great many more berries found their way into her pretty mouth than into the pail. She picked on for perhaps an hour, but even then one pail was still empty, and the other only half full. She had forgotten all about her father and Tom, she was so interested in crushing the largest and plumpest berries between her lips, when all at once she was startled by a great snort from Ned.

Springing to her feet she looked wildly around. Ned was pulling at his halter, rearing and plunging, snorting and trembling. His eyes seemed to be starting from their sockets. Bushy's heart was beating fast, and something seemed to be choking her. In a soothing tone she called: "Whoa, Ned! whoa, old boy! nothing is going to hurt you."

She had just started toward him when suddenly her heart stood still and she stopped, for over the top of a bowlder she saw two gleaming eyes fastened upon her. For a second they disappeared, but were soon followed by a huge dark-brown bear. He came shambling toward her, his wicked white teeth gleaming in his open jaws. He was grunting with satisfaction, like a pig expecting a good dinner.

Bushy stood as if she had been turned to stone; her face was as white as the snow that covered the tops of the tall mountain peaks. All this time poor Ned, who was tied not more than a dozen yards away, had been trembling in every muscle. It seemed as if he appreciated Bushy's danger, and he stretched his long neck as far as he could in her direction and opened his mouth wide as if he wanted to snatch her from the path of the dreaded animal. At last he could bear his suffering no longer, and his agony found vent in a peculiar cry which sounded much like a human shriek.

This drew the bear's attention away from Bushy. He uttered an angry growl and raised himself upon his haunches, the hair about his head and neck standing erect. He looked steadily at Ned a few seconds. His angry eyes glowed like coals and his teeth snapped together after every growl. It seemed to Bushy that in the twinkling of an eye the bear had covered the distance between him and Ned, but he had not been quicker than Bushy herself.

The little girl, who had been unable to move in her own defence, was all courage when she saw her poor horse in danger. Quickly reaching for the revolver which hung by her side, she fired rapidly three shots at the bear. One of the bullets evidently took effect and wounded him. This only served to enrage the bear still more. Ned gave a wild leap and broke his halter, but it was too late. The bear had reached him, and there ensued a sight that Bushy will never forget to her dying day. The savage growls of the bear, poor Ned's pitiful neighs and cries of agony as the cruel claws tore through his flesh—ah, she hears them yet !

Bushy ran up quite close to the struggling animals, never thinking of the danger to herself, and kept on firing at the bear. Mr. Sukolt came tearing down the mountain-side, for he had heard the reports of the revolver, and reached the scene just as the bear fell from Ned's back, mortally wounded.

" Keep away, keep away, Bushy ! Don't go near him; he may tear you to pieces even if he is dying," screamed her father, as he came in sight and saw her danger.

" Hurry ! " shouted Bushy. " I'm afraid Ned is dreadfully hurt."

Tom came bounding over the rocks and fallen timbers, spilling berries at every jump. Mr. Sukolt fired a shot at the bear, but this was useless, as Bruin was already quite dead. Poor Ned, it was all over with him. He turned his head feebly toward Bushy as she knelt by him, and in his intelligent eyes there was a look that was pitiful to see.

"Oh, Ned! Oh, poor dear, dear Ned!" cried Bushy, the tears streaming down her face. "Padre! Tom! can't you do something for him? See, he is all torn and bleeding. Ned, old fellow, Bushy loves you so! Bushy was wrong to tie you so you couldn't get away. Ned, Ned, Ned! Don't die, Ned!"

She held his head in her lap and kissed his big, sorrowful eyes.

"Padre, can't you do something?" she cried again.

Mr. Sukolt and Tom both sadly shook their heads. Bushy threw her arms about the neck of the dying horse and wept bitterly. Then she tried to lift his head, talked lovingly to him, coaxed him, and kissed him, but Ned made no sign that he heard his little mistress's voice, for he was dead—poor, dear Ned was dead!

SHE HELD HIS HEAD IN HER LAP AND KISSED HIS BIG, SORROWFUL
EYES.

CHAPTER XVIII

It was not very long before another pony was brought to the little girl.

" Don't believe you will do at all," said Bushy, " but I'll try you." Jip, for that was the new horse's name, turned his head and looked appealingly at the child who thought he was not good enough for her.

" I don't mean that you are not a fine pony," continued Bushy, patting him lovingly on the nose, and then turning to continue braiding his mane, " but you will never be bright like poor Ned. You can't imagine the wonderful things that Ned took me through. Why, there was the trip up Stone Gulch, when poor Spott was killed by that Indian who thought he was going to get Padre's scalp, sure; then at Cross Roads he helped me save the soldier's life by standing so firm when I lariated him. But you are a stupid little Indian pony and don't know anything about lariating. Oh ! I know you won't ever do. You are stupid and haven't heard one word I have said." She grabbed him by the head and shook him with all her might.

Bushy had a big comb that one of the miners had made out of a piece of pine shingle, and with it she was combing out the long, silky mane that almost swept the ground. Tom said he had never seen so long a mane on any of the Western ponies.

"Oh, listen to me, Jip; you are so impolite! Padre always punishes me when I don't look at him if he talks. I tell you that Ned was much smarter than you, because just think how he took me through the snow to the very edge of the shanty when it was under the snow-slide! You couldn't do that. Now, could you, Jip?"

Bushy threw her arms about the Indian pony's neck again and putting her lips close to his ear, whispered: "He carried me safe to the blacksmith's when the wolves were after me. Do you think you could do that, Jip?"

Jip gazed wonderingly in Bushy's face and neighed as much as to say he could.

"Why, you dear old fellow, you do understand me after all, and I guess you are half as good as Ned! But would you save me from the big mountain bear? Ned did. He snorted and screamed so that the bear attacked him instead of me. If Ned had not been the best and loveliest horse in the world I would have been scratched to death. Ugh!

"Oh, Jip, dear, do stand still and don't look at

me all the time; it crooks your neck so that I can't see if the braids are all made. What a funny pony you are ! Sometimes you won't look at all, then you are licking my hand all the time. I bet you want sugar. We are out of sugar. I put the last bit in Padre's coffee this morning, and we are not going to send for any more, because we are going away. Oh, Jip, I must tell you all about it."

With one spring she landed on Jip's back, and then stretching herself at full length she clutched his mane and said: " Do you know how you came to belong to me, Jip ? It's a long, long story, but I tell it to myself every day. I loved Ned next to Padre, and after the wicked bear had killed him, I cried until Tom carried me home. I can't bear to think of anything turning over on its side and shutting its eyes that way. Oh, Jip, dear, will you do that, too, just when I get to loving you so hard ? "

Bushy cried softly to herself and Jip grew uneasy. " Never mind, Jip; I am coming to the nice part soon. When we got home that night after the berrying, Shanks and the boys and the wagons were all there, and you were tied to the feed-box at the back of the train-master's wagon. You broke your halter and came right up to me. You thought I was your little mistress—your poor little mistress that was killed. Do you think I will do, Jip ? Maybe you don't like me half as well as you did the little Indian girl that the wagon-master said was dead and hanging to the funny kind of a saddle you had on your back. Do you think you can like me a wee, tiny bit, Jip ? "

Bushy anxiously reached out her hand and twisted Jip's head about so she could look into his large, intelligent eyes.

" The wagon-master's name was Bill, and he said that you were wandering over the valley at the foot of the mountain range with this dead girl dangling across your back. When he tried to lariat you you were naughty and ran away. The morning after they saw you first, Bill woke up early and went out to see what was disturbing the train horses, and there you were, eating out of one of the feed-boxes, just as if you were starved to death. Bill slipped up behind you and threw the bridle over your head, and it was no good to try and get away then.

" The little Indian girl was a very pretty little girl, so Bill said, and you must have loved her very much, Jip, 'cause Bill said you pawed the ground and cried and cried when they took her off your back. You almost killed one of the train boys, but that was because you did not want them to take her away, I guess. They buried your princess by the roadside and tied you to Bill's wagon. He said you made friends with no one until you saw me.

You broke the strap and bounded up to me just as if you thought I was the Indian Princess—poor Jip! You had lost your little girl and I had lost Ned."

Again Bushy gave way to soft crying, and Jip grew unhappy and whinnied and pawed the soft dirt beneath his feet.

"Bill told me he guessed the little Indian girl belonged to a tribe that passed up north on the west side of the range, and he heard some miners over there say they had caught them driving off their stock, so they sent out ten men to get back the horses. Ever so many Indians were shot before they would run away and leave the stock, and he thinks that is the way the little girl got killed. She had tied herself on with a rawhide whip and some strips made of her buckskin skirt. Bill says, that shows she was not killed outright, but lived long enough to fasten herself on your back. Poor little girl! Maybe she thought you would take her back to her father. Bill thinks you did not know where to go because the tribe was moving north.

"And now you are mine, all mine, Jip," said Bushy, brightening into her old self again. "As soon as Bill heard that Ned was up in the mountains, never to come down any more, why, he just put the rope that was about your neck into my hands and said: 'There, Bushy, I knew Jip was meant for some special thing. He was sent to us in such an odd way. He is yours, Bushy, with my compliments.' Ha! ha! that is the way he did it, Jip. Do listen! You are growing stupid and are not taking in half I say."

Slipping off his back she pounded him in play on his head and then kissed his eyes and patted his nose.

"I am going to ride you all the way to the new home. Padre is going and I am going and so is Tom and so is Shanks. We are going because Padre has sold the mine to a rich man who came with the train of freight wagons, and we are going back—back—oh, I don't know where it is we are going, but Padre knows. Then he will 'tend to some mining business and maybe we will go into Mexico, where Ned was born, and maybe I'll get some books and some clothes like the little girls Tom tells about, but, Jip "——

"Bushy!" called a voice from the shanty, "where are you, and what are you thinking about? It is way past the time to take the lunch to the miners!"

"Gracious! It is all Jip's fault; he kept me talking so long," replied Bushy as she bounded into the shanty. "Say, Tom, I like Jip. We have made up," and snatching the pail of hot dinner she swung it on her arm and jumping on Jip he made his first trip to the mine. Next day they started away in covered wagons—two of them, with three old saddle-horses, Bushy's Jip, and old Rover trotting on behind.

CHAPTER XIX

Imagine for yourself the covered wagon that was to be Bushy's home for several weeks. She called it " a little house on wheels."

" Just look at it, Tom," she cried the morning they left Great Pine Mine. " See, I have fixed the room up beautifully, quite like a true house ! " The conveyance had been packed full up to the top of the wagon box; all the valuables were put in there. Over the top was laid a smooth pine floor, with a step cut out in front for the driver to sit on.

A very thick cover was drawn over the wagon hoops that ran up from the sides of the box, and, as Bushy said, made a complete little house. A small stove was set up in the back, and the pipe ran out of a hole in the cover above. This was fixed so that the pipe could be taken out and the hole covered, if there came a severe storm. Mr. Sukolt had put up four posts, one for each corner of the wagon, and these were so strong that Tom hung up a hammock, made out of a good, warm blanket, for Bushy to sleep in.

Her father made his bed into a roll in the day-time and used it for a seat, and at night he slept on the floor of the wagon. Shanks, who was very handy with carpenter tools, made a hinged stand that would shut down and lie against the end of the wagon in the day-time when not wanted, but during the meals was raised and turned into a low table for the four to sit about. All the provisions and dishes and cooking utensils were carried in the provision boxes, fastened something like a feed-box at the back of the wagon.

The horses were tied to the end of the wagons, and trotted along all ready to take the place of the mules should any of these get hurt or die.

"Jip would not be of much account to pull a wagon, would he?" said Bushy, looking at his trim body and slender legs; but Tom had great faith in Jip.

"He is a true Indian pony, and I have an idea he is a prize. Suppose you try to ride him by hanging on his side as the Indians do!"

Bushy thought it a great scheme, so she and Tom ran races all day long—that is, at every place where the road was good enough to let them. Bushy got some very bad tumbles, and once her father was tempted to forbid her playing circus, as she called it, but Tom had good reason for wanting her to learn all the tricks he had seen the Indian children do.

" Now, Bushy, let Jip stand still, and try to swing yourself about his neck on to his back without falling off." Oh, what a time they had ! Bushy would fall, and try again and fall, and still keep at it. Jip looked at her as if he thought her very clumsy, yet he knew his business and did not move. She would get on his back and put her arms about Jip's neck and swing under, catching his stiff mane with her right heel, and there holding until she had swung far enough under his neck to throw the other foot over his back. As she would let go with the right she was on the upward swing with the left. It took a very sudden swing to keep from falling and landing bump on the ground instead of regaining her seat, but she did it finally.

That was the most difficult thing she ever tried to do, but she learned to ride on the dead run with her whole body hanging from Jip's side, so that anybody on the opposite side could not see that there was a rider on the horse. Bushy learned to be an admirable horseback rider, and being naturally cool-headed in all circumstances, both Shanks and Tom grew to think her quite as capable of taking care of herself as they were of themselves. The Indian pony was not so high as Ned had been, and it was an easy matter for Bushy to place her hands on his back and leap over him. Then she would amuse herself by letting him run at the top of his speed. Clinging to his mane she would leap to the ground and back, again and again, as he dashed madly on. She taught him to kneel for her, and if she would not climb on his back while he knelt, he would get down lower still. Mr. Sukolt also would often spend the greater part of the day with Bushy training Jip, who turned out to be a most wonderful horse. It seemed as if he were almost human in his intelligence. If they could make him do a thing once, he would repeat it when he received the same signs.

It took Mr. Sukolt a long time to teach him that he was to pick Bushy up by her belt and carry her home. They began to teach this in a kind of play, and he and Rover got to be fast friends. Rover could not carry Bushy now, because she was too heavy. Mr. Sukolt would send Bushy out somewhere to hide, and then her father would tell Jip and Rover to go find her. At first the horse simply followed the dog, and, of course, Rover found her every time; but Mr. Sukolt thought Jip ought to be able to find her, too.

"Now, Padre, don't let Rover come," said Bushy, "send Jip all alone."

"Now, Jip, find Bushy," said Mr. Sukolt, and Jip started, but waited in the road for Rover, and Rover would break bounds and dash after her. Sometimes Jip would find her, and then there was great glee on the part of the whole family. The next thing to teach him was to bring her home. He was taught to kneel and neigh for her to climb on his back. If she pretended she could not do it he would get down on his side, and Bushy would crawl on, and cling to his mane while he got up and dashed back to Mr. Sukolt.

It was lots of fun for several weeks. Both Bushy and her father forgot all about her lessons. Bushy thought it was all fun, but her father was preparing for a time when he perhaps might not be at hand to help his little daughter.

All this was preliminary to the job of teaching the pony to pick Bushy up by the belt and carry her home to her father, something as a cat carries a rat. Oh, it took a long, long time to get that idea into Jip's head. He would kneel, then get down on his side if Bushy paid no attention to him, then he would neigh and make a great fuss. Finally Mr. Sukolt fastened her to Jip's bits, and he and Tom would help carry Bushy home to show Jip what was wanted. Bushy would keep still as if she were dead. Little by little they would leave the weight on Jip, and finally he carried her himself. Now the question was how to make him pick her up. They slipped her belt over his lower jaw and let him carry her that way, and at last he would nose around and find it himself. It was a time of great rejoicing when he first did this. Bushy had to wear mittens and strong moccasins, because he would sometimes drag her along on the ground. She was now over thirteen years old, very small for her age, but slender and agile like a cat.

"Where are we going, Padre?" asked Bushy one morning, after they had been some weeks on the way.

"Down south on a prospecting tour. A freight-train of wagons will start from Georgetown. We are not out of danger from the Indians until we get within ten miles of that place. There will be more danger of our running into Indians along here than anywhere else, because the soldiers are all the time driving them back. The Indians go there for their rations of food and clothing, and if they are not in the most pleasant humor they may do us harm when we meet them. In case we do get into trouble," said her father, "you must try to get to Hold Up Fort and give warning. That can't be more than five miles from here, straight ahead."

Noon-time came, and as there were no signs of Indians about, Mr. Sukolt very unwisely had the mules unhitched and lariated them in the middle of a patch of fresh tender grass. Jip was with them, too, though he still wore his blanket saddle, as Bushy had ridden him all the morning and had left his back only to assist in getting the noon meal.

"Merciful heavens, there are the Indians!" cried Shanks, in a frightened whisper. Everybody looked up with a blanched face, for coming down the mountain road, way off in the distance, could be plainly seen about a dozen of the redskins, dashing pell-mell toward the covered wagons.

"They have been refused rations at the fort and have spied us from the high road!" exclaimed Mr. Sukolt. "They mean to steal our freight and drive off the mules and horses. We are four against ten or, perhaps, twenty, there is no telling how many there are in ambush. Oh, if it were not for Bushy!"

"Can you three keep them at bay for half an hour?" cried Bushy, her eyes almost starting out of her head in her excitement and fright. She had followed her father out after the horses, and when assured he could fight the Indians off for awhile she threw herself flat on her face, and, crawling on the ground, she reached Jip, who at the first signal, knelt, then she caught his mane in one hand and wound her foot some way in the rope that circled Jip's body, and then let him bound up and away at a keen jump toward the fort. The Indians saw him go, but supposed he was a frightened pony or a runaway because they could see no one on him. They did not shoot, but watched Mr. Sukolt driving in the mules and horses, trying to get behind the

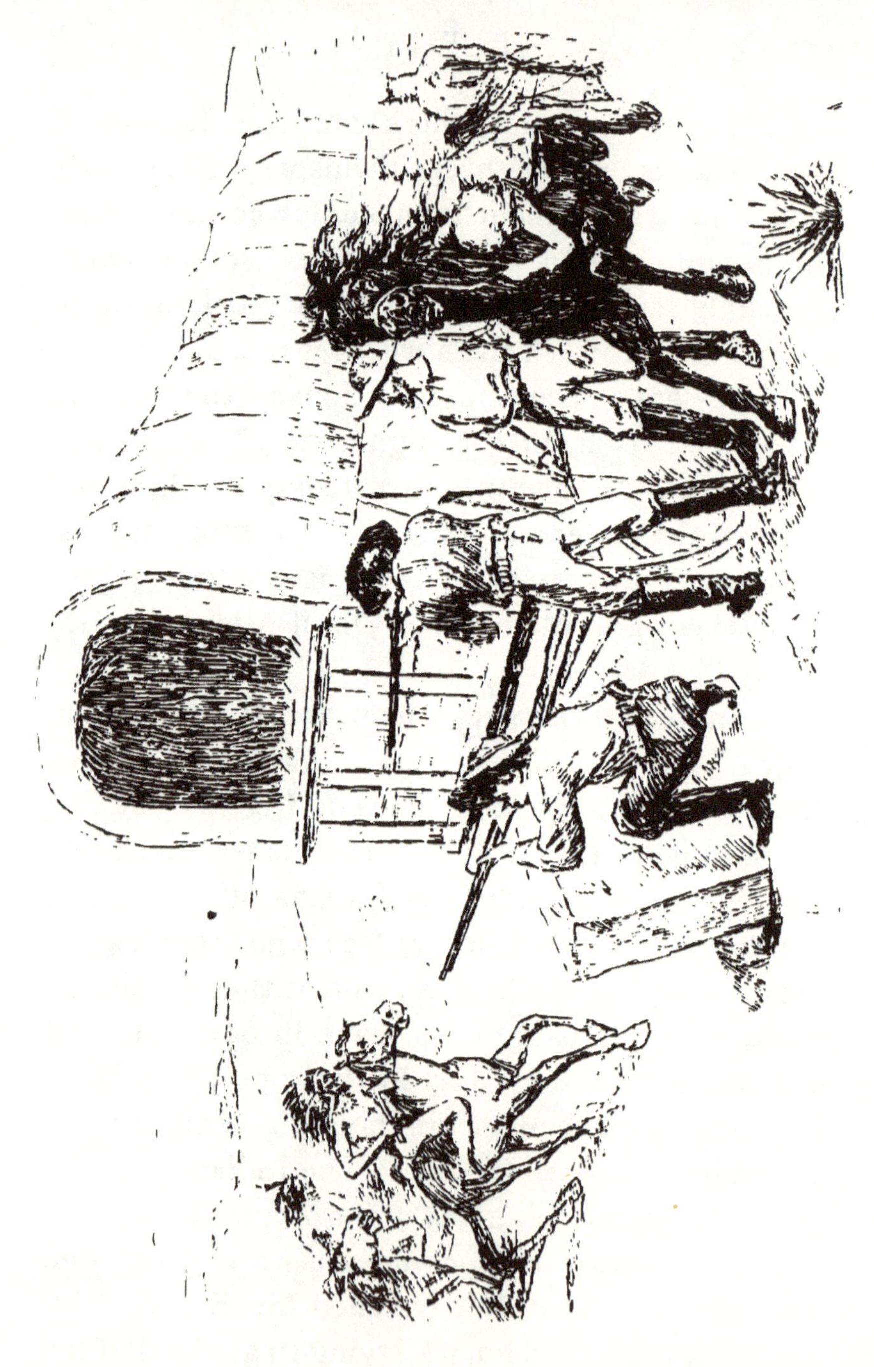

two wagons that Tom and Shanks had drawn up to form a kind of breastwork. The men threw the buffalo robes, bedding, and as much of the freight as they had time to get out, all about the wheels, making a safe place for them to crawl behind to give a warm reception to the Indians as they came down. It was all done in much shorter time than it takes to tell it.

"Where is Bushy?" exclaimed both Shanks and Tom, as they took up their places behind the wheels and arranged their revolvers and extra ammunition for use.

"Gone to give warning, thank God!" said Mr. Sukolt. "She went to bring help from the fort, and I sent her, hoping she would escape harm; but there is little chance that she can bring reinforcements in time for us; it looks pretty tough just now."

The Indians came on at a full run, yelling and brandishing their tomahawks, but when they got within eighty yards of the white men the three opened such a volley upon them that they held up and began to circle about and close in. This circle did not take in Bushy. She was already out of sight and, no doubt, riding with all her might toward the fort.

Each of the men picked off an Indian before five minutes had passed. One mule was killed, and Tom drew nim up to add to their breastwork. An arrow pierced his hat and just scratched his skull-cap. This made him livid with rage, because, you remember, Tom had lost his scalp through one of the wicked redskins. He rose up, took good aim for the leader of the gang, and fired. The Indian fell from his horse. On perceiving this the others probably came to the conclusion that they would have some difficulty in getting the freight, and so drew off and gave the men a short rest. This was a fortunate thing, for Bushy would have more time in which to make the trip, and the men would have a chance to load and prepare for a new attack. It soon came.

"They have been reinforced!" cried Shanks. "We are lost if they rush upon us, for we are three against fifteen or twenty." They made the circle as before, and then, giving warwhoops that chilled the blood in every vein, dashed up to the wagons. The three men picked out each an Indian, and dropped him. The savages were too close now for much of a plan to be carried out—it was a hand-to-hand encounter.

A tomahawk was raised over Mr. Sukolt's head, when a bullet from some unknown source killed the holder of it. Tom had been stunned from a blow on the side of his head, and lay helpless across the dead mule. Shanks was close in the embrace of a dying redskin, and seemed doomed to death from a blow of a tomahawk in the hand of an Indian back of him. Mr. Sukolt struck the axe with the butt of his gun, and received an arrow in his left arm from an Indian who had slipped behind the wagon and had shot from under cover.

"Thank God, Bushy is safe!" he murmured as he felt the cold knife in an Indian's hand seeking for his scalp line.

Crack! crack! flash! bang! sounded the welcome reports from the soldiers' firearms. The Indian who was in the act of scalping Bushy's father fell across him dead. Mr. Sukolt went down with his weight, and it was well he did, for an arrow came whizzing by which would have ended his life without doubt.

"We are here, Padre!" called out the voice of Bushy, who, in spite of the warnings of the soldiers, rushed ahead and into the thickest of the fight.

It was Bushy's quick action that had saved the lives of the campers, but she could not claim that it was her shot that laid low the villain who was trying to scalp her father. The few Indians that were not killed fled like cowards when they saw the soldiers. Bushy had come across the detachment out scouting, and that was how she reached the camp so early, and just in time.

Tom was only stunned, and, but for a lump on his head, was all right in half an hour. Shanks was not hurt at all excepting a few black and blue spots. Mr. Sukolt had his arm done up, and Bushy almost went into hysterics after everything was over.

CHAPTER XX

"Hello, Rover, Rover! Where are you, Rover?" called Bushy, suddenly stopping her crying and rushing about wildly for her dog. Nobody had seen Rover. Several soldiers were helping Mr. Sukolt and the men get the wagons into order to move toward the fort. Five soldiers had followed the Indians some distance and chased them back behind the hills. The others were keeping guard for fear they might pick them off, one by one, by slipping back and getting within shooting distance without their knowing it.

Everybody stopped and called Rover. A low whine directed them to Tom's wagon, and there, underneath a pile of clothing, the poor dog was found, trembling and frightened.

"Dear Rover, I thought you were killed sure," said Bushy, hugging him and crying with delight. In her anxiety over the dog she forgot her own troubles, and taking Rover by the collar dragged him out and up into her wagon, where the two snuggled down on buffalo robes. The men hitched up one of the horses in place of the dead mule and then they all started for the fort, the soldiers dividing, some riding in front and some behind. But the Indians watched from ambush the movements of the soldiers, and formed a plan for the destruction of the whole band. The redskins seemingly fled, but instead they made a circuit of the mountain and got between Mr. Sukolt's party and the fort. They hid behind the trees that grew in the fork of a stream and there they waited until the wagons came quite close. The soldiers were on the lookout; nevertheless, they were much surprised when the warwhoop suddenly sounded in front.

The wagons were again turned into means of protection. Indians are cowardly and not good riflemen, as a general thing, and when the soldiers with their deadly aim picked off every red man that showed himself, the others quieted down and no doubt wished they were safe out of the fight.

" Bushy, you and Rover crawl under the bedding and lie down flat," cried Mr. Sukolt. He piled about her the three hams and several great pieces of bacon that had been brought along to be eaten on the trip.

Bushy could not see out on the side where the Indians were. It was growing dark and the fight being in a little grove of trees the red men concluded to take advantage and crawl stealthily, tomahawk in hand, upon the enemy.

Bushy, from her elevated position in the wagon, was almost on a level with the heads of the redskins, as they rose to flourish the tomahawk.

" I'll lie down flat," said Bushy to herself, " and be ready to fire if any Indian comes on my side of the wagon."

She had no more than settled well down into a comfortable position when she saw the headdress of a redskin bobbing up and down in the tall grass close to the wagon tongue. Without any ado whatever she fired and laid him low. With a yell that was appalling, another Indian rose out of the grass and made an attempt to drag away the dead man, but Bushy fired again, and he, too, fell and rolled out of sight in the darkness.

" Bravo ! " cried the soldiers.

" That's two for me," said Bushy, softly to herself.

The soldiers continued fighting, determined on the destruction of the few Indians that remained, when suddenly Bushy heard an anxious cry for powder. " I am out of powder ! " cried Tom. " So am I, almost," yelled Shanks from behind the nearest tree. " Here take my can," called Mr. Sukolt, as he crawled through the grass and divided with the boys.

" I know where there is more," thought Bushy, and scrambling from under the hams and sides of bacon, she immediately proceeded to open the box and fill her skirt with as much as she could carry.

" I'll slip along down and furnish the men with all they want," said Bushy.

She crawled from under the wagon-cover and fell, with a soft thud, to the ground below.

" Here Tom; help yourself," she said a minute later, as she nudged him on the elbow.

" Bless your heart, child ! how did you get here ? You must not run such risk," but before he had finished talking she was off to Shanks, and after supplying him she started for her father who was hidden behind a bowlder on the left, but he sharply ordered her to drop the powder on the ground and climb again into the wagon.

Just then a dusky cloud settled over the trees, throwing the grove for a moment into complete darkness, and the captain of the soldiers called out:

" Everybody be on guard and draw near to the wagons. When all are in, make a grand rush and try to get out of this wood."

Tom jumped to hitch the horses to the wagons, the soldiers kept guard, shooting at every move in the grass outside of their circle, nevertheless, two

horses were killed and three soldiers wounded before Tom succeeded in making everything ready.

The three men were put tenderly into the freight
wagon, as Tom called the second vehicle. Shanks
suddenly called to them to " lay low." They fell flat
on the ground, and thus were saved from an arrow
that came whizzing through the darkness.

" All aboard ! " shouted Shanks, as he jumped
to the wagon-seat, and taking the reins, declared
he was ready to start.

" I killed that fellow," said one of the soldiers,
after shooting at a face that had gleamed at him
through the still darkness. " I think he is the last
of them."

" Are we ready ? " called out the captain. " If
so, to the fort ! "

Tom struck his horse a most cruel blow; the
team bounded like mad down the road, followed
closely by Shanks and his load of wounded men.
The mounted soldiers dashed after them, each with
loaded gun ready for the slightest sign of an Indian.
On they went, never stopping until out of the
woods and some distance into the valley.

" Bushy ! " called Mr. Sukolt, and a loud bark
from Rover proved him still under the pile of hams
and bacon.

" Mr. Sukolt ! " then called the captain, " I need
your help here, one of my men has fainted." Mr.

Sukolt jumped out and helped the soldier into Shanks's wagon. Tom had received a gash on his face that was setting him wild with pain. He drove madly on, dreading every minute that he, too, would fall helpless. To make matters worse, Jip suddenly broke the halter and ran back to the woods.

"Only one quarter of a mile more," cried the captain; "let the pony go, no time to bother with him now," and in a few minutes the wagons were hauled up before the fort. Tom fell staggering into the arms of an officer, which incident again distracted Mr. Sukolt's attention from his child, and it was some minutes before he turned, half frightened by a sudden thought, and again called, "Bushy!"

There was no answer.

"Smothered under the hams, maybe," said one of the soldiers, as he hurried with Mr. Sukolt to tear away the coverings and throw the smoked meat to the right and left.

Rover gave one yelp of joy when he heard his master's voice, and bounded out, and down to the ground.

"Bushy!" called her father, throwing down the last ham and then making a hurried search through the bedding, and feeling of the quilts in the hammock. "Bushy! My God, boys, she is not here;

"BUSHY! MY GOD, BOYS, SHE IS NOT HERE!"

she is gone !" He gave a gasp and fell into the outstretched arms of Shanks, who for two minutes had given up the search and stood with face whiter than death, dreading the time when Mr. Sukolt should realize that his daughter had been left behind.

CHAPTER XXI

Bushy had poured the powder on the ground as her father had ordered her to do, and was wishing that the stuff were not so dirty.

"I have spoilt my skirt. It is all mud and powder, and I wish Padre would not put his head out so often, he may get hurt." Thus she went on thinking to herself and crawling slowly through the grass to the wagon's side.

It was a brave deed for Bushy to take the powder to the men, yet it did not seem possible that she could get hurt going no farther than she did, and when Mr. Sukolt ordered her to go back to the little fort made of hams he dismissed all idea of danger from his mind. The wagon was watched by soldiers, and Indians were picked off the minute they showed themselves. Nevertheless, with all their watchfulness, a young savage succeeded in getting through the grass and lay under the wagon waiting for someone whom he could use as target for his arrows. To his surprise the very first object that came in sight was Bushy crawling to him.

The young Indian's eyes snapped. He grasped

his tomahawk and crouched still nearer the ground, his eyes shining like balls of fire.

Bushy saw the eyes and halted, still on her hands and knees. "It's a panther," she thought, and she made a move for her revolver.

The Indian was as much amused as astonished at finding a little girl in the fight, and never once dreamed she knew how to shoot. There would have been little danger for her had he not feared she would scream and bring the whole force of soldiers down upon him.

When he realized that she saw him, quick as lightning he raised his tomahawk and struck her a blow on the head that stretched poor Bushy flat at his side.

"Scalp little squaw!" muttered the Indian, gleefully. Then he drew his half blanket about her, sling fashion, and began to drag her slowly back to the thick trees beyond.

Unfortunately for Bushy and fortunately for the Indian it was then the sky clouded over, and it grew so dark. It was at that moment that the captain called for the soldiers to close in and prepare to rush from the woods. The Indian made the best of the darkness, but it was his dragging Bushy through the grass that had attracted Shanks and had made him call to the men to "lay low." The bouncing over the ground after awhile brought

Bushy to her senses enough to realize that she was in the hands of an enemy.

"I cannot see," said Bushy to herself. "Poor Padre! what will he do when he misses me? I wonder if I will lose my scalp like Tom, or will I be roasted alive, like the poor trapper Padre tells about who used to hunt with him."

Bushy finally got her revolver, and though the blood was so thick in her eyes from the gash the tomahawk made on her head that she could not see, she waited until she felt herself drawn close to the Indian, then pointing the weapon toward where she knew he must be crouching, she fired.

Bushy heard nothing but a low groan in response to her shot. "I am afraid to move," she thought. "If he thinks I shot at him he will surely kill me. Perhaps he is playing dead like I am. Oh, Padre, Padre! if I dared scream!" Then the cramped position she was in renewed the pain from the cut in her head and she must have fainted, because she remembered no more until she felt the warm nose of some animal pushing against her. Her heart stood still with fright. "Panther, or maybe a bear! No, bears would not come so far down from the mountains, but a panther might," she reasoned, as she held her breath and shivered every time the nose touched her.

"Padre, I am here in the tall grass," she tried to

say, but the words stuck in her parched throat. " I must have been here a long time," she thought, " or panthers would not be prowling about."

One eye was so clotted with blood that she could not open it. Again the nose and hot breath frightened her. " I'll shoot if I can find my revolver," but she could not get herself disentangled from the blanket for fully a minute, and in that time, which seemed ages, she suffered more than she had in her whole life before.

" Padre ! " again she screamed, and this time it was loud enough to be understood by the animal that was nosing her about, and what do you think was the reply ?

A soft neigh of delight from the Indian pony Jip !

Bushy screamed with joy, and with renewed strength floundered in the blanket until her head got out, and then followed her hands and arms, which she flung crazily about trying to clasp them around the neck of her faithful friend.

" Jip, Jip ! You dear old darling ! you will take me to Padre ? Down on your knees, old fellow ! help me, because the redskin has done something to my head that makes me feel so queer; and I am all over blood, Jip, so I can't exactly tell whether I am Bushy or a dead bear."

Jip knelt and patiently waited for her to mount. Bushy staggered to her feet, and all the world turned black and the stars came out, she said, and shot all about in such strange fashion.

"Keep still, Jip, old man. I don't think I can stay on your back if things cut up in this way. Jip, dear, where is the Padre? Did the Indian catch him, too?" She then tried to climb on Jip's back, turned, and thus faced the Indian who had been carrying her off. The sight was a great shock. He sat up stiff and straight and his eyes were staring at her wide open in death. The horror of the picture came upon her with such force that in her weak state of mind she became flighty—quite out of her head.

She lost her balance, tumbled off Jip, and rolled down a slight incline away from the Indian, calling "Jip, come Jip! Let us play circus!" then lost consciousness.

Jip may have been extraordinarily intelligent, or may have thought this only a repetition of the circus games that Bushy had so often played by the day with him, but he did his part remarkably well.

The Indians had all fled and carried with them their dead, with the exception of this one who had tried to carry off Bushy. The only other redskin who had known of his crawling under the wagon was the one that fell dead from the last shot fired by the soldier. The other Indians had taken the latter, and under cover of the darkness that had fallen so suddenly upon them, they all had hastened north while the soldiers and miners had hurried to the east. Thus Bushy and the dead Indian who had held on to the blanket-swing in which she was bound were the only beings left on the field of battle.

When Jip could not rouse Bushy by his second nosing about, he must have concluded that she wanted him to carry her as he had done in the play days. I sometimes feel that Jip knew everything and fully realized the condition that Bushy was in, but Mr. Sukolt, who was a particularly wise and learned man, said afterward, that the horse had no thought beyond that of pleasing his little mistress in performing the trick that he had been taught.

He evidently had much trouble getting her up the slight incline, down which she had rolled, for there were left great gashes in the green grass showing where his hoofs had dug and cut into the ground on both sides of the spot where she had lain, and the sward was marked with blood that had flowed from the fresh bleeding of her head after she had fallen from the horse.

The soldiers, on learning that the miner's little daughter was missing, immediately formed one band for searching the ground where they were attacked last, and another for a continued journey until the escaped red men should be killed, or Bushy rescued. There was no doubt in their minds that the little girl had been carried off.

Mr. Sukolt could scarcely sit on his horse, yet he was the first in the band to strike out for the woods. Tom and Shanks carried lanterns to be used in the search, though their hearts told them that there was little hope of finding her alive.

" It will kill the old man," said Tom. " Just look at his face; it is twenty years older already."

" Something coming this way," cried the leader, turning his horse and riding back to where Tom and Shanks brought up the rear. The three men got down and listened, placing their ears to the ground.

The captain ordered a halt. Mr. Sukolt so far had not uttered a word; his heart seemed broken; he only looked wistfully at the soldiers, and seemed to pray that the delay might not be a long one.

" It is one horse walking so irregularly that 1 imagine it is wounded," said one of the soldiers.

" Well, there's no danger for us in one horse," said the captain; " forward !"

They dashed around the bend, and soon, far in the darkness, they could make out the form of a horse coming slowly toward them. He had stopped the odd trot which the soldiers thought he must have been in when they heard the sound of his hoofs. Rover was capering like mad about him and the object he carried in his mouth.

"Thank God!" burst from the lips of Mr. Sukolt, and with one wild leap he left his horse and ran to Jip, for it was Jip, carrying Bushy by his teeth. He had slipped her belt over his lower jaw and was holding his head as high as he could, so she would not drag very much on the ground.

"Is she alive?" asked the whole group of men at once.

"I don't know," answered her father as he clasped her in his arms. "God help me if she is not."

CHAPTER XXII

Rover went almost wild over her recovery, even if she did look more dead than alive, as they tenderly put her in Mr. Sukolt's arms and hastened back to the fort for medical aid. She soon recovered consciousness. Though she was dizzy and faint from loss of blood and fright, they saw, to their great relief, that their darling would be all right in a few days.

Her father sat by her bedside all night, keeping her little hand in his and listening to the babbling words she spoke in her feverish sleep.

The glaring eyes of the Indian and the hot breath of what she had thought a panther seemed to be ever in her mind. It was not until the following morning that he heard all the story about his little girl's escape.

" I was so afraid I would have to part with my scalp, like Tom, and have to wear a black cap, instead of my hair, for the rest of my life. Oh, I am so glad I shot him before he could take it," she concluded, with a smile and a sigh, as she nestled closer to her father.

Mr. Sukolt took her in his arms, thinking how near he had come to losing her, and what a lonely life his little girl was leading.

They had been at Hold Up Fort three days when Mr. Sukolt called Bushy to him and said: " You must not go far from the fort. It is unsafe now, on account of more Indians moving northward."

" Oh, Padre, how could I stop here all day long while you are away drawing your old maps ? " replied Bushy, with the most woe-begone face. " Jip and I will both die, sure as we live." This funny remark sent Mr. Sukolt on his way, laughing most heartily.

For three days Bushy obeyed very faithfully, and did not lose sight of the wagons. When she stepped out into the sunshine on the morning of the fourth day, however, she felt as if she could not endure the imprisonment any longer. The wound in her head did not trouble her very much; it had been done up so carefully that now it seemed almost well. Why should she stay in the fort all day ? The singing birds were free, the insects buzzing in the air were free, even the trees were free to wave their branches as they liked, and she, the most active of all the busy beings about, was told to sit down and keep still. She, who had such swift feet, and a swifter pony when she got tired of walking—was a prisoner.

"Ah!" argued Bushy, as she walked out to the stall where Jip fretted and pawed and snorted to get out, "this is very wrong, indeed. Padre has forgotten all about his little girl, Jip," she murmured. "Don't you wish we could go out as we used to? I should like to go after some flowers. The soldier captain said such beauties grew at the foot of the mountain, and I am sure that Padre would like some to press in his old botany book. I don't think he would mind it much if we went out there, do you, Jip? You know that Padre just loves flowers. I think that we can go; shall we Jip?"

Jip neighed, stamped his feet, bowed his head, and showed such anxiety to get out that it quite settled the question. So Bushy jumped on his back, and tried to buckle her revolver into her belt, but in her hurry broke the clasp. "Oh, well, never mind!" she said aloud. "I don't need a revolver to pick flowers, anyway," and she thrust it into her blouse waist and let it fall to the belt line, where it swung as if in a pocket.

They galloped through the long grass, scaring the birds and chasing the rabbits before them, both hilarious with joy, at their recovered freedom.

"We have been in jail, Jip, haven't we? And the sun seems brighter and the grass fresher and greener than when the Indians played us the bad tricks. And, oh, look, Jip, at the blue sky out there! It is beckoning us to come on."

She gave the reins to Jip, and he fairly flew forward. Not a twinge of remorse disturbed Bushy, for was she not out solely to gather specimens for her father's botany book? In the woods she dismounted, and, leading Jip by the bridle, walked briskly over the velvet moss, and ran and skipped from stone to stone, often making it difficult for Jip to follow her. She adorned the pony with flowers and then made a crown for herself, keeping up a constant chatter, Jip answering in his own peculiar way.

" Now, Jip," said Bushy at last, as she sat down on the mossy mountain side, " I am going to make a trimming of wild flowers to go all around my blouse." The joy of her freedom had blown Bushy's usual good sense to the four winds. Without realizing it she had wandered far out of sight of the fort and the place was strange to her and time seemed to fly on wings. It was not until the trimming grew into yards and yards that she stopped to think.

Jip was making for the grass growing at a little distance—his dinner was all ready for him, but little girls can't make a dinner on grass; and oh, she was so hungry! For some minutes she sat very still. All was silent about her, with only the insect buzzing, and Jip nibbling the grass, and a bough cracking here and there as a squirrel passed over it. The sunbeams fell through the leaves overhead and drew ever-varying patterns of light and shade on the grassy mound at her feet. Bushy thought, " I can't see the fort anywhere," and she began to feel uneasy.

" Jip," she called, and the pony, ever watchful, trotted up to her.

" Guess we had better run home, old fellow, and get something to eat besides grass. I am awful hungry." Jip neighed a yes and knelt for her to mount him. Off they went again, right down toward the valley; at least, that is what Bushy thought. But after they had gone on and on to her great surprise she came to a brook that leaped merrily over the stones, making beautiful little waterfalls that Bushy could never have seen before and forgotten. " How lovely ! " she exclaimed; yet at the same time her face grew serious, and checking the pony she looked all about her.

" I do declare, Jip, we have taken the wrong way ! Oh, of course, we ought to have gone to the left of the pine-tree. How stupid of you, Jip, to let me go wrong. Didn't you know we were trying to get back to the fort ? "

So back they went, but no pine-tree was to be found.

"Where is it, Jip? It was here a few minutes ago. We must have gone wrong again. How very careless!" It was something new to Bushy to be in a country where she could not travel as far as she wished yet never be out of sight of some landmark that would point out to her the location of Great Pine Mine. But now, after endless turning and walking, she confessed that she was hopelessly lost.

"Oh, Jip," she sobbed, "how I wish I had minded the Padre! After dark the bears and maybe other dreadful animals will come after us, and I have nothing but one revolver and no belt to carry it in to be ready to shoot quick." Remorse and grief such as she had not felt since she carried Pete to the fort against her father's orders now stormed her heart.

After a few minutes' thinking, some of her good sense came back to her, and she understood that she would never get back to camp unless she trusted to Jip or stayed where she was until some one came out to hunt her. "If Jip doesn't seem to know what to do, I'll stay just here and trust to Tom's hunting me in the right place.

"Jip," she said, patting his head and talking distinctly, "go home, go back to the Padre, do you understand? Go back to your dinner and stall; go hunt the Padre and take me home!" She jumped on him, threw down the bridle and gave him a smart cut with the whip, a thing she had not done ten times in the months she had possessed him. The horse whirled about as if frightened; danced and capered as if undecided what to do.

"Jip, dear old Jip, see if you can find the way back to the Padre now. I am sure you can."

He whinnied intelligently, and Bushy, taking this as a token that he understood her, trusted to him and good fortune.

Bushy soon felt faint with hunger. It must be about four o'clock, she thought, looking at the sun. In two hours her father would come home and miss her. Her heart beat loud. What would he think?

All of a sudden Jip stopped and began sniffing and neighing joyfully, but before Bushy could think what was the matter with him off he started at a flying gallop, faster and faster, hardly touching the ground with his feet. Bushy clung to his mane breathless, never had the pony acted in this way before. A feeling of relief came over her. "Jip has smelled the way back and is running for dear life to get me home safe," she thought.

But surely that white mass in the distance with dark figures walking to and fro was no soldiers' fort. A cold shiver ran over her as they drew nearer. Jip was taking her to an Indian camp!

" Whoa, Jip, whoa, old fellow ! " but Jip did not seem to hear. Bushy knew that she was lost. The pony had evidently scented some old friend in the group, and was taking the little girl with him, a prey to her enemies. She was unable to get at her revolver, even should there be any good in defending herself. What service would killing one or even two Indians do her, she quickly reasoned as Jip dashed onward. Nothing would be gained by jumping off, for already her approach was observed.

Jip galloped in among the wigwams, Bushy clinging to his mane, pale with fright, and staring wildly at the redskins she feared so much. What a commotion followed ! What jabbering ! How the Indians crowded about ! What caresses Jip got, and how surprised the savages were over the child's appearance. The squaws fingered her blouse and pulled off some of the flowers. The young bucks noticed her saddle and felt of the bridle and bits. She was lifted from the pony by the young chief, who had evidently at some time been the master of Jip, and he handed her over to a cross old squaw, who was to hold her in safe-keeping.

" Oh, Jip ! " wailed Bushy as she disappeared into the wigwam and faithful Jip tried to go to her, but the chief prevented him. Night was closing in and the thought of her poor father's anxiety made her tears start afresh. Her sobs stirred the pity of a young Indian girl, sitting near the entrance of the wigwam. She gave Bushy a drink, and reassured her as much as she could. Bushy was soon left alone. The excitement of the day had made her feverish, and the wound on her head began to sting, but notwithstanding the grief and pain she began to plan to get away. She didn't want to be roasted alive, or pierced with arrows. Of the loss of her scalp she was almost sure, so she thought it was no use fretting any more over her fluffy hair.

The more she thought the less she could conceive of any way to escape. The Indians set a watch over her—this seemed very serious. If they didn't kill or scalp her now, they would certainly take her with them in their first attack on the miners and kill her before their very eyes. Indeed, now that she came to think of it, she was sure they would do that.

Fatigue and pain had exhausted her, and the sickening fear of a cruel death was too much. Brave Bushy for the second time showed weakness and fainted away on the little bed of leaves where the squaw had placed her.

CHAPTER XXIII

Bushy was very much surprised when, in the middle of the night, she woke up. Generally when once she was asleep it required a good deal of shaking to wake her before the usual time of getting up.

" I am feeling awful queer ! I wish I knew what's the matter with me. There is something, but I cannot remember," she thought drowsily.

Then by and by the dreadful truth came home to her. She was a prisoner among the Indians !

The night was very clear, the bright moonshine made it almost like twilight. She could distinguish the dark forms of the people in the wigwam; they were all fast asleep, their regular breathing proved that. Bushy's heart gave a great bound. Oh, if she could only get out of there ! Suddenly in the silence her ear caught the sound of a rustle outside the wigwam, as if some one were cautiously coming through the long grass. She grew frightened, but soon all her fears changed into great joy. A well-known sniffing and snorting betrayed to her that Jip had been nosing about for his little mistress and had found her.

" Jip," whispered Bushy, ever so softly.

To her unutterable alarm Jip neighed loudly and repeatedly; the Indians in the wigwams moved uneasily.

Bushy kept motionless, almost breathless, for some minutes. Would the Indians wake up ? If she could only get outside. But creeping past the sleeping savages was by no means an easy task, and Bushy almost despaired of getting to the pony. But out she must go; it was her only chance of escape.

She rolled over, her face downward on the floor, and lay perfectly motionless for some time to make sure that the rustling of the dry leaves had not been heard. Then she began to crawl cautiously along the uneven ground. The entrance to the wigwam seemed miles off. She had almost reached it, and could see the moonlit camp through the opening, when the young Indian squaw who had been so kind to her the evening before stirred in her sleep.

" She is going to wake up, and she will murder me sure for trying to run off," Bushy thought, pressing herself closely to the ground. Her heart beat like that of a frightened bird, and cold perspiration stood in great drops on her forehead. But good luck attended her, and a few minutes afterward she crawled out into the long grass, free, and outside of the wigwam. Jip trotted up to her.

"Sh ! Keep still," whispered Bushy.

He thrust his cold nose in her hand and welcomed her with his best tokens of affection. A piece of halter, showing that he had broken loose from some tree, was still hanging about his neck. Bushy was as yet in danger. She had to pass all the red-skins sleeping around the camp-fire; and without a decent revolver, too, what could she do to defend herself !

"I'll go round by the edge of the camp," she reasoned, "and hang on to Jip and ride out side-ways, so they won't see me. They may let Jip roam about, even if they should wake and see him.

In her joy at the slight prospect of deliverance she had been a little off her guard, and had not noticed an Indian boy stealing up behind her. The boy was frightened. The mother squaw had told him the little girl was dead when she fainted and fell over so still on the bed of leaves early in the evening. This explains, in a measure, why the Indians did not watch her more closely. They thought she was dying, hence they curled up care-lessly in the different corners of the camp and went sound asleep.

Jip, moving uneasily, made Bushy turn her head and face the boy, who with wild and frightened eyes gazed upon her. Her heart sank, but freedom was worth another effort, she thought. With a rapid movement she drew the revolver out of her blouse and threw it at his head. He staggered and fell back without a cry, disappearing in the long grass that surrounded the tent. Bushy then jumped on Jip's back and whispered: "Home, home ! Jip; let us hunt the Padre. Quick !"

Bushy hung on one side, the side away from the Indians, and clung desperately to Jip's mane and to an old rope lariat that she had dexterously and quickly thrown about his body. She had tied it with a slip knot, thus making a surcingle to which she clung with her feet. In the white moonlight, as Jip's hoofs sank deep in the moss, they looked like spectres moving noiselessly about at midnight.

Whether the Indian boy was dead or only stunned, and whether the other Indians waked up, Bushy never knew, but when at last she was miles from the camp, she felt that there was some hope of again embracing her father. She resolved to stay in the bushes till daybreak, knowing that neither Jip nor herself could find their way back in the pitchy darkness. The moon had by this time disappeared, and she could scarcely see her hand before her.

"I think I had better not lie down and sleep; wild beasts might come, and I could not get away if I were not on the watch. I'll just slip off you, Jip,

"SH! KEEP STILL," WHISPERED BUSBY.

'cause I am so tired, and sit down against the tree a little while and keep my eyes open. I wish I had my revolver, I would not be afraid then.

"There is no use crying over spilt milk," Bushy murmured as she found a good seat and firmly resolved not to go to sleep.

"Don't leave me, Jip; keep right here."

When Mr. Sukolt came home the day before, he had thought it rather strange not to find Bushy waiting for him at the door of the fort as she usually did.

"Playing hide-and-seek with the old Padre, little girl ?" he exclaimed, giving a merry whistle to let her know he was there. "Wait, I'll find you, you rascal !"

He went all over the rooms and through the passages, looking in every corner and behind every barrel and bag, but no Bushy was to be found. None of the soldiers knew where she had gone and no one remembered seeing her all day.

No answer came to his repeated call. "Perhaps she is in the stable with Jip," and off he started for the stable. Just imagine his alarm when he not only failed to find Bushy, but missed Jip, too !

"She has gone off, though I expressly forbade it ! I am afraid the child is running wild. All those Indians are abroad, too !"

Night began to close in and no Bushy came. Half mad with alarm, he called the captain and told him about his little daughter's absence.

" You had better let me send out some soldiers in search of her," said the captain.

" Thank you," said Mr. Sukolt, his voice full of gratitude, and they were soon on their way. The shifting lights of the lanterns and the cries of " Bushy ! Bushy !" disturbed the quiet of the sleeping birds. At eleven o'clock the searchers returned, and all had the same sad message to tell— the little girl was nowhere to be found—and the hunt was given up until daylight.

For more than an hour Mr. Sukolt sat in dumb despair, too dispirited to think of anything but his lost darling.

It was three o'clock when he walked out into the darkness and wandered aimlessly about. As he approached the bushes on the east side, perhaps a quarter of a mile from the fort, he was suddenly startled from his gloomy reveries by the neighing of a horse, a neigh that sounded like heavenly music in his ear.

" Father in heaven !" he exclaimed, making great strides forward. " If that is Jip, Bushy must be near, too."

At the same moment Jip made his way through the bushes and trotted toward Mr. Sukolt. The pony circled about and galloped back to the spot where Bushy sat against the tree, sleeping as soundly and quietly as if she had been in her little bed in the fort. Mr. Sukolt gathered her in his arms and covered the face of his naughty little girl with kisses.

"My darling! my darling!" was all that he could say.

Bushy woke up with a start, and could not at first make out what had happened.

"Oh, I say, I went off to sleep, after all. Jip, you stupid fellow, could you not keep me awake?" Then the memory of what had brought about this adventure came back to her, and she clasped her arms around her father's neck, sobbing in shame and penitence.

"Oh, Padre, I have been so naughty! I got lost. I do not deserve to be found by you or anybody else. I guess you will never trust me again as long as you live!"

"Softly, softly, my little girl," said her father, soothingly. "Let us first go home. You were very near the fort, without knowing it. I cannot understand what Jip could have been thinking about."

"Oh! Padre, it was not Jip's fault, because I climbed off his back and told him to keep close, and he did, I guess, until he heard you coming.

But, Padre, he took me straight into the Indian camp and they made me a prisoner and "——

" My God ! Bushy, dear, what is it you say ? " exclaimed her father, drawing her closer to him. His emotion frightened Bushy more than all the peril she had that day gone through. Between sobs and fitful laughs, half hysterical, she spent the remainder of the night telling her adventures to her father and the boys as they gathered about.

CHAPTER XXIV

" Come, my work here is done, the maps are all finished, and I want to go to Central City as soon as we can get away. How long does my little girl think it will take us to pack the wagons ? "

" Oh, Padre, how jolly ! I think it won't take more than one day. Let's begin now."

Bushy was so glad at the prospect of a change that she danced around the room and finally ran out to tell Tom and Shanks and Jip of the journey before them.

It was almost a week after her last escapade, and in all that time Bushy had not once moved from the immediate neighborhood of the fort. She knew now that even the cleverest little girl can get into trouble when she is disobedient.

After a warm farewell from the kind captain and the soldiers, they left; Bushy riding Jip and waving her calico handkerchief till they were out of sight.

" Here we are going again, Jip, old boy ! Hurrah ! " she cried, and Jip, thinking it fit to express his approval, made a wild caper and set off for a run in front.

Mr. Sukolt called to her: " We are going to have company, little tomboy, two wagons from a California immigrant train are to join us soon. I think we shall see them to-morrow or the day after." Bushy was thoughtful for some moments. She did not receive the news very enthusiastically. She was perfectly happy with her father and Tom and Shanks and the pony, and did not wish for more company.

" I hope there will be good men in those wagons," was all she said. She had not seen a white woman or any but redskin boys and girls for years, so the possibility of meeting travellers other than men did not enter her mind.

That same night the other wagons appeared, and Bushy was anxious to see how the men looked. The neatest looking of the two vehicles, however, was kept closed, and though Bushy went around twice she could not get a peep at its inmates, so she went to bed very cross.

" If they don't show up and make friends to-day I'll bombard their door, sure as I live," said Bushy to herself, when she woke up the next morning. There was no necessity, however, for this extreme measure, for when she looked out there was a woman, not an Indian squaw, but a real live white woman in plain sight. She was very tall and gaunt, with projecting jaws and sharp elbows. Her hair was of a dull brick-red and on it she wore a grass-green sun-bonnet. Bushy gazed upon this picture in the deepest admiration.

"What a beautiful woman," she said; "and what a beautiful hat ! I wonder if Tom can make me one like it." Bushy locked her arms behind her and sidled around to get a better view of the latest style in head-gear, when her eyes opened wider than ever in surprise.

"Jimminy ! There's a little woman, too," she cried, suddenly. Hastening up to the wagon she called out: "Say, did you know I was in the other wagon ? My name's Bushy, and I've got Tom and Shanks and Padre along with me."

"Hello, if there isn't a little boy, sure as I live ! " cried the woman. "Why "——

"Oh, I'm not a little boy," screamed Bushy, turning a hand-spring in the road in her great delight. Then, with one jump she landed on the tongue of the wagon, and, clinging to the box with her hands, looked at the two new-comers curiously.

The woman was still laughing at Bushy's hand-spring, and the child had not yet stopped clapping its hands when Bushy astonished them with another cry.

"You sweet little woman ! I love little women

and big women, too. Such a pretty scalp ! Awful long, aren't they ? " She lifted the golden curls to her lips and kissed them again and again. " My mamma had long curls, and they were yellow, so Padre says. My hair sticks out. It won't wind around my fingers this way."

" I'm a boy, and my name is Willie," exclaimed the child, " and I can beat you in a horse-race. Mamma and I are going out now ahead of the train, and I'll run a race with you if you've got a horse."

" If I have a horse ? Well, I just guess I have ! " replied Bushy as she drew away and felt a little bit offended. " But, of course, you don't know Jip yet. I'll run and get him. Oh, how jolly to have a race with a real boy ! "

She started to climb down from the wagon when she saw Willie's mother smiling at her. " I've got a real dress, but I can't wear it any more, because Rover spoiled it years ago by dragging me through the muddy pond when I had it on. The pink has all run into the white, and it's shrivelled up now."

" I wasn't laughing at your boy's suit," replied the woman. " It's just the thing to wear on a trip like this, and I am glad you are along. I had a little girl once, but she is dead."

" A little girl like me ? " exclaimed Bushy, springing up and clasping the woman about her

BUSHY GAZED UPON THIS PICTURE IN THE DEEPEST ADMIRATION.

neck. "Maybe you are like my mamma, and I'll grow up to look just like you. I love mammas, but I never saw one before."

"Bushy, child!" cried her father, coming forward just in time to see her kiss Willie's funny looking mother. "It seems to me you are rather familiar on such short acquaintance."

"It's a woman, Padre; such a beautiful woman, with long hair, see?" She patted the heavy coils of reddish hair fondly.

"Don't scold her, please," said the woman to Mr. Sukolt. "We are fast friends. I want to get some cactus pears, and your little girl can go with me, if you have no objections."

Bushy and Willie hurried away, each so happy and full of admiration for the other that they could scarcely separate to saddle and bridle the ponies.

"A beautiful woman," said Bushy in a hurried whisper to her father, as she swung her rifle over her shoulder. She gazed again on the lank figure, half shutting her eyes in the ecstacy of her delight. Her idea of the beautiful was very amusing to her father.

"Do you think I will ever grow to look like that?" she asked, with enthusiasm.

"I hope not," answered her father, dryly.

Bushy went on: "The little boy with the long curls is dressed 'most like me. A real live little boy!

Oh, Padre, won't I have fun beating him in the race ! He says he's ten years old."

The three rode off on the keen jump. Astride on a bony horse sat the woman, tall like a man, and with coarse, masculine features. The large green sun-bonnet flapped in the wind, and her hoarse voice could be heard telling the children not to run far at a time and then wait for her to catch up. Her poor beast stood no show with Bushy's and Willie's.

" Do you see that great tall tree far off there ? " cried Bushy to Willie.

" Yes," he answered and his blue eyes snapped with delight. " I'll get there first," and away they flew, Jip and Bob—Willie's horse—both in for the run. Bushy won this first heat, but it was only the beginning of a series of races in which success was about equally divided.

At last they came to where the cactus beds were laden with pears, and the mother proposed dismounting. While she gathered the prickly fruit the children picked flowers, Bushy selecting choice and strange blossoms for her father, who generally could tell her what they were, and Willie filling his hands with everything he could find. Suddenly Bushy heard the woman's voice crying " Great heaven, what will become of us ! " She looked up and both mother and boy were out of sight. She could see no one, yet could hear shriek after shriek, first from Willie then from his mother. For a second Bushy's heart stood still with fright. "A snake, maybe! perhaps a bear!" She did not move from her position, but quickly examined her rifle and found it all right.

She crawled on her hands and knees to a little bend around which Willie and his mother must have wandered. The screams continued, and Bushy at last caught a glimpse of Willie in the clutches of a big redskin, who was getting ready to use the scalping knife artistically on that beautiful hair. The mother was on her knees endeavoring to drag the child away.

"Ugh!" grunted the Indian angrily, and he gave her a blow with his tomahawk that stretched her at his feet. Bushy stood up. The Indian saw her. Not fearing the child he did not drop poor Willie, but instead, hastened to gather up the curly hair for the scalping.

"He is going to kill me," screamed Willie in terror, and his little legs gave out. He sank to his knees, still held up by the curls that were clutched so firmly in the Indian's red fingers. The savage drew Willie roughly to his feet again and turned his back on Bushy. She raised her rifle and fired. The aim was good and the Indian fell, but Willie had been badly cut. A great gash on one side of his head had sent the blood running down his white face and it covered his buckskin blouse.

" It don't hurt very much," said Willie, trying to wipe the blood from his face. " Look, Bushy, and see what he did to me."

She took some grass, wiped round the cut and cried with joy: " Oh, Willie, he has only cut a slit; your scalp isn't off at all."

" But mamma—she is dead !" and the boy began to cry.

" Sit down by her, Willie, and I will ride back for Shanks; Shanks knows everything." Bushy was on Jip and out of sight before Willie had time to say he was afraid to stay alone. Bushy's frantic riding told her father that there was something wrong, and before she had reached the wagons, Mr. Sukolt, Shanks, and Willie's father were on their horses and on their way to meet her.

" Willie's all right, but his mamma looks dead," gasped Bushy, turning and leading the men to the spot where the woman lay so still.

" He's all right," said Shanks after examining the cut on Willie's head; " and your wife, Mr. Goodwin," he added, turning to Willie's father, " will be herself in a little while; I imagine she fainted more from fright than from the blow on the head."

" Who killed the Indian ?" asked Mr. Goodwin, gazing with astonishment at the dead redskin.

"I was too slow, Padre, but they were a long way from me when the Indian grabbed Willie. Will the beautiful lady be angry with me, do you think, because I did not shoot quicker?"

"I don't think so," was all her father could say as he clasped her to his breast.

"My brave little girl must be taken out of this kind of life," he added, after they had returned to the wagons and Bushy had fallen asleep with her arms clasped tight about his neck. "I'll send her to school in Central City if I ever get her there."

CHAPTER XXV

Three days after Willie's narrow escape, Mr. Sukolt and his party arrived at Silver City, a mining
camp consisting of seven cabins and one paying
mine.

" I must stay here one day to give the horses and
mules a rest and have a chance to look over this district," said Mr. Sukolt to Tom and Shanks early in
the morning as their wagons drew up to the spring
about which were gathered all the men of the little
place. The animals were unhitched. The miners
were only too glad to have Mr. Sukolt examine the
property. They wanted the children to go along
with them to the mines, but both preferred amusing themselves in their own way.

"We will take Rover with us and have some
fun," said Bushy to Willie. "Tom says there is
no fear of Indians about here, because they are
afraid of the white men when there are a lot living
together."

" They did not get me and my mamma, did they,
Bushy ? " laughed Willie as he felt for the tender

spot on his head where the cruel knife had slashed through the skin.

"You look awful funny, Willie, with two big curls gone. Why don't you cut them all off and give me half to remember you by?"

"I like you, Bushy, and will give them all to you; won't you cut them off?"

Willie looked so pleadingly into Bushy's face that she tried to think she ought to take them, yet in her heart she felt guilty over coveting the fair hair. "If you want them cut off very, very much, why I can do it for you, but they are awfully pretty curls, Willie."

Bushy felt better after saying that.

"Never mind, you cut them all the same," cried Willie. "Let us go up the canyon where nobody will know it before it is all over with."

"Perhaps we had better tell the Padre," remarked Bushy, timidly. But Willie had fled around the corner of the wagon and diving his hand into the provision box that was still on the camp ground had secured a pair of dull scissors that the men used for cutting canvas and rope fastenings. "Here," he cried, thrusting them into her hand; "now, let's hurry. Rover, come Rover, we want you!"

The children ran off, chasing butterflies, gathering flowers, and forgetting all about the hair-cutting scheme.

It was fully half an hour before a peal of thunder announced that, as Bushy put it, " the clouds were fighting." The children were now following a path which led close to a precipice. Great trees grew on the mountain-side a little way above, and Willie broke from Bushy's clinging hand and sought shelter underneath the branches of the largest one.

" Oh, Willie, Willie, don't do that. Don't you know if the lightning strikes, it will surely take the tall trees and you would be killed. Come away ! do, Willie; don't be afraid of the rain; it won't hurt you."

By this time the water was coming down in great sheets. Bushy could scarcely see Willie. The thunder roared and bellowed, and though Bushy called to the boy again, she knew he could not hear her. The lightning kept up a continual flashing. Willie cried and clung with both arms to the trunk of the pine-tree.

" I'll go pull him away; he must not stay there," thought Bushy as she started up the mountain-side. Just then there was a flash of lightning that not only blinded her but threw her flat upon the ground.

" Ah, that struck somewhere close." A scream from Willie relieved her, yet it seemed a long time before she could get on her feet and look for him.
" Oh ! Willie, that is worse than ever," she cried,

as he, in his fright, fled from the first tree and sought shelter under one close to the path. Another flash, accompanied by a cracking and crashing and a whirl of wind, told Bushy one of those awful mountain wind-storms was on them.

"Throw yourself on the ground," screamed Bushy, but Willie could not hear. In his alarm he started again to run and Bushy ran after him, begging him to stop and let them hide behind some of the great rocks near. A deafening peal of thunder made him seek a tree again and throw his arm around it.

The wind now rushed upon them, and at times would lift Bushy entirely from her feet and hurl her roughly against the rocks; once she almost went over the cliff.

"Oh! if Willie would only mind," she thought as she struggled on to overtake him; "we may both be killed if we keep in the open path this way."

"Padre mio! what was that?" she tumbled all in a heap and could not get up. Something heavy had rolled down upon her buckskin jacket and held her fast. It was the heavy limb of a tree broken off by the wind. Peal after peal of thunder rattled until she could not think, and lightning played around her in the most alarming manner. "The scissors! the scissors!" she screamed. "They are doing all this." With an effort she cast them from her belt.

A loud barking filled her heart with joy. " Rover, has come ! Rover, here, Rover ! " she called, and he came bounding upon her with his shaggy coat wet and dripping.

" Go to Willie ! Hunt Willie ! " she commanded, at the same time freeing herself from the limb with a sudden effort.

She turned and looked down the path where she had seen Willie last. " He is gone ! " she gasped, and her heart stood still in terror. Rover leaped to the edge of the precipice and began to howl dreadfully.

" The tree has been struck with lightning," was her second exclamation. " Padre, Padre, I wish you were here," wailed Bushy, running with all her might to the place and looking down to the water below.

" Willie ! " she screamed.

There was no reply except the thunder, which continued to roar. Leaning way over and looking down the precipice she got a glimpse of Willie's blouse as he lay on the very edge of a jutting rock that extended out into the water below.

" Willie, can you hear me ? " No answer. " Hush, Rover, you make me want to cry," said Bushy, as Rover set up another series of mournful whines.

Bushy realized that the water would gradually

wash Willie into the swift stream, and he would be carried away never to be seen again.

"Oh, why have I neither rope nor revolver!" she cried. "Three shots from my revolver would bring any of the men to us. Padre always knows by three shots that I want him. No rope, nothing!"

She stopped talking and worked her way back to the place where she had thrown away the scissors. "If I can make a rope by cutting my jacket and skirt into strips I can get to Willie and hold him on the rocks till some one comes to find us."

To make the rope long enough she used every bit of her clothing, except her little flannel pants and waist. Her stockings were both knotted in. It took her a long time to tie the strips together, because the wind was strong and the rain pelted her, but finally she fastened the improvised rope around the trunk of the blighted tree and began to let herself down. The buckskin held strong.

Carefully, carefully she descended, until at last her feet touched Willie's body. She caught hold of his golden curls, and thus securing him, she succeeded in moving about over the rocks until she got a safe place to stand on.

"I'll hold you, Willie, dear," she said, and after tying the rope about her waist, so she could not be washed away, she drew him closer to her, and thus with her arms wound about him and half chilled, her father found her an hour later.

Rover's barking as he kept watch above had attracted the miners to the spot. Mr. Sukolt had not worried about the children, thinking they were with the wagons.

" Give me the rope," cried Mr. Sukolt, in a husky voice, as he took in the situation. A miner handed over a lariat which he had taken along to lower the bucket into the mine, and before the men realized what had happened, Mr. Sukolt had swung down beside the children. Then balancing himself by clinging to Bushy's rope he called for the men to haul up the other, attach the bucket and lower it immediately.

Willie, limp and unconscious, was put in first. The storm was now over, and an almost dreadful stillness reigned. The bucket slowly ascended. The men said not a word when they lifted out the little boy and again lowered the bucket for Bushy. Bushy had only murmured, " I could not help it, Padre; he would go under the tree and the lightning struck him." Her white face set with pain and cold, grew whiter as her father tenderly lifted her from her cramped position.

Silently she was hoisted to the top. One of the miners wound his coat close about her while another rubbed her chilled feet in his warm hands.

"I'LL HOLD YOU, WILLIE, DEAR," SHE SAID.

Mr. Sukolt then came, hand over hand up the rope, and the little procession moved down toward the camp at Silver City.

"Any hope?" anxiously asked Bushy's father as he placed Willie in Shanks's arms. "Bushy says he was struck by lightning."

"He'll be all right to-morrow," came cheerily from the miner's lips; "no doubt he fell backward, and that explains how he happened to go over the cliff. He is hurt more by the fall than by the lightning."

Bushy cried herself to sleep that night. When it was learned how Willie had meant to divide his hair with her, his mamma cut four of the longest curls from his head and gave them to Bushy, saying: "It is all I have to give for saving Willie from the wicked stream."

Bushy had the curls made into a beautiful neck-lace when she got big, and often looks at it now, put away so carefully in a little square box, lined with soft blue cotton, and wonders where Willie is, and if he knows how much she loved her first little boy playmate.

CHAPTER XXVI

" Jip, if you don't keep still I will come out and whip you," called Bushy next morning about four o'clock. She raised the wagon-cover and peeped out to see why the horse should make such a clatter that she could not sleep. An odd light in the sky made her lift the canvas higher and put her head outside so close to Jip's nose that he snorted with surprise.

" What is it, Jip ? " she asked, kissing his cold ears and patting him lovingly. " Why, you are all of a tremble ! It looks awfully light and queer; not a bit like sunrise ! It is the reddest we ever saw, Jip."

Rover uneasily crawled under the wagon, and, throwing up his nose toward the bright sky, gave a little howl and then seemed to forget his distress over whatever it was, in his joy at seeing Bushy.

" Keep still, Rover," she cried in a loud whisper; " you will wake everybody up. How queer it smells ! Why, that's the wrong side for the sun ! It is smoke, I do believe ! She sniffed the air and raised herself high on the side of the wagon and leaned far out to get a better view.

" Padre, the mountains are on fire ! " was the cry that went like an electric shock to the heart of every sleeper in the wagon, and roused all instantly.

Tom looked very funny without his skull-cap, and, had Bushy ever seen a clown in a circus, she would have called him one then, because in his alarm he had not stopped to protect his head, and without any hair and his face white with fear, he made a very odd-looking picture. Shanks had long hair, and it was all tousled and standing up almost straight, as if it never meant to lie smooth again or be combed into curls about his neck. Bushy burst into a laugh, forgetting the seriousness of things.

But the laugh died away on her lips, for one glance at the face of her father, who was looking over their heads at the lurid sky, made her remember all.

" See yonder, boys," he said, and he pointed to the north. The broad heavens now seemed fairly on fire. The men turned and gazed in wonder, then in fear. Tom hurriedly remarked: " We must get out of here. These pine-trees will burn like paper."

" What is to be done ? " cried Shanks, smoothing down his tangled locks and fastening his belt snugly about his waist as if preparing for a fight.

Bushy was already dressing herself in a buckskin suit, exactly like the one she had cut into strips the night before. "It will stand fire better than any cloth," she said to herself.

"Great Scott, boys! we are in greater danger than I imagined; see there!" exclaimed Tom. He pointed to a jack rabbit that was making its way down the ravine toward the stream. "That is a bad sign. There goes another. There is something leaping on the other side of the cliff. There it goes; it looks like a deer! The fire must be very close!"

By this time the other people in that little camp had been roused by Tom's loud calling, shaking at the wagon fronts, and pounding on cabin doors. There were only seven cabins, and the inmates were all miners.

"Where do you go in case of fire?" asked Mr. Sukolt of one of the men, as he hurriedly saddled Jip and ordered Bushy to roll up two horse-blankets and then jump on and await his orders.

"There is no place of safety this side of the mines," said the man addressed. "The long tunnel abandoned six months ago can be utilized for the horses and cattle if we can get them there, but "——

"Padre," ventured Bushy, "don't you remember the wide place in the stream just below the mine, and don't you remember how, back about two hundred feet, a high ledge of rocks juts over the water—just below where Willie fell yesterday? Maybe all of our wagons can be got under there."

" I did not notice it. Perhaps we had better try, if you are sure of what you are talking about. The tunnel will not hold all of us."

" Hi, Shanks," he called, " Bushy will lead us to the shallow spot in the stream, or where the water spreads, and "——

" I know I can, Shanks, because Willie and I waded almost across yesterday, and the great ledge of rocks we called our fairyland. I know we can get under, but I don't know how we can get the wagons down."

" If you two children got down we can, and we will let the wagons go if the fire proves a bad one. I would much prefer the water and rocks to the tunnel."

So off they started, Bushy on Jip leading the way.

" We are going to take to the water," called Mr. Sukolt, as one of the miners came back for a last look at the cabins, now deserted.

" All right," said the man, " but you are welcome to join us in the tunnel. The wind is coming from the north, and will sweep down from the back, and we have pumped up a lot of water, and will pump more in hopes to keep the woodwork at the mouth of the tunnel from burning."

" Don't go back far into the mine under any circumstances," called Mr. Sukolt. " I rather wish you would come with us; Bushy says she knows the place is large, and the ledge is on the north side."

" No," the man called back, " we are all right," and he hastened after the other men; Mr. Goodwin deciding to follow them to the tunnel because of Willie and his mother.

The wind began to rush upon them, bringing with it hot smoke and fine cinders. Sheets of flame lighted the air for miles about. Great clouds of smoke began to rise and darken the sky, until sudden day would turn into sudden night. Then, as if the fire had attacked some new group of pines, the light would burst up in the north and clouds of sparks would shoot high, piercing the blackness like forks of lightning.

" Hurry, drive faster, for heaven's sake ! " cried Mr. Sukolt to Tom, who was in the lead. Shanks drove the second wagon, and Bushy and her father rode horseback.

" It's coming close, Bushy," cried her father. " You know we are placing our lives in your hands, child ! " He rode near and anxiously gazed into her flushed and frightened face.

" I know, Padre, that the water is shallow, and

not so very rocky, and that we can all get under the rocks, and that no trees grow close."

"Let her alone," cried Tom, assuringly. "She never forgets a place; don't you know that, old man? I'd trust to her to lead me even in the dark."

On they went, up and down, over rough places that almost upset the wagons, and down steep pathways that scarcely allowed the passing of the wheels.

"All I fear, Padre, is that the wagons may not get through," she cried, once, when it was only by holding on to the wheels that Shanks and Tom succeeded in keeping a wagon from tumbling over the edge of a precipice.

"Here we are at last," joyfully called Bushy, pointing to a place where the water spread out like a fan. "We are safe now, are we not, Padre?"

"I think so," he replied, and he reached over and squeezed her little hand. "What a blessing to us you remembered this spot! Go ahead to where you and Willie were yesterday."

Now, light-hearted in the thought that she had done the right thing, Bushy dashed down into the water and called for Tom and Shanks to follow.

Jip would not go farther; his head was turned to face the red sky. He snorted and reared and pawed the water all over Bushy and her buckskin suit, until she leaped from his back, and gripping his bits, scolded and urged until he slowly but still resentfully followed her, Bushy wading knee-deep in the water. Ofttimes he fairly lifted her from her feet when the wind howled loudest and the flames seemed to roll over their very heads.

"Come on, Tom!" she called, "we are almost there." Tom and Shanks were obliged to lead their horses also, and the wagons went bumping over the rocky bottom of the fierce little stream.

"At last!" they all cried as the wagons were placed close under the overspreading rocks and the horses were hitched and well tied.

The air grew hot and the cracking and snapping and roaring of the angry blaze made the animals snort and plunge.

"Take out your blankets, dip them in the stream and throw them over the horses," cried Mr. Sukolt. The men did so, and then with buckets kept the coverings saturated with water. Bushy had all she could do to hold Jip. He was determined to rush across into the bright red flames. "Jip, poor Jip, don't be afraid. There, now, old fellow, keep cool; keep cool, sir!" were the odd words that kept him in control.

It was hours before the danger was over and the little group made their way up the hill. A spot was selected where there had been few trees to burn, and there they camped for the day. The horses and

"THERE, NOW, OLD FELLOW, KEEP COOL; KEEP COOL, SIR!"

mules were tied tight to the wheels of the wagons, as there was danger of their getting badly burned if they wandered about. Silence reigned, a dull smoke hung over their heads, and it was still hard to breathe. The wind had rushed on with the fire, leaving all quiet and gloom-stricken behind.

The party in the tunnel had suffered dreadfully. The wood-work about the mouth of the excavation had caught fire, and to save their lives the miners had fought the flames with all their strength. Mrs. Goodwin and Willie had been carried back around a turn in the tunnel where the flames could not reach them, but they came very near suffocating. The mules and horses had become unruly, and in the stampede, when the fire was raging about them, two of the men had been badly kicked. Mrs. Goodwin had fainted and lay like one dead for hours. Little Willie was frightened into insensibility, and the men who were striving to save the wood-work at the opening of the tunnel got sadly burned about their hands and faces.

" It was well that you took to the water," called out one of the men who was first to meet Mr. Sukolt when Bushy's father came to investigate the condition of the people in the tunnel. " Just look at the fix we are in ! "

Bushy hastened back and searched for Willie and his mamma. The men had placed them on a kind of shelf made of the walls of rock, and there they lay white and still, with Mr. Goodwin frantic beside them.

"Padre," Bushy cried, "let me go back and hitch up one of the wagons."

"The way is covered with fallen trees," he said. "It would take all night to clear a road for a wagon. You must take Jip and bring Shanks's medicine-bag and the roll of bandages, while we get something to eat and drink. What a blessing we are unhurt and able to help these poor fellows!" He threw off his coat and so did Tom and Shanks, and those who were most badly injured were soon resting on a temporary bed made for them out of the half-burned clothing in the wagons.

"We saved what you see by dipping blankets in the water and throwing them over the side exposed to the fire," said one miner. "But I believe I shall die from the burns I got doing it," and the poor fellow groaned aloud with pain.

"Oh, no, you won't!" said Bushy, kneeling down close to him. "Shanks can cure everything, and when you get something to eat you will be all right."

Shanks soon revived Mrs. Goodwin. Then he gave little Willie some medicine. "When he wakes up he will be all right," said Shanks, in answer to Bushy's anxious inquiry. Shanks had been thoughtful enough to bring a small medicine-box which answered their temporary needs, but Bushy was sent back to bring the large one.

"Hurry, child," called Mr. Sukolt. "It will soon be dark, and we must do all we can before the light goes. Look out for the burning trees."

"Here, Bushy, wait a minute!" called Tom, running after her. "Buckle on my revolver, and should any of the horses be tangled or broken loose, fire three times and I will come down. Perhaps I had better go along, anyway," and he started with her.

"No, no, Tom," insisted Bushy. "You make a big fire and get the supper started. Everybody is starved. And by the time you get ready for me to help you I'll be back with the medicine-box. Why, I can put it in front of me on Jip and be here again in no time. Jip can go anywhere I can."

So away she hurried down the path out of sight, on past the place where Willie fell over the cliff, then down to the lowland, where the wagons, mules, and horses had been left. No horses or mules were there. The spot was bare, and only the deep cuts in the ground made by the animals' hoofs told that the place had ever been occupied.

"Rover," called Bushy. "Rover, where are you?"

A joyous bark from the wagon, in which Rover

had been chained ever since the fire had been discovered, announced that he was all right.

"Ah, I am not afraid with Rover and Tom's revolver," she said, advancing to the first wagon and climbing in.

Rover almost ate her up, he was so glad to see her. "Poor fellow," she called, "did you try to keep the horses, or did you untie their halters?"

This gave Bushy a new idea. "I wonder if they did get away by themselves, after all." She set Rover free; he was out of the wagon as quick as she was, then she began to examine carefully the imprints in the ground.

"That's queer," she finally exclaimed, kneeling to look more carefully at a man's footprint. "Neither Padre, nor Tom, nor Shanks ever wore a boot like that. Rover, has anybody been here?" she cried, fairly shaking the dog off his feet in her anxiety to know.

"Bow-wow!" answered Rover as loud as he could, and then bounded off toward the creek and sniffed and howled on the bank.

"Horse-thieves, as sure as I live!" she said to herself; "and poor Rover was tied so he could not defend even Jip.

"I'll just take a look about, so I can tell the Padre which way they have gone," she thought, and ran after Rover and looked down the stream.

" They tried to follow the creek, Rover," she
screamed at last in delight; " but look, old fellow,
they had to come out just below; there are the
tracks ! Come, let us see what they did afterward."
Her heart was almost broken to think Jip was
stolen, too.

" What's that, Rover ? " She paused and listened. Rover's nose went high in the air as it always did when he thought he understood. Bushy
put her ear to the ground. " It's only the falling
branches, Rover. They are breaking all the time
and burning, too, in some places." Rover, every
now and then, howled with fright and pain as he
would step on some hot stick or brand. They
managed to make their way to a sudden turning
around a sharp rocky bend. The scene that they
then witnessed was startling. There was a Mexican greaser, as the half-breeds are called, riding one
of the mules and leading the other animals. Jip was
ugly, and every few seconds would pull back and
almost unseat the Mexican. They were going
slowly, yet no doubt would get out of the burnt
woods soon, and then there would be no hope of
ever catching the horses or the thief.

" Rover, we must get the horses," said Bushy,
softly, shutting her mouth with a snap that meant
she would fight for them if necessary.

" I am so far away now I don't think Tom or any

one at the tunnel would hear the three shots, and then I may need them myself, if the Mexican is mean. I'll shoot him if he doesn't give up Jip."

Even in all this danger a smile came to her lips, and her eyes for a moment sparkled. " Sh ! Rover, lie down; we will fix the Mexican."

She dodged behind the huge bowlder that had so long kept the horse and horse-thief from her view, and gave a peculiar whistle. Jip pricked up his ears as if he thought he had heard something, then as if in doubt, trotted on with the rest of the horses. The path was now wide and quite clear of fallen trees, so that the Mexican was trying to make good headway.

" Now, Rover, watch ! " said Bushy, and she gave the whistle three times, so loud and shrill that it seemed to pierce the very heart of both Jip and the thief. Jip gave a sudden bound backward and followed with a decided jump toward the place where Bushy lay hidden. The Mexican, with a curse, fell to the ground, and before he could drop the halter by which he had been leading Jip, he was dragged some distance.

With a soft chuckle Bushy grabbed Jip's halter and sprang on his back and was down upon the Mexican horse-thief before he had well regained a standing position. Tottering and blinded, he looked up, expecting to be killed on the spot.

"Throw up your hands, sir!" called out Bushy in her childish voice. The man was so surprised that he merely gaped at her.

"Throw up your hands!" she cried again, and this time he looked into the muzzle of a revolver. "You were stealing my father's horses, and the miners hang men for that. You must help me take them back to the tunnel. Where are your revolvers? Are you unarmed?"

"I lost everything while fighting with the fire. The belt broke and I have nothing, señorita," was the bland answer. "I am badly burnt and "——

"But not too bad to stop you from stealing my father's horses and my Jip," interrupted Bushy. The stealing of Jip incensed her more than the taking of the other six animals.

"I will not shoot you so long as you behave. But I must take you and the horses back to the Padre. If you are burned, Shanks will doctor you. Padre never hangs people, so you need not be afraid; but now take up the halters of the animals and lead them back to the wagons. Take the two mules first; tie the others here so they won't wander."

Bushy kept the revolver pointed at the man's head and never took her eyes off him. When he had the two mules ready to lead, she ordered him to go ahead. Slowly he advanced, and in cowardly fashion gazed back every few seconds into the muzzle of the revolver.

"I can shoot," cried Bushy once, when she thought the man looked as if he were going to try and run. "I will drop you as sure as you live, if you try to get away." The odd glitter in her eye advised the thief to obey, and he slowly led the mules to the end of the wagon and tied them securely. "Now," said Bushy, "we will not go back for the horses, they can stay there until Tom goes after them; we will go to the tunnel where the men are."

Bushy was growing a little bit frightened. The revolver began to shake in her hand. She realized that the Mexican might get the advantage of her, and now she wished she had fired the three shots for help.

"Go right up that path," she said, indicating the way with the nod of her head. The man started, but began fumbling oddly about his flannel shirt for something.

"What's the matter?" she asked in a very brave voice, though her heart was full of fear.

"I am burnt badly," he answered. Then looking up he saw two men hastening down upon them. They were Tom and Shanks, who had started out to learn why Bushy delayed bringing the medicine-box. The Mexican's eyes flashed wickedly, and, with a sudden, lightning movement, he turned and made a dash at Bushy, with a bright dagger in his uplifted hand.

Simultaneously with his yell of defiance came the report of a pistol, and the man fell headlong under Jip's legs.

The instant Bushy realized her danger she had fired, and when she saw the man unable to get up her arm sank to her side, and the revolver fell to the ground.

Jip jumped to one side and gave a neigh of recognition as Tom and Shanks ran breathlessly toward him.

No word was spoken until Bushy was held safely in Shanks's arms. Then Tom stepped over to the writhing Mexican, and asked, in a trembling voice, though he tried not to show his agitation: " What was the row, Bushy ? "

" He is a horse-thief, Tom," she answered, raising herself out of Shanks's embrace long enough to take a good square look at the man. " He had stolen every one of the horses and was driving them down stream. Oh, Shanks, wasn't it awful to have to shoot him ! But he rushed at me, did you see ? " Bushy buried her face in Shanks's buckskin blouse, and Rover took it upon himself to guard the wounded man, and snap and snarl at his every move.

THE INSTANT BUSHY REALIZED HER DANGER, SHE FIRED.

Three shots soon brought Mr. Sukolt and one of the miners to the scene. It was another long hour before they all got back to the tunnel again, and it was two days before everything was in condition to proceed on their journey. Mr. Goodwin and his family remained at Silver City.

CHAPTER XXVIII

" Central City ! Here we are," cried Tom as the wagons reached a high point in the road, from which the travellers could look down on a small town; its little shanties scattered along the side of the mountains.

" It is beautiful," exclaimed Bushy. " I never saw so many houses in my life. Oh, look ! there is a little girl, and there goes a boy ! Oh, what a lot of them ! One, two, three—Padre, there are six, sure as I live. Hurry the horses, Shanks; let's catch them before they get away."

" You don't think they are mountain sheep, do you, Puss ? " said Shanks, with a wink. " I have an idea that they live down there the year round, and you can get a look at them any time."

" That's so," said Bushy, with a laugh. " I forgot things didn't run away in a great city. This is a great city, isn't it, Padre ? "

" The largest about here. Bill Shoemaker said there was to be a school opened, and that is why we came this way."

" Perhaps school will disagree with me," murmured Bushy. "Maybe I won't take to children. Most likely Rover and Jip will be homesick, and you will send for me to come home again."

"Home! You don't know what the word means, child."

"I don't know just what you mean when you say home, but I know what I mean. I mean wherever the Padre is, that is what I call home."

Bushy did not know how near her chatter came to bringing tears to her father's eyes, and she kept right on, scarcely stopping for breath in her excitement over entering a real town.

It did not take the party long to unhitch the horses and pitch the tent on the outskirts of Central City.

"We must get Bushy some clothes," said Shanks, who was more thoughtful about her looks than any of the others. "She looks funny even for a mining town. She must have shoes first."

"Of course she must!" exclaimed her father. "I will go with her and pick them out."

"Oh, Padre, let me do it. I never was in a big store in my life. I want to go alone, just for fun."

"I don't see any fun in buying shoes, but I don't object. Go down to where you see the bend in the road. A Fourth of July flag still waves in front; do you see it?"

"Yes," said Bushy breathlessly, as she fairly danced about in her anxiety to be off.

" Go into that store and say you are Mr. Sukolt's daughter, and that he will pay for the shoes you select."

" Yes, yes, I can do all that," and off Bushy flew down the road.

" Please, sir," said Bushy walking up to the counter—her head coming not so very far above it—" I want a pair of real shoes, like the folks about here wear."

" What kind did you have last. Let me see and then I can get some idea of what kind you want."

" I never had any last," sighed Bushy, gazing down at her moccasins.

" Oh ! you are Mr. Sukolt's little girl, are you ? " inquired Mr. Richards, the owner of the store, and he smiled and leaned over to shake her by the hand.

" Yes, sir; I am not so awfully little though," she replied, half offended at the word.

" You shall have your pick of my stock just the same," said the shoeman, and he set before her all kinds of foot-wear.

Bushy gazed upon them with a critical eye and shook her head. " Once I saw what was awfully pretty and I want something just like it."

" Tell me about it, do," said the shoeman. " I'll have a pair made for you."

" This girl was in a picture that hung in Shanks's cabin until a fire came and burned it up. Her shoes came up awfully high and had buttons on the side, and a lot of pretty marks all around the edges."

"What do you want such shoes for?" questioned Mr. Richards, and he laughed softly as if much amused.

"To wear to school; I am going to stay here and learn to study."

"I have only one pair of button shoes and they have buttons on both sides, but, by jove! you shall have them if you want them. They are a sample pair that we could never sell here."

He brought out a pair of delicate kid boots that laced up the front and had a beautiful embroidered piece that buttoned on one side and lapped over the lacing, and then buttoned down fast on the other, making an ornamental front that extended from the toe of the boot to the top.

Bushy's eyes beamed with delight. Her moccasin was off in a jiffy and her plump right foot settled itself into the kid boot with a determined thud, meaning to stay there.

"It just fits, and I'll take these," she said, though the shoe was much too large. "Two rows of buttons are prettier than one, anyway; and won't the Padre be proud when he sees me?"

"I think he will," answered the shoeman; "for I am sure he did not expect you to buy kid boots to wear in the Rocky Mountains."

"Oh, yes, he did. He said get just what I wanted," insisted Bushy putting on the other boot.

"All right then; shall I do them up?"

"Do them up? What for? Can't I have them?" Bushy's eyes opened wide in fear. "I am sure the Padre will pay for them; he said so."

"Oh, that's not it. Don't you want paper around them to carry them?"

"I am not going to take them off," she persisted, and by the time the shoeman understood what she was going to do she had laced both boots and was struggling with the buttons.

"You are going to wear them?" he asked, bending to help her.

"Wear them! Why, what would I do with them if not wear them? What a funny man you are! I must hurry and show the Padre," she said; "I won't ever wear moccasins any more—no, what do I want of them? You can throw them away."

"I would rather you would do it," said the shoeman, handing her the neat bundle containing her leggings and moccasins which she had discarded. She flung them down on the floor disdainfully.

"Oh, how light I feel; it seems as if I could fly," she murmured as she darted like a deer up the rough street—not knowing, of course, that kid cannot stand knocks against sharp rocks.

The shoes made her oblivious to everything else.

The people were looking and wondering who in the world she was, but it did not take them long to find out she was Bushy Sukolt. Many of them had heard about her, and especially well known was the fact that she could shoot and ride like few other little people in the world. They came out of the stores and watched as she darted by.

"I wonder how they look going," thought Bushy, and she lifted her skirt high and stooped over to watch the boots as they ran along.

Bump she went, into a post—she lost her balance and fell over into a deep ditch by the roadside.

"Are you hurt?" asked a man as he climbed down and helped pull her up.

"Oh, no, sir. I have just got a pair of new shoes, and I am going to Padre." On she went, this time looking back as she ran, to get the effect of her boots.

"Take care!" screamed a man with a pick on his shoulder, but he spoke too late—over she tumbled into the ditch on the other side before the old miner could catch her.

"I'm not hurt, thank you!" she exclaimed, trying to rub the dirt off the boots with her petticoat. "Do you know my Padre? I am going home to show my shoes. Now, you stand there and see how quick I can get to the tent."

Bushy did not know what the word stranger

meant; she had seen so many miners—new ones almost every day—and the idea of introduction had never entered her head. She never doubted that the miner would enjoy hearing of her shoes when he learned they were new. "They go very well, but I wish I could see just how they look. Do you like two rows of buttons better than one? My foot looks awful little, doesn't it? Padre won't know me; now watch!" and not waiting for a reply, she started again up the hill on the keen jump. Her arms swayed from right to left, and she would lean this way and then that, to get a glimpse of her shoes when they were going. Forgetting all about the miner, who smiled and went on his way, she bounded into the tent and found it empty. "Padre has gone out. Hello, who are you?" she cried, as a little girl came in.

"I am Bessie Gray, and I live up there on the hill. We are going to play steal sticks and want you to go on our side. Can you run?"

"I just guess I can! See my new shoes! They are dirty now, but Tom can clean them. What is 'steal sticks?' Are there a lot of children in Central City?"

Just to the right and around the bend were eleven youngsters—six boys and five girls.

Bushy made the twelfth, and they were delighted to have the full number for "steal sticks."

"We must stay on this side of the long line across the road and the boys on the other, and ten feet from the line on each side we put six sticks, and there is a circle on each side of the sticks, on each side, called the jail. Now, what is your name?" asked the girl, turning to Bushy. Bushy told her. Then Bessie went on explaining the game. "We girls must try and steal all the sticks on the boys' side, and the boys will try to get ours. If we are touched on the other side of the line we are put in jail, and must wait there till one of the girls can run and touch us, but you can't keep a stick unless you steal it, and get across the line again without being touched by the boys. Everything depends on how good a runner you are."

"Oh, my!" said Bushy, "we'll beat the boys. I'll bet my new shoes on it."

"Huh," said Mike Shaker, "we'll see about that!"

The game began and the game ended, and Bushy had stolen five out of the six sticks that the girls had added to their six in store.

"You beat us, did you?" cried Bushy, as she shook the whole bundle at the boys. She stood bareheaded, with her blouse opened from her neck to her belt; her cheeks were red as roses, and it was indeed a pretty picture that met Mr. Sukolt's eyes as he came around to find her.

" We beat the boys, Padre," she cried, running to him, and the eleven crowded about, to say she was the best runner they ever saw.

" Oh, I can run so fast in shoes—in shoes," she stammered, catching sight of her shoes for the first time since she began the game—they were in rags ! The tender kid was cut so that the sole clung to the tops only by narrow strips.

" My shoes ! my shoes ! Oh, Padre, what has happened to them ? " She dropped her sticks and burst into tears. " They looked so grand coming up the hill. Oh, Padre, they were such beauties. What will I do ? "

" Better put on the moccasins and we will try again," said Mr. Sukolt, finding it difficult to suppress a smile in spite of his little girl's distress.

" I left them in the store and I'll have to go barefooted," she cried. Mike slipped out and soon brought the missing bundle, and by invitation of Mr. Sukolt the whole team of " steal sticks " went to the tent, where the children remained an hour to console Bushy on the disaster that had befallen her first pair of shoes.

" Never mind, Bushy," said Mike, " you are the champion ' steal sticks ' runner, and to-morrow we'll give you a party for beating us so."

" How much am I to pay for Bushy's ' steal

sticks ' shoes ? " asked Mr. Sukolt of the shoeman that night, after Bushy had gone to sleep.

" I could not prevent her taking the boots," he said; " she simply bossed us here. I never enjoyed anything in my life like watching her efforts to see how they looked while she was running. It is a marvel she did not break her neck when she rolled into the ditch."

" How much ? " asked Mr. Sukolt, again.

" Just $4.50 they cost me, but not a cent will I take," answered the shoeman.

Mr. Sukolt then ordered a strong pair of calf-skin shoes to take their place.

Not so very long ago Bushy was in Denver, and met the shoeman, who is now a great politician. Mr. Richards had been Congressman and a lot of other things, but he had not forgotten Bushy's first pair of shoes, and asked her if she was still the champion " steal sticks " runner.

CHAPTER XXIX

"This is the school-house," said Mr. Sukolt, as he and Bushy neared a low, long building situated in the thickest part of Central City. "It has been opened only a little while, but one of the smartest men in the country is the teacher, and I would like you to attend and learn something, like other little girls. We will see how you and school get along."

Mollie, Mike, and Jake, of the "steal sticks" team, came up, and escorted Bushy into the school-house. There we will leave her and call at Mr. Sukolt's tent in the evening to hear Bushy talk to her father and Tom and Shanks of her day's experience. It is more interesting to listen to Bushy telling it in her own way, than to follow her all day long through the school-hours.

"Well, what have you learned?" asked Mr. Sukolt, as Bushy came bounding into the tent at twenty minutes after four o'clock. She threw her sombrero in one corner of the tent, her slate on the table, and before her father could expect a reply she was turning somersault after somersault from the door toward him, landing on her feet right under his nose. Clasping her arms about him, she cried: "I can't help it, Padre, I am too full of joy; I had to find vent in a little exercise different from what they gave in school—just for relief, you know." With a quick movement she unclasped her arms and reached for the guitar and, playing it herself, danced at the same time a Spanish fandango, until at last she dropped on the buffalo robe at her father's feet and laughed. The little birds stopped their singing on the trees outside to listen. "There, I am run down enough now to talk!" she said. "But crickets and grasshoppers! wasn't I buzzing? Why, Padre, I have felt the springs getting tighter and tighter every minute since you left me. Oh, Rover, old fellow," she continued, grabbing the dog by his shaggy coat and dragging him down on the robe beside her, "you must go to school and learn something; we are great greenies —you and Jip and Bushy."

"Well, I am glad you stop to take breath and give me a chance to ask what it all means," remarked Mr. Sukolt, while Bushy was hugging Rover. "I must confess you are more giddy than ever; school has had a queer effect on you."

Tom came in with provisions for supper, and while he got the meal, and Shanks mended the surcingle of his saddle, Mr. Sukolt put aside his figur-

ing, and they all listened to Bushy, who talked fast
and excitedly.

"I am not going any more," was her astounding
remark to begin with.

Tom stopped peeling potatoes, Shanks almost
fell off his chair in astonishment, and Mr. Sukolt
looked seriously at his wild little girl.

"It's all right, Padre; I have learned all I can
manage for a year."

She pinched Rover's ears till he howled, and then
she began and talked so fast, Tom said it made him
drunk.

"'If you are a gentleman, you will remove your
hat when you enter a house,' said a little man just
as we got inside the door," began Bushy. "I
thought my sombrero was the thing meant, and
whipped it off my head. Then a lot of boys and
girls giggled and acted so funny. 'Oh, it's a boy,'
said a skinny chap with a prairie-dog mouth and
eyes like a ground-squirrel."

"I did not like him and I told him so. Then the
teacher—the little man—came from behind a table
and said: 'You must be Bushy Sukolt. This is
Bushy Sukolt, children.'"

"Everybody grinned at me, and they made me
think of a lot of little owls—you know the kind that
live with the prairie-dogs and rattle-snakes. They
all nodded their heads just like the owls do when
I call 'How-de-do.'"

" ' What a funny dress,' said a mean little girl. ' If you attend to your own dress you will have quite enough to do,' said the teacher, ' and, besides, I wish you to remember that personal remarks about anybody's dress or manners are forbidden in this school.' "

" I felt sorry for the little girl, and told her I didn't mind one bit. And when she began to cry I said I was the best shot around, and if she would come over to the tent I would teach her to shoot with the bow and arrow."

" ' Bushy Sukolt, we do not allow loud talking in school,' growled the little teacher, ' and it would be better for you if you would not boast of your superior knowledge. If you are smart in anything your friends will find it out without your blowing your own horn.' "

" Oh, Padre, I felt littler than a minute, and here is what the teacher said. I have written it down on the slate as one of the things I am to remember forever."

Bushy got up and handed the slate to her father. It was covered with writing beginning with lesson No. 1 and running along with things she had jotted down, until both sides were completely covered.

" You see, Padre, when the tall boy in the corner squinted at me, and told Jake that I was his ' girl ' I heard it and forgot there was a little man teacher. I went over and shook the tall boy till his teeth

jingled, and when he tried to slap me I boxed him
on both sides of his face, and was going to tell him
what I thought of him; when the little man teacher
marched me off to a stool in a corner of the room,
and put a pretty paper cap on my head, and said I
could sit there for awhile.   I got my slate and
learned just the same. Now, see this number "—she
put her finger on No. 3—" I put down when the
teacher told Mike to stop picking his teeth. ' You
must make your toilet before leaving your home,'
he said, ' and cut your finger-nails, too !'   Jimminy ! I asked if I could come home to cut mine,
but the teacher said for me to wait till to-morrow."

Bushy's finger followed each number on the
slate, and she told each story that had caused her to
jot down a memorandum.

" Just behind me sat a wee bit of a girl in a pink
dress, like the one Rover spoiled for me. She had
such a tiny mouth it looked like a catfish mouth.
I couldn't look at her without wondering what she
would do if a fish-hook caught her. The teacher
told me to study, and she made a face at me. Big-
mouthed Tom I like better than any of the children,
but blue-nosed Lucy was good, too. She took me
on her side at recess, and when we played ' pull-
away ' we won, of course. Recess was a few minutes for us to go about in and stretch our legs and
try our voices.

" It was twenty minutes long, so big-mouthed Tom took me into the bowling-alley back of the school-room and we watched the men bowl. They didn't play any great game. The teacher doesn't allow the scholars to play in the bowling-alley. I can't see why.

" A little girl named Libbie got in a swing and a bad boy tried to push her out. I tripped him, and he told the teacher on me, so I had to sit on the funny stool again after recess. It was a nice place. I could see everything that was going on all the time. They called it the dunce-cap that I wore. I didn't mind it. It was red and pretty.

" Libbie stuck her gum on the side of her desk, and when she was reading for the teacher the big boy hooked it. He winked at me and whispered, ' I am going to keep it.' That was very mean, I thought, and forgot I was to sit on the stool. I walked over and took it away from him.

" The teacher said he would punish me if I moved again.

" Billy Sholtz had the nose-bleed, and his face got awful white. He kept blowing his nose all the time. Now, Shanks, you know that makes it bleed worse. I told the teacher so, but he paid no attention to me.

" It bled and bled and bled until poor Billy got frightened and white, and began to cry. The teacher sent after the doctor, but he was in Eureka Gulch. I couldn't stand it any longer. I left the stool and ran to him and held his nose tight between my thumb and finger.

" He began to caper about the room, and I kept saying, ' I can stop it if you will just hold still.' He ran away to the other side and fought me, but I clung to his nose, and by the time he fell down, tired out, I knew the blood had had time to clot, and sure enough it bled no more. Then, of course, the teacher put cold water on the back of his neck, and made him sniff it up his nose till he was well. When I went back to the stool the teacher looked sorry, and all the children laughed because I held Billy's nose.

" A girl who chewed gum in school divided with me, and we chewed all day. The teacher made us both march up and chew for the school. I didn't see any great fun in that, but the other children did.

" I almost died when we had to sit ten minutes with our hands folded. Oh ! oh ! it is dreadful to stay all day in school."

" But what did you learn ? " asked Tom, as he put the kettle of water on and dropped the potatoes in one by one.

" Learn ? Why, look on my slate. I have got enough to keep me going for a year. I tell you,

Tom, I'd have fits if I had to remember any more until I get this all perfect."

She pushed Rover away with one foot, reached for her slate and read aloud, so they all might know what she had considered her lesson for the day.

" Take off your hat when you go into a house— if you are a boy.

" Don't talk about anybody's clothes before them.

" Don't play smart and tell what you can do; let people find it out.

" Don't fight a boy bigger than yourself, if there is a dunce-stool and a dunce-cap in the room. You will have to sit on it all day.

" I must not pick my teeth or cut my finger-nails when away from the tent.

" Children with little mouths are not so good as boys with big ones.

" Blue-nosed people are not so hard to get along with as red-nosed ones.

" Children must not play in the bowling-alley; it is not nice.

" It is all right to disobey the teacher if a boy gets the nose-bleed.

" I had better not go to school unless I can run home and turn somersaults at recess. It makes me fidgety to sit still all day."

" That will do," called her father, as he joined

Tom and Shanks in a loud laugh; "come, let's eat supper. I have an idea you were not a promising pupil—no doubt you were naughty; I shall have to see the teacher."

"I just ran over," interrupted a voice at the tent door, "to see——"

"Oh, Gee! It is the little teacher," said Bushy, softly to Rover, and she lifted the edge of the tent and dragged the buffalo robe and Rover both out on the other side, and there, in the soft light that fills the mountains just after the sun goes down, she stretched herself to listen.

She was in great dread that her father would make her go to school again. "We will run off, Rover, sure as we live, if the Padre sends us to read a poky book, and get the fidgets by sitting on one chair all day." Bushy listened.

"Ah, what is the little teacher saying? He won't get us there again." She rolled up close to the flapping tent and lay still, but her heart beat very loud, so loud she could not catch a word. This is what the teacher was saying:

"It was quickly done, Mr. Sukolt. It was little Mary, the pet of the school. She had been out where some boys were burning brush, and her calico skirt caught fire. Of course, she was frightened 'most to death, and set up such a screaming and crying that the other children were panic-stricken and fled for the school-room.

" Your little girl was on the dunce-stool. It was just at the beginning of the recess, and I had told her to sit still until she got permission to get up. From the window she saw the child with the burning dress. Before I knew what had happened, Bushy had thrown her slate on the floor, and grabbed a coat belonging to one of the big boys that hung on a nail near the window. She did not stop to go through the door, but jumped out of the window, eight feet to the ground. Like a cat, she fell feet-first. Little Mary was by this time running up the path to the bowling-alley door. Bushy headed her off and threw her down on the ground, rolled her in the coat, holding her face near the ground, so the flames, which were rising, might not get into her mouth and nose. She left Mary's head out and threw herself across the body, tucking in her own skirt about Mary's neck. Then, working from the neck down, she wrapped the coat tight and snug about the body.

" By the time we got to the spot little Mary was on her feet and laughing—the child was too small to realize her danger, and, hence, received no shock, for which I am thankful. Bushy and the older children knew what a risk the little one had run, and when I examined her and found only two small burns on her fat legs, my relief was intense. The children were soon playing ' pull-away,' and Bushy,

I noticed, was one of the leaders in the game. I suppose she is all right, but I thought I would rest easier," added the teacher, " if you assured me the child received no burns and is perfectly well. I fully realize that little Mary's life was saved by your daughter's prompt action. Had she run five minutes in the stiff breeze, nothing could have saved her from being burnt to death."

The three men looked about for Bushy. " She may be burnt badly," said Shanks, and he started around the tent. " She is a trump," said Tom, and he forgot his potatoes and went hunting around the other side of the tent. Mr. Sukolt lifted the flapping edge and was at Bushy's side by the time the two men were there. She was asleep, with her head resting on Rover.

She still clung to the slate that held the memoranda of what she had learned the first day at school. The teacher leaned over her and read the last line which Bushy had forgotten. It was this: " Little girls must not play near fire when they wear calico dresses. They may get burnt up. Everybody ought to wear a gunnysack one, like the kind Tom makes for me."

" Although Bushy has spent the day on the dunce-stool," said the teacher to Mr. Sukolt, " if most of my children were half as observing as this slate proves your Bushy was to-day, I would indeed be proud of them as pupils."

CHAPTER XXX

" Would you be very unhappy, do you think, Bushy, if I were to leave you here to attend the school for six months ? " asked Mr. Sukolt early the next morning, after Bushy had tried her one day on the dunce-stool.

" Oh, Padre ! " cried Bushy, as she stopped washing dishes, and, with her hands still wet, stepped out of the tent to talk with her father, who was on his horse ready to ride off for the day. " I will stay if you really want me to, but—" her lip trembled and two big tears trickled down her brown cheeks —" I think I would die, away from you." She leaned against the horse and tried to stifle the sobs that would come up to choke her.

Mr. Sukolt was serious, and his face looked troubled and sad. " It is very hard to tell what to do," he murmured, half to himself. " I must not allow you to grow up in ignorance; and still, little girl, I feel something like you—that is, I would die, away from my daughter; away from my tomboy, my little wild girl."

He reached over and patted her head. " Come, tell me what you think we ought to do."

Bushy's face brightened. She had thought and thought about it during the night. Not for a minute did she intend to disobey or be naughty; still she had formed a plan, and now was her time to make it known.

" Padre, you know a lot—Tom told me so—and why can't I get some books and take them along with us into the mines ? You can teach me, can't you ? I will study harder than I would if in school. I'll promise to get every lesson you give me. Shanks can hear me if you are not home. Don't you think I would study, Padre ? " she questioned, not understanding the expression of her father's face.

" If you promise, I think you would," he said. " I am sure you wouldn't mean to break your word; but there is the association with children. I think you ought to have some of them about you, instead of always serious old men, like Tom and Shanks and——"

" And the best man in the world ! " cried Bushy, leaping behind her father on the horse.

" I don't know what to make of children. They are always in trouble, and some way I feel it my fault. Their legs and arms are so little I'm frightened all the time. I'm sure they are going to get hurt. I'll go down to the school and buy some books, like Mike's, and ask the ' little teacher ' how to do, and, then when you come home, I'll be all ready to start in with you and Shanks as my teachers. Oh, I am so happy ! Do you know, Padre, I love you more than school or anything in the——"

" There, go back to your dish-washing. Who ever heard of a little girl making love to her father like that ? Skip out, you fly-a-way ! and see that you have everything all ready to pack. Much depends on my business trip to-day. We may start away by four in the morning to catch the wagon-train that is in camp ten miles north of here." Bushy waved the dish-cloth at him. He cracked his whip and was soon out of sight.

" Rover, come here ! " called Bushy, " and listen to what I say. We are going down to the school very early to buy some books and then we will take a run. I will ride Jip and you can keep up if your legs don't give out." Rover wagged his tail and barked disdainfully at the mere suggestion that he would give out in any one day's run, even if he was growing old and stiff.

The dishes were washed and Bushy put on her great, wide hat, one that used to be Tom's. " Now for a race," she said. Rover understood, and away they scampered, raising a great dust in the wide path that led down the gulch into Central City.

" Good-morning, Mr. Teacher," said Bushy as she bounded into the school-room at eight o'clock and landed in front of the funny desk, behind which the little man sat writing.

" I thought you were not coming to school any more," he said.

" Oh, my father sent me here to ask if you will please tell me what books to get, for I am going to study with Shanks and the Padre so I won't have to be left all alone in the big city. I will go with them and learn, too."

The teacher told her to take a seat and wait until recess and he would go to the store with her and help her get a good slate, some soft pencils, and the books she needed.

Bushy was delighted, and she sat down to await the children. Children were a great curiosity to her. One must not forget that it was a new thing for her to see little girls and boys. She had never played with children, and had always talked as grown people do, because she had never heard anything else.

" I'm awfully fwaid," lisped a wee child of five, as she hurried into the school-room and sat down close beside Bushy. " Big Snooks and Bully Boy are coming here to hurt the teacher. Bully Boy is my big bruvver, and Snooks is such a bad boy ! The teacher won't let them tum to school, and dey

is goin' to sew him up in a sheet. I's so fwaid !"
Margarette, for that was the little one's name, hid
her face in Bushy's lap and began to cry.

"What is the matter with her, Bushy ?" asked
the teacher, leaning way round his high desk to
look at the child he heard crying.

"Oh, don't tell him ! Bully Boy will whip me
if you do." She clutched Bushy nervously with
both hands, and shook with fright. The teacher
was busy and did not notice that he got no answer,
but bent closer to his desk, and the pen went
scratch, scratch, scratch over the paper before him.

Bushy was trying to think what to do, when
Margarette drew closer to her and whispered, " Dey
is comin', see ?" She pointed with her trembling
finger out of the window, and immediately two
boys with evil faces looked in.

"I wanted to tell," whimpered little Margarette,
"but I's so fwaid of Bully Boy; he licks me so hard
every time." Her lips trembled, and she silently
petted a black and blue spot that disfigured her fat
baby arm.

"Sew teacher up in a sheet ?" thought Bushy.
"I wonder what that means ? Maybe it is a game of
some kind."

The little teacher behind his high desk was quite
out of sight, and the two boys slipped softly up the
aisle. There was no one in the school-room but

Bushy and Margarette. What big boy would think of being on his guard against two girls—one a mere baby and the other a new scholar !

Bushy's heart gave a leap and she drew her breath hard and quick. Neither of the boys had seen her before. Big Snooks was raw-boned, tall, and slouchy-looking; his mouth turned down at the corners, and his eyes were small and kept ever on the move like a monkey's. Bully Boy was half intoxicated. He had drunk enough whiskey to make him ugly tempered, and his face, which at other times was good-natured and gentle, was screwed up into queer grimaces and wrinkles that made him look extremely wicked. He carried a sheet and Snooks had a lot of short rope and string.

Softly and silently they advanced, being careful to keep their heads bowed, so the teacher could not see them. They had taken their shoes off outside, and, catlike, moved on to catch their prey.

Bully turned and shook his fist at Margarette and Bushy, as much as to say he would smash their noses if they made a noise.

It was fully half an hour before school-time, and the boys had planned to have the teacher tied up and stood in the corner for inspection when the children marched in. The bowling-alley did not open until ten o'clock, so there would be no men to hear if the teacher cried out.

Before Bushy could collect her thoughts, Bully Boy had caught the teacher from one side and Snooks from the other. They tried to pin him down and throw him full length on the platform, but he struggled fiercely. They all staggered off the platform into the middle of the floor, quite close to where Bushy and Margarette sat.

"Ah, I understand," said Bushy at last, and quickly she carried Margarette to the door and pushed her out, saying, " Run home as fast as your legs will carry you; you'll get hurt here ! " She looked up and down the street, but not a soul was in sight. The boys knew well when to make the attack. Every miner had long ago gone to work, and the grocery-store was a long way off, and nobody happened to be out when Bushy looked for help. A great thud shook the frame-house and Bushy knew some one of the three had fallen to the floor. She hastened back, and, sure enough, it was the teacher, and his head had struck on the corner of the platform, stunning him. He lay perfectly still and the boys hastened to tie his hands and wrap the sheet about him.

Now, Bushy knew how to wrestle, and her quick eye had detected that the boys were stupid blunderers, only succeeding in overpowering the teacher because he was taken unawares.

"I'll tackle the two of 'em," she soliloquized.

Many and many a time she had wrestled with Shanks and Tom and her father. She had grown to be very skilful in the exercise, and even in boxing and fencing her lessons had been quite thorough. Her father had always blended the useful with everything that was taught her. One day he had said: " If ever the need of throwing your opponent comes into your real life, be sure and use all the knowledge you have on the subject of wrestling, and win." All this now came to Bushy, and she eyed the two boys for a second, and in the next, both of the strapping fellows lay sprawling on the floor. While they were scrambling to their feet and looking about to see what had happened, Bushy stooped for the rope, and another movement sent them again full length on the floor. She took the nearest boy and attempted to tie his two hands. He resented, and she sat upon him, giving him at the same time a blow with the flat of her hand that dazed him. Bushy knew how to tie a good knot, and before he could collect his senses he was secured to the leg of one of the desks. Snooks was on his feet by this time, and realized that only a girl was making the great commotion.

He roared at her like a lion, and struck out with his big fist, missing her, of course, for she ducked under, and at the same time brought the great overgrown body down again very hard on the floor.

The teacher now tried to free himself and called aloud for help, not knowing what was going on, because the sheet was over his face.

"You are all right, Mr. Teacher," screamed Bushy. Then, turning her attention to the big boy, said: "You had better give in or I will finish you." Snooks was kicking and yelling now with fright. He lost all courage when Bully could no longer help him, and, though he knew if he got loose he could whip a dozen little girls, he was anxious to get out and hide. So he doubled himself up, and using all his strength, freed his arms and legs and made a dive for the doorway. Bushy was prepared for that, and had given him warning once that he had better "give in." She cut him off just as he got on the step, and while he was trying to strike her she used her right foot in throwing him on his back. He received a hard slap in the face, too, and the next thing he remembered was the cord cutting into the flesh of his wrists. He was tied to another desk, and, as the desks were nailed fast to the floor, the boys could not possibly get away. Bushy left them and went to unwrap the teacher, who was calling wildly for help.

Little Margarette in her fright had run up the street, screaming at the top of her voice. From her broken sentences the owner of the grocery store gathered enough to understand that there was trouble in the school-house. Some children seeing him run, chased after him, and as a result, by the time Bushy had the teacher sitting up, the school-room was crowded with people—men, women, and children. The scene needed no explanation. Two men took charge of the bad boys and marched them off to the cabin used as a kind of jail, where they were kept two weeks as a punishment. The teacher, as soon as liberated, bathed his head, and said he was ready to continue school.

He stroked Bushy's fluffy hair and looked at her in wonderment, as did everybody else. But Bushy hurried back to the tent, and, saddling Jip, went off on a wild ride to stop her heart beating so queerly.

"Oh, Padre, do let us go away from the big city; it is a dreadful place," she said to her father that night when he returned to camp. Central City was talking of nothing but Bushy Sukolt, and almost everybody called at the tent and wanted to see her. She did not quite understand why they should make such a fuss. What else could she have done?

"It was not because I was brave, as they say," she explained to Tom, later. "I had to do it, because there was nobody else around, and I feared they were going to kill the little teacher. I just had to do it; but oh! Tom, old fellow, can't you hurry the Padre away? I don't like the city; let

us all go back to Great Pine Mine, where everything is so still and lovely, and the birds sing and
the squirrels whisk about. Let us go where things
are not in such a flutter," and much to her joy they
did leave the place, starting the next morning at
four o'clock.

CHAPTER XXXI

" I think I ought to take him up; don't you think so, Tom ? "

" I declare, Bushy, I have not heard a word the old fellow has said," answered Tom, with a start. " I was 'way back in Iowa in my mind, you know, having a good time at the foundry again."

" Then listèn to him now; do, Tom, because I am going to take the bet."

This positive statement, accompanied with several wise nods of Bushy's head, awakened Tom thoroughly from his dream of being in Iowa. He looked about him to realize again with a sigh that he was only one of many men on a prospecting tour for gold, hoping every day to " strike it rich and go home."

The sun was setting behind the mountains, and the round red ball sent its good-night glances through the great high peaks on to the camp, making the decline of day gorgeous by tingeing the clouds above them a deep red and gold. The miners had stopped here for the night because there was good grass for the horses and a spring of water not far distant. Mr. Sukolt, Shanks, and the wagon-master had ridden on to a place two miles ahead where mail was delivered once a week. There was only Tom in the camp who possessed the least bit of control over Bushy, and he felt sometimes unable to cope with her when she got her head set on doing anything. She needed a lesson, for she was without doubt growing too wilful, and this day she got a good one.

" What is it all about, boys ? " called out Tom to the crowd that sat cross-legged around the blazing pine-log camp-fire. Tom was sitting on a feed-box, leaning back against the wagon-tongue, smoking a huge clay pipe. Bushy had found a comfortable seat in a big pile of harness close to Tom, and there, half lying, she rested her chin on the palms of both hands, and listened to the miners as they talked and told stories. Rover had snuggled as close as possible to Bushy, and Jip ate his dinner from the feed-box on one end of which Tom sat. Everybody was waiting for the three men to return before they would sit down to the evening meal. A savory side of bacon simmered on a stick close to the fire; a pot of potatoes with their jackets on, steamed on the other side; a Dutch oven, which is something like a skillet with an iron cover, was still hidden from sight by red-hot coals that had been piled over it, to bake the choice biscuits that were to prove a great treat for the men that night.

"Why, I was saying," spoke up a tall, raw-boned miner, "that my mustang might as well be killed, because she is so beastly wicked that none of us is willing to ride her. We know she bucks like all get out. Several times we have saddled her, but gone no farther. I will bet the first good strike that I make, that nobody can stick on her as far as from here to the creek yonder!"

"And I'll bet the first good strike that I make that I can ride her even farther," sang out Bushy, in a clear, loud voice that brought the men to their feet in admiration.

"Heigh-ho! What do I hear?" cried the old miner. "A challenge from a midget of a youngster like you! I'd take your bet but for the danger attached to the carrying of it out. You might get hurt, and then I'd mourn the rest of the days of my life—sure I would!" The old miner hitched his blue overalls high up on one hip, then on the other; tightened his revolver-belt and fidgeted about, feeling annoyed as well as amused over having his bet taken up by a mere child.

The miners crowded about Bushy; Rover was excited, and Jip neighed uneasily, but Bushy only laughed and said:

"I won't get hurt if I look out, and I do want the

first claim you find. I know you will make a great strike, and to think how rich I can become just by riding a wild mustang several hundred yards ! I'm not afraid, for I have broken a lot of 'em, haven't I, Tom ? "

Tom looked worried, and said he wished Bushy would stop talking so foolishly, because it always made him ill to see her on any horse that was not perfectly gentle.

" But I'm not fooling. I'm in earnest, and I'm going to ride her." She got up and walked toward the mare, followed by the men—some anxious and others jubilant.

" I'll not give my consent to it, Bushy, and I ask you to wait till the Padre comes back. We don't want to hand over to him a little dead girl, or a little girl with a broken leg or a broken neck, either."

" Now, Tom, dear old fellow, you know I can ride. You are always so squeamish ! It makes no difference what I do, you never think it is right. I'm going to win the bet." Then she leaned over and whispered in Tom's ear: " I heard Shanks tell Padre last night that this man, Daddy Bob, was the luckiest and most skilful miner in the camp, and he never failed to find the richest veins of ore whenever he went with a band to any new field. Now, he gives his first rich strike if I can ride the mare.

Why, Tom, you wouldn't be so silly as not to want me to take the bet, would you, when you know I can win it as easy as rolling off a log ? "

Tom still protested, but Bushy ordered the saddle put on, and a great time the men had in doing it. One old fellow, who simply looked on as he puffed away at his pipe, said if the wagon-master was there no such doings would go on.

" The child will get killed," he repeated over and over, but no one paid any attention to him. Tom got out his horse and saddled it, to be on hand to follow the bucking mustang. If she acted dreadfully, and Bushy should be in danger of being thrown, he must be near to lift her on to his horse. There is always danger in getting near a bucking animal, yet Tom was going to be prepared to aid the headstrong child in case she did need his help. That was all he could do, for he could not make her let the animal alone.

Most everybody has seen the bucking ponies in the Wild West Show. This unbroken animal acted in the same manner. She shivered when the saddle first touched her; then she squatted and jumped sideways, leaving the saddle on the ground where her feet had been pawing the soft earth. Again and again she played the men the same trick. It was given up as a bad job, but Bushy asked them to try once more. The surcingle this time was caught

and tightened before the lunge was made that had
hitherto sent the saddle flying to the ground.
Quickly the pony was girted and the straps buckled,
so there was, after that, no danger of the saddle
coming off.

The mustang was blindfolded and kept so until
Bushy was ready to mount.

" Now, ready ! " cried the men who held the rope
bridle, and Bushy was lifted lightly to the animal's
back. Clinching her legs tight to the mare's sides,
she settled herself for the stiff-legged jump that is
generally the first effort a horse makes to get the
rider off. The blind was slipped off. The horse
shivered, sunk down until her back swayed like a
hammock, then bringing her four feet together she
humped preparatory to the jump. Bushy was
ready, and with a stinging whip, or quirt as they
called the small rawhide out there, she lashed
the mare's sides with all her might. The pony was
not prepared for such treatment, and though she
did jump, it was not such a terrible stiff-legged
bound as she would have made had she not flinched
under the whip-lash. She then started on the dead
run. The camp was in a valley between two high
mountains, with a pretty good road extending for
fully three-quarters of a mile up grade. Bushy remembered this, and determined that since the pony
would run, she should not stop until tired out.

Bushy applied the whip with all the might that lay in her tough, brown arm. Tom followed, for he was on a good horse and it was an easy matter to keep right behind the infuriated mustang.

"Can you stick on?" he yelled. Bushy said nothing, only whipped the harder.

"I guess you have taken the right course, Bushy," he again screamed, but Bushy did not hear; she kept her seat with difficulty, for the mustang would shy from one side of the road to the other, so quickly that often Tom stretched out his arm to try and save Bushy, supposing she was going off sure. On they sped, leaving the miners far behind; finally nothing could be seen but the stately mountains on both sides and the rocky road ahead.

"Free yourself from the stirrups," called Tom. "The little beast may stumble, and look out not to fall under her."

There was no time to scold, though Tom regretted that he had not taken Bushy by force and shut her up in one of the wagons until her father should arrive.

"Can you stick it out till she gets tired, do you think?" asked Tom when he got near again.

"Oh, yes, I can stay on if she just runs," answered Bushy with difficulty, because the wild runaway was trying to slacken her speed, and Bushy, in her determination that she should not have an opportunity to get her feet together to buck, kept plying the whip. " Help me whip her, can't you ? "

They had run a mile, mostly up hill at that, but Tom saw the science in her treatment and whipped from behind, and the poor pony started on with greater speed—up and down, up and down— stumbling now, once in a while.

" I think you can let up now, Bushy," advised Tom, but Bushy foolishly wanted to make the mustang run till she couldn't go any farther; she knew that White Face, as the mare was called, would be gentle as a lamb ever afterward if she could get her thoroughly tired out. Bushy had taken her feet out of the stirrups—she rode astride, of course, for it would have been sure failure to at- tempt to ride a bucking horse otherwise—and thinking the pony needed just one more good whip- ping began again to use the quirt. White Face, sud- denly rebelled and turned off into a deer path that led from the main road. The rope bridle was no use to her, for the pony did not know what it meant, and Bushy now realized that she was in great danger of being dashed against the tree-trunks or dragged off by the low limbs. Before she had time to jump, or even prepare to jump, she saw ahead of them a sudden drop in the path. It was like a deep ditch or gorge. Bushy understood in a second that her only hope was in the horse leaping safely over. If she tried to stop her they would both roll bodily into it, and that would undoubtedly mean death. Quick in her instinct, she determined to try the leap, and lash after lash fell on the fat side of White Face, the rawhide cutting into her flesh now as if applied with a man's strong arm instead of a little girl's.

"I am in for it!" she murmured, and shut her eyes as she felt the horse nerve herself for the spring and got a glimpse of the black strip right under them. In much less time than it takes to tell it, Tom understood the situation. He brought his horse to a halt, shaded his eyes, and listened for the awful scream and thud he thought must follow such a leap. There came the thud, but no scream. Tom looked up, and, pushing his horse to the very edge, saw that Bushy lay in a heap ten feet beyond, while White Face, who had safely covered the break, sank on her knees and then with a groan fell over on her side, almost rolling over the edge into the water below. Tom sat like one stupefied, his face white as death. Not a word escaped him, but his eyes were riveted on the little bunch of buckskin clothes that now passed for Bushy. In a minute it straightened out, and Bushy staggered to her feet. After pushing back her hair from her eyes she looked about and saw Tom still and motionless.

"Oh, I am not hurt one bit," she called, "but I was tangled up awfully ! I fell on my shoulders and feet, and for a long time, Tom, I could not tell how to stand up. Can you come over ?"

Tom reached her by going by the roadway, which had a bridge lower down across this very opening. Together they got the horse on her feet, and found that she was not hurt, only wearied out and shaking with fear. Plucky Bushy led her back to the road and insisted on mounting her again. Tom made no objection, because he well knew that White Face could not make her tired legs go fast again for some time.

"Are you certain that you are not hurt ?" asked Tom, anxiously.

"There is a funny pain in my neck," answered Bushy, as she twisted about, trying to determine what was the matter; "but it's not an awful pain, so I guess I got off easy; and my foot aches a little, too. I fell so in a lump—just like a ball, wasn't I, Tom ?"

They both laughed, and Bushy rode proudly into camp a half hour later to tell the tale to the men.

"Well, you have won the bet, and I'll keep my word; I wager my head I will !" said the old miner as he lifted Bushy off the drooping horse.

"If it is a million dollars will you stick to it ?" asked Bushy as she limped to a camp-stool and tried to look brave—her foot was paining her dreadfully.

"I solemnly promise, do you hear, boys!" he called, and then Mr. Sukolt, Shanks, and the wagon-master rode up and dismounted. It did not take Shanks long to see that Bushy was hurt. He took her into the tent and there was much mourning over the supper that night, when Shanks came out to tell them that Bushy had cracked her collar-bone and cut her foot so on a sharp stone that she would not be able to ride horseback or walk for several days.

"It serves me right," said Bushy when her father looked at her reproachfully. "I should have minded Tom. I am learning, Padre, that every time I do foolish things I get punished."

Although Bushy took the whole blame on herself, every man in camp who had seen her mount the bucking mare felt in his heart that he, particularly, was the cause of the whole thing; yet nobody felt quite so badly as did Daddy Bob, the miner who made the bet. Late in the night he came to the tent and awakened Mr. Sukolt, to be assured again that Bushy would be all right in time. "I'll pray that my first find be a good one," murmured the old man as he finally turned in for a few hours sleep, "and by thunder! she shall have every gold nugget in it."

CHAPTER XXXII

Two weeks after Bushy's ride on the bucking broncho the train of miners reached Whitestone, a place in the mountains where it was reported that great gold strikes had been made. It was pretty high up, and nothing but what was absolutely necessary to the maintenance of life had so far been freighted there. The miners were living principally in tents. A few log cabins had been built, but they were given up to the men with families. Bushy was full of joy to learn that a Mr. Delaney had two girls and one boy in his family, and that Mr. Hogan, with his wife and a beautiful blue-eyed girl of seven, lived only a few yards from the place where Mr. Sukolt pitched his tent. The nights were very cool, and often it took both camp-fires and buffalo robes to keep the people warm who lived in tents. Mr. Sukolt and Tom and Shanks concluded that their first duty was to build a cabin.

"What good would a rich find do us if a storm came and caught us without a house, and any of the four should get sick and die?" said Mr. Sukolt. So, while the other men in the party went off and prospected for gold, Bushy's people cut pine-logs, and spent the first three days in building three small cabins close together. One was for Bushy to have all by herself and to be used in the day-time as a kind of sitting-room. The other two were, one for a kitchen and one for a sleeping-room for the men. The beds were made of pine-brush and autumn leaves, with buffalo robes spread over them. Bushy had never lived in such a beautiful home, for there was more room here than they had had at Great Pine Mine. She was quite well now, and delighted in the work of fixing up the room.

"Come over and help me," said Bushy to Mollie Delaney on the third morning. Mollie and Bushy had, until this time, simply looked at each other; but Johnny, a boy of eight, had made up with Bushy on the first day, and helped carry the leaves, and drove nails, and tagged after Bushy wherever she went.

Mollie disappeared for a second; then came out of the cabin with a roll of something under her arm.

"My father is a baker; don't you want a loaf of bread?" said Mollie as she reached Bushy. She thrust the loaf into Bushy's hands, and then, evidently thinking she had made friends, sat down on the bed to see if it were as soft as hers.

It was a great thing to give a loaf of bread in those days, because flour was at this time $60 a sack, and white bread was a luxury. Mr. Delaney was baker for the camp.

" Your father must be a nice man," murmured Bushy. She remembered the time she had tried to make biscuits, and knew from experience it was a rare art to be able to make bread well.

" He is a nice man when he doesn't drink," said Mollie. " He is awful when the miners sell him whiskey. We all have to keep away from him. That's why I am glad to come over here now. Bill Murphy got a big bottle of whiskey, when he went for the mail yesterday, and he sold it to my father for ten loaves of bread. Dad's drunk now in the cabin, and when he wakes up we are going to keep him locked in till he gets sober again."

Bushy felt very sorry for Mollie, because her own father never drank, neither did Shanks. Tom took a little once in a while, but not enough to " kill a mosquito," he said. The two girls played in the cabin, fixing up everything they could find to make the place pretty, and had forgotten all about Johnny and little Belle Hogan and the drunken father. The mother had died of mountain fever months ago, so Mollie was the housekeeper. Suddenly little Belle's voice in a shrill scream brought both girls to their feet, and with blanched faces they rushed to the door and tried to get outside to see what was the matter. The door stuck, and even with their united force would not open. Scream after scream rent the air. Then came curses and growlings in a man's voice, followed by sharp cries from Johnny.

"Father is doing something dreadful!" gasped Mollie, and again she tugged away at the door, but it would not open.

"The window!" shouted Bushy. She pulled Mollie toward the opening in the wall that passed for a window and said, "Climb on my back and jump out."

"But aren't you coming, too?" asked Mollie.

"Yes, yes!" answered Bushy, and when Mollie had jumped to the ground, her playfellow was by her side in an instant.

"Oh, Dad! don't, Dad!" cried Johnny.

"Mollie! Mollie! where are you?" wailed little Belle.

That was all the girls could hear as they ran in the direction of Mollie's home. They were obliged to go the full length of the three new cabins, then around a jutting corner of rock that marked the flat mountain top on which the few cabins had been built.

A terrible scene met the eyes of the two little girls as they rounded the rock. Mr. Delaney had wakened up with his brain on fire from the dreadful whiskey he had taken, and without saying a word he had softly slipped up behind little Johnny, who was busy whittling. His father gripped him with both hands, and before he knew what had happened Johnny was astride a wild colt that one of the miners had tied to a tree, meaning to break him for hauling logs the next day. The colt could not get away, but kicked and jumped about, throwing Johnny, of course, just as soon as his crazy father let go of him. It was a miracle how the lad escaped being danced upon by the colt, but he did, and started away on a run. Mr. Delancy was swifter than the boy, and with a fiendish yell clapped his poor little son on the wild animal again, saying: " It is capital fun; begorra, and it is, Johnny ! "

It was just as Johnny was forced on the horse the second time that Bushy and Mollie came in sight. The colt raced like mad, around and around the tree. Finally, when he came near the log cabin where Mollie lived, he bucked and kicked his hind feet so high that he almost went over on his head. Mollie and Bushy stood still, almost paralyzed with fear. Little Johnny flew high up in the air and then came down on the slanting roof of the cabin. Bushy realized that something must be done right away, and when Johnny rolled off and fell limp and

still on the rocky ground, she started to run as fast
as she could in the opposite direction. One would
have thought that she was afraid, but Bushy had a
plan already formed, and she had to run if she hoped
to carry it out. Mr. Delaney went up to Johnny
and tried to make him stand up, so he could " ride
the pretty horse again."

"Oh, don't leave us !" screamed Mollie, when
she saw Bushy start for the cabin.

"I must get a knife to cut the colt loose. Hurry
and get me a lariat; don't you see he is going to
put Johnny on again ?"

Mollie was a brave girl when she knew what to
do, so she started for the rope. Little Belle had
heard Bushy's order as she stood trembling like a
leaf in the cabin door. She got the butcher-knife
and met her half way, but, quick as they had been,
the crazy man had already tried to throw Johnny
once more on the colt's back.

"If he gets Johnny on I must not cut the rope,"
thought Bushy, "for then the colt would surely
kill him." Ah ! the colt jumped and left Mr. Delaney still holding the unconscious boy in his
hands.

"Hold up, Mr. Delaney, and let me help you !"
called Bushy, and she slyly slipped near the frightened colt and scared the animal farther away.
Then running to the tree she climbed it by grasping

the sides of the trunk with her knees and lifting herself up to where the rope was tied. With one quick cut the halter was half severed. Another and another made it so weak that a hard pull by the colt broke it in two, and the creature dashed away down the mountain as much frightened as any of the people he left behind.

"So that is your game, my little lady!" cried Mr. Delaney, and his fiery eyes glared and his bloated face grew black with rage. He dropped Johnny and started for Bushy. She had expected such a movement and fell like a cat to the ground, screamed for Belle and Mollie to take Johnny into the cabin and bar the door, then stuck the butcher-knife in her belt, snatched the lariat out of Mollie's hand and made ready to defend herself. The lariat was of no use unless she could get room and time to swing it. She decided to lead the frenzied man around the cabins, mixing him up if possible, so she could get far enough away to make the right swing and finally catch him in the loop. Mr. Delaney was not "drunk in his legs." He could run and walk as well as he ever did; his drunkenness was in the brain, and he imagined that Bushy had cheated him out of some fun, and he was going to punish her for it. While he and Bushy were playing that awful hide and seek around first one cabin and then the other, Mollie and Belle carried

Johnny into the cabin and barred the door, leaving little Belle inside and Mollie on the outside, for Mollie wanted to help Bushy—she was no coward. There were no holes big enough in the Delaney cabin for a person to climb in or out, and feeling safe about Johnny and Belle, Mollie grew braver. She rushed over to Mrs. Hogan's cabin and pounded on the door, but got no reply. It seemed very strange that there should be no one except the drunken man and the three children in the camp.

"Bushy! Bushy!" she cried, "we must get into the cabin."

" I dropped the butcher-knife and he has it. He is just as apt to hurt himself as he is us," Bushy panted, as she ran up to Mollie.

Mr. Delaney was not in sight, but could not be far away.

" You go back in the cabin and get a gun; is there one there ? "

"Yes," cried Mollie, excitedly; "but you wouldn't shoot my father, would you ? "

" I could lame him, Mollie, just so he could not kill Johnny or any of the rest of us. Where are all the people, I wonder.

" Get the revolver or gun or anything that will shoot, and be ready with it at the door if he chases me there, and "——

A scream from Mollie made Bushy turn, and there close behind them was the furious madman. Mollie ran toward the cabin, and little Belle, who was watching through the cracks between the logs, opened the door and let her in. Mollie grabbed the rifle and waited at the door for Bushy, who, she supposed, was immediately behind her; but Bushy, who was a faster runner, had got far enough away already and was swinging the lariat preparing to catch the crazy man if possible. Mr. Delaney caught sight of the rope as it swung toward him, and instead of dodging it, he stupidly stood still and waited for it to fall. Bushy could scarcely believe her eyes when she saw the loop quietly settle over him. With a quick jerk she tightened the rope, and with another she threw the man to the ground.

"Mollie, Mollie, come quick!" cried Bushy, in her fright and excitement. She wound the rope about Mr. Delaney, binding him fast to a tree, which he had gradually backed against. Mollie got an extra rope, which the two girls added to the length of the lariat, and when at last the man was safely bound, the children looked up to see the whole camp hurrying toward them.

The miners were puzzled at first, till the girls told their story. Then old Bob looked at the raving drunkard as he stood bound to the tree—Bushy, still held the end of the rope—and then turning to the crowd that had gathered so suddenly around her, he said: " The find is Bushy's, by George ! You don't need to congratulate me any longer, boys.   There stands the owner of my first strike. Bless her ! "

Bushy did not know what this meant until it was explained that old Bob had struck a rich vein of gold-bearing quartz that very afternoon. The news had travelled like wildfire, and even Mrs. Hogan had gone to see the find. That is how it happened that the children and the drunken man had been left alone in camp.

CHAPTER XXXIII

" Good-morning," said Miner Bob to Bushy, as she opened the cabin-door the next day. " I've been waiting here since six o'clock for you to wake up. You see, I want to take you along with me to look at the new find."

" Why didn't somebody wake me up ? Where is Padre ? Where are the men folks ? Why, I never slept so late before in my life !" Bushy rubbed her eyes hard, for she was yet very sleepy and could scarcely see old Bob, though he sat on the step, right at her feet.

" Shanks said you were 'most played out lariating Delaney, and gave orders for nobody to disturb you till you came out on your own account."

" Shanks is always afraid something will happen to me," said Bushy as she dipped her head in a great tin basin of spring water.

Bob leaned back against the logs and laughed till he showed all his yellow teeth—teeth so much like Rover's that Bushy could not help noting the resemblance. He took out of his pocket a plug of tobacco, and cutting off a square piece, tucked it in his left cheek before answering her.

"How long have they been gone?" asked Bushy, as she warmed up the breakfast that had been left her, and Bob busied himself fixing the fire and keeping it burning.

"About half an hour."

"And you waited for me?"

"Yes, because I wanted to show you the gold myself. Why, Bushy, it is a clear white quartz, and I dug down three feet and the prospects are fine; there is a great fortune! Just what I have been looking for these twenty years."

In the beginning of the conversation Bushy's eyes danced and she ate so fast the potatoes almost choked her. Bob was going to give it all to her. How rich she would be! "The first thing I'll buy," she thought, "will be a wig for dear old Tom."

But when the old man said: "It is just what I have been looking for these twenty years," Bushy detected a sad tone in his voice that startled her. "Perhaps he is sorry he made the bet; maybe he wants to back out?"

"Don't you make a lot of good strikes, Bob? Tom said you were one of the best experts he knew, 'cause you always got ahead of everybody else."

"Oh, I've had many good finds, but none like this one. Just come along, Bushy, let us hurry; I'm anxious to hand it over and get it off my mind."

They started out, Rover following close at their heels. Mollie Delaney met them at the door. She had come over to carry a message from Johnny, who could not go to sleep until someone would tell him Bushy did not get hurt and was " good as ever " when she woke up in the morning.

" You tell him," said Bushy, " that I will come in and see him after I visit the mine that Bob has given me for winning the bet on the broncho. I'll bring him a specimen with free gold in it. How is your father ? "

" Oh ! he is being watched by his partner, Bill Sattler, so we are not afraid any more. Bill says Dad may have the delirium tremens next time he takes whiskey. He is in bed now, and Bill is making him take the medicine Shanks left for him."

Mollie went back to the cabin and Bushy and Bob travelled toward the mining gulch.

" Have you got a family, Bob ? Little girls and little boys and a mother and father ? "

" I don't think they are very little now, because it has been years and years since I saw them. My old mother is dead and the last letter the boys wrote me said father was ailing. Guess he ought to be, for he is eighty-five years old."

"They would like to have you come back, wouldn't they, Bob?"

"Better believe it! My old wife would cry her eyes out with joy, and the little boys and girls, who are men and women now, would never know their old dad, I am so grizzled and weather beaten." Bob slyly wiped a tear from his eye and Bushy pretended not to see.

"I am sorry I took you up, and now I wish I hadn't won," murmured Bushy, half aloud, and Bob heard and straightened himself with a jerk that meant "steady, old man, don't you weaken!"

"You needn't feel one bit sorry, Bushy, because it would have been the same had one of the boys picked me up. A bet is a bet, and not to pay an honest bet is just as bad as horse stealing. I'd feel just as uncomfortable not to pay a bet as a horse-thief must feel when the rope goes curling about his neck."

"I won it fairly, didn't I, Bob?" asked Bushy, as they came in sound of the miners' picks. "If I did not win it perfectly fair and square I don't want you to give the mine to me."

"But you did, and I am going to have all the boys who saw you ride the broncho be witnesses to my turning over the new lead to you. I would never sleep easy again if I didn't pay the bet."

The excitement of Bushy and her companion was

considerably increased by the appearance of two strangers who caught up with them on the road, one of whom said to Bob, " I'll give you $40,000, here and now, for that find,"and Bob shook his head rather mournfully. Bushy said nothing.

" Hello ! here they come," cried Shanks, which was the signal for everybody in hearing to draw near the rich quartz. All were curious to know if Bob would really keep his word—everybody but the Padre, Shanks, and Tom ; they were more curious to see how Bushy would receive the gift.

" I don't think it a wise thing to have her so tempted," said Mr. Sukolt, and his face looked troubled.

" Oh, pshaw ! " cried Tom. " It was a square thing. If it had happened between two men there would be some tall fighting and perhaps a little lynching if the affair wasn't done up in business fashion."

" That's so ! that's so ! " chimed in several of the rough men, " and we will see that she gets the ' lead,' too; Bob was a darn fool to make such a bet, but, by George ! he must pay his debts."

" It is a very unfortunate affair," said the Padre. " This will test my little girl's nature in a way I would much have preferred to have avoided."

" Let her alone," cried Shanks, who was watching Bushy's every move. " Old Bob is superstitious, and would think the stars would fall on him and kill him if he broke his word."

Mr. Sukolt felt Bushy's hand slip into his, and turning he saw her face fairly aglow with happiness.

"Padre!" she cried, "come quick. There is a man here who wants to buy the lead. He has offered Bob $40,000 in cash this minute. It is my mine, you know, and he can't have it for $40,000, do you hear, Padre?"

"Bushy, child, Bushy! what has gotten into you; do you really intend to hold the old man to his foolish bet?"

"Of course I do, Padre," and she dragged him hurriedly to the fresh-dug hole that was causing such excitement; Tom, Shanks, and seven other miners following.

"By rights it is not my mine," old Bob was saying, with a dreary little smile on his bronzed face. "If I considered it my lead you could have it for that amount, sir, and I would start for the States at sunrise to-morrow." The tremolo in his voice seemed to strike a sympathetic chord in everybody's heart but Bushy's. She shocked them all by her sudden interruption with:

"But it is not his mine, sir, and I'll not take a cent less than $50,000. I know enough about veins, sir, to feel certain that rock will yield the owner who works it $100,000 in no time. Look at the width of the white quartz vein, and see, it branches out in two great arms, big tunnelling to the right and left, then following the main vein down. There will be three mines in one. Is it not so, Padre?"

Bushy talked so excitedly and seemed so oblivious of the fact that the greater she made the mine out, the more poor Bob suffered for his folly; that Mr. Sukolt was stunned by this new evidence of avarice in his little girl's heart.

"You are right as to the three veins," answered Mr. Sukolt, after digging about awhile with his stick; everybody closing about to see and listen. "Are you an old miner, sir?" he asked, turning to one of the new-comers, the one who had offered the $40,000.

"We are both Californians and working our way home with success in our pockets. I did not intend to mine any more, but it's as fascinating as gambling. I offer $40,000 for this strike. I have the amount here," and he tapped the great leather belt that girdled him, which seemingly carried nothing but revolvers.

"Bob, it is my mine, is it not?" cried Bushy, running to him and throwing her arms about his waist. "Remember, Bob, bad luck will come to you if you don't pay your bets."

"Yes, yes, I know; and I was only weakening

because I just thought for a minute how near I had come to seeing my old woman once more."

" I can't understand, Bushy," said Mr. Sukolt. " I think I had better send her back to the cabin; she seems to have lost all feeling."

" Let her alone," said Shanks, " the child is up to something. I see it in the peculiar glitter of her eye. She would tell us if she had a chance, I think, but she can't here, you see. Let her alone. It is like playing euchre when she has called for her partner's best card, and will play it alone."

" Yes, let her alone," grumbled the miners, some of them ugly with jealousy, and others with drink. So, while Bushy and Bob were having their talk, the miners flocked about the fresh-dug hole and gossiped on the value of the find.

" Boys," cried old Bob at last, as he and Bushy joined them, " I want you all to be witnesses to the fact that I now give up all claim to the mine and hand it over to Bushy Sukolt, in payment of the bet, lost two weeks ago, when she rode my wild colt, White Face."

" Hurrah for Bob !" shouted the miners.

" You are a fool," said the two Californians.

" Can't help what any of you think !" muttered Bob, as he signed a written statement made out in pencil, on the leaf of a memorandum book, by one of the boys who insisted that Bushy should have something more than their word for security. " I feel better, any way. I may have been a fool to make the bet, but, by Jove ! I don't agree with you that it is acting the fool to pay it."

" I'll prove to you that it is," said the man from California. " I'll give the little girl $50,000—that is her price, I believe."

Every eye was turned on Bushy. Mr. Sukolt's face was ashen white, the excitement was intense. Shanks walked over and stood close to Bushy, but said nothing. Tom got shaky in his legs, and squatted down on a rock near the mine. Bob trembled so that when he handed the paper to Bushy, she took his hand as well as the paper, and held it fast. Thus, clinging to his arm and hand, she replied, in a clear, firm voice: " I'll take it, sir, if you can pay me this very minute."

" You are all witnesses that this is no child's play," spoke up the California miner as he began to unbuckle his huge leather belt.

" I'll see that it is not," said Shanks, who immediately tore out two leaves from his note-book and made out the necessary papers to render the sale legal.

" Fix it so he can't back out, Shanks," said Bushy.

" Fix it so she can't back out, Shanks," said the California miner, imitating Bushy's voice as best he could. This made everybody laugh, even old Bob smiled faintly—he was literally being held up by Bushy, who for some reason would not let him sit down as Tom had done.

" Will you hurry, please !" said Bushy, and the man counted out: " Thirty, forty, forty-five, fifty—there, young lady, is the $50,000 in cash, for which I shall take, in exchange, the Bushy Mine, for that is what I shall call it."

Bushy evaded the eyes of her father. She felt his disapproval all the time, and even when the cheer went up as the gold and greenbacks were placed in her dress-skirt, which she held up to receive the money, she dared not yet look up to him; for the glad light, that always covered his face when pleased with her, was not there.

" Now, Daddy Bob," she said turning to the old man, who still trembled at her side, " I want to buy White Face, for that wild animal brought me all my good luck."

Daddy Bob looked puzzled, but Shanks threw up his hat with a regular war-whoop. He saw at last through Bushy's way of doing business. He brought out his note-book again, and with a face beaming with delight, said: " How much do you intend to offer for White Face ? "

" Just $45,000 ! "

Daddy Bob sank in a heap at her feet. Tom

tumbled off his rock and went rolling into the new mine. Exclamations of surprise burst from the lips of every miner. Bushy raised her eyes and glanced at her father; he was watching her and only smiled, but that was enough for Bushy. She knew he was pleased.

"Make out the bill of sale, Shanks. Be quick, please," said Bushy, and she stooped down to help Daddy Bob to his feet again. With one hand she clung to her dress, full of gold and money, and with the other she led the old man to a rock near the Padre, and there they counted out the cash—Mr. Sukolt looking smilingly on.

"Thirty, forty, forty-five—there, Daddy Bob, is $5,000 more than what you would have got, had you not paid the bet, for I heard you tell that man you would take $40,000 if the mine were yours. I held on, you see, and can give you $45,000 and keep $5,000 for myself, which is good pay for riding on a bucking broncho. Don't you think so, Padre?"

Mr. Sukolt put his big hand over Bushy's brown one, and squeezed it, but he said not a word, he was watching Daddy Bob. Bushy took the bill of sale, and piled the money into Bob's shaking hands.

"Don't forget, Daddy, that you go East by sunrise to-morrow morning." Daddy could not stand it any longer, he bent his aged form, and kissed Bushy on the forehead and burst into tears.

" It is quite fair, is it, Mr. Sukolt ? " he stammered at last as he dried his eyes on his coat-sleeve and looked wonderingly at the money.

" Quite fair," spoke up the Padre, who now held his daughter on his knee, and had both her arms about his neck.

" Boys, do you think it fair ? "

" She's a brick," cried one.

" A jolly business woman," said the travelling companion of the California purchaser to Bob. " She managed to make you pay the bet and at the same time hand you $5,000 more than you would have got at your own bargain, and she pockets $5,000 for herself. Of course it's fair ! "

Thus assured that it was all right to sell the colt for so much money, Daddy Bob put away the $45,000, and told the boys he would really start next day for the East and his family.

The miners gave three cheers for Bushy before going back to work, and Tom whittled out the words, " Bushy Mine " on a pine-log and stood it up as a mark for the new owner. Mr. Sukolt told Tom to go back with Bushy and take care of the $5,000, and then get dinner and bring it out to the boys in tin buckets. On their way home Tom said:

" How did you happen to be so smart, Bushy ? It didn't seem natural," and he laughed heartily.

"Well, Tom," she replied, "I heard one of the California men say to the other 'bid $40,000 and go up as high as $50,000 before giving it up.' That is what made me so brave. You didn't think I was going to keep the money, did you, Tom?"

"Darned if I knew!" said Tom, and they both laughed.

"Well," said Bushy to the California man, as he passed them on the road a few minutes later, "Daddy Bob was not such a fool as you thought to prove him, was he?"

"Oh, Daddy was all right," replied the man, laughing aloud, "the little girl was the one who gulled me."

Bushy talked it all over with her father that night. He did not tell her he had feared that she would give way to the glittering temptation.

CHAPTER XXXIV

A year later, and we find Mr. Sukolt and his party still at the same camp.

"What is it ?" asked Bushy of her father, who was reading attentively a letter that had come to him by the last mail-wagon. "What is it, Padre ? You look so serious."

"They want me to come back to Great Pine Mine and bring three men with me. The offer is a good one."

"Three men," cried Bushy; "why, Padre, then you can take Big Bill, can't you ?"

"What do you think about going, boys," asked Mr. Sukolt, turning to Shanks and Tom.

"Oh, Tom," said Bushy, almost pleadingly, "we are going back to Great Pine Mine—you and me and Padre and Shanks and Big Bill, and there is a lot of money waiting for you there—the letter says so, and "——

"Hold on and take a good breath, chicken," cried Tom, as he pinched her ears. "You are going too fast altogether."

After considering everything, Mr. Sukolt de-

cided that if they could dispose of their mining property they would go. Big Bill had not been at all fortunate in finding gold in this camp, and was glad to be made one of the party.

Little Belle heard the news and came running into the cabin, carrying her new hood that her mamma had just finished. "You must take it, Bushy, because when winter comes it will keep your ears from freezing, and it is much better than any kind Tom can make."

" Well, I like that ! " cried Tom, who turned just in time to hear his skill deprecated by pretty little Belle.

" Oh, Tom," they both cried, and more hearty laughing followed. " We know you do a lot of things, but you do sew so funny ! " put in Bushy as she caught him by the hands and whirled him around and around.

It was a busy day, and yet there was not much work done in the mines. Every man seemed to prefer lingering about the Sukolt cabins rather than digging ore. Without being asked, they assisted in sorting and packing, and cleaning wagons and mending harness, splicing ropes, brightening firearms, dividing ammunition, and adding little necessaries, like a sack of salt, a plug of tobacco for Tom, a side of bacon, a round of ammunition, all taken from their own little stock.

Mr. Hogan said he would try and sell the "claims," should any Eastern gold-lover with a lot of money wander into camp. They were good mines and would pay well if anybody had money enough to work them. The only one being worked was the Bushy Mine, which had turned out to be one of the greatest finds that year.

It was a sad day when the two wagons and the four miners and Bushy rode out of the old camp. Mr. Sukolt had sent a reply to Great Pine Mine by the same man who brought the mail, saying he would accept, so when, three days afterward, they started on their journey the word that they were coming was four days ahead of them.

They had along with them a cow and four oxen. The men walked most of the way, only riding when it was down grade. Big Bill drove the cattle. Bushy rode Jip, of course, and was a kind of scout. She went ahead and warned them of any coming teams, or bad crossings; hunted for water, and looked out for good camping grounds and grass spots where the horses and cattle might get a little grazing as a luxury. On the third day they reached a very high place in the mountains. They actually rode right through the clouds to get there. The mountain-peaks rose high and sharp all about them, and the scenery was magnificent in its sudden changes from storm to sunshine. Bushy had never seen anything equal to it before, and she kept wishing all the time for Mollie and the other children to look at it with her.

" It makes me think of two big buffaloes fighting —butting their heads together," cried Bushy, as she sat on Jip and watched two black clouds rushing toward each other.

Bushy, in her delight over this new phase of nature, urged Jip on ahead, and was soon high up and far in advance of the two wagons and Big Bill with his cattle. Still she could hear the men behind distinctly, and often understood their calls one to another. " Oh, oh ! " she screamed as she reached the very tip-top of the divide, " those two black fellows roll about like they were alive."

She checked Jip and sat like one entranced, watching the play of the two clouds in the sky to the left of her. They took all kinds of funny shapes, first long, with queer waving tails, and arms stretching out, then they would roll up in a ball and appear to bump angrily against each other. The sky assumed all colors and shades imaginable, and for a while Bushy wondered if the world was coming to an end—everything suddenly looked so strange. " Jip, oh, Jip, they are coming this way ! " she screamed as a tremendous thunder-clap almost startled her into falling off the horse. Peal after peal rent the air and Jip trembled so that Bushy dismounted, thinking he would sink under her. "Crack! flash! bang!" went the lightning, "boom! boom! boom!" sounded the thunder like a thousand cannons going off at once, yet the thickest clouds were far below. The sun was shining overhead.

" If it comes any farther this way, Jip, old fellow, we are in for it," said Bushy, looking back anxiously for the appearance of the two wagons. " Surely they will get up here soon, I cannot be so very far in advance ! "

The clouds seemed to be rolling down the mountain-side. Bushy watched with wide-open eyes and soon saw beneath her nothing but the big buffaloes, as she called them, and the noise was deafening. Crash! fell the trees. Bang! boom! and then a bellow like that of a wounded grizzly. " Gee! whoa! haw ! " would come to Bushy's ears now and then from the darkness below. Then she heard, " Hold your horses, they are slipping down the mountain-side ! " " Ah, that was Tom's voice," murmured Bushy. " Jip, we are left out of this entirely." She tried to make Jip go down the road, but no force could drive him one step in that direction. While Bushy and Jip were standing in the bright sunshine, the men and wagons below were being drenched with rain. To them it was all dark, and the rumbling thunder and quivering lightning, coming upon them almost every instant, made it imperative to stop where they were and try to keep the animals from dashing down the precipice in their fright. The rain did not fall in drops but poured, as if out of buckets.

"I am all right, Padre!" but though she could hear the men, they could not distinguish her voice, for they were in the midst of the storm.

Still pressing forward, the little party were brought to a sudden standstill by a tremendous report of thunder, which startled them even after their experience of the last half hour. As suddenly as the storm had come it settled and drifted downward, giving a few departing groans and disappearing in the valley below. With streaming faces and hair, and drenched bodies, the little group looked about them to ascertain if anyone of their number was missing.

"Bushy!" they all screamed, as the sun burst upon them in its glory and made their dripping forms seem grotesque and out of place.

"Here! here! Jip and I are all right," she cried, and when the wagons reached her a more astounded set of men never gazed upon a little girl.

"Dry!" they all cried. "Not a drop of water on her!" It was a wonderful experience for them all, and the miners never got tired of telling the story.

CHAPTER XXXV.

They got to Great Pine Mine all right, and, after a warm welcome by some of the old miners, they soon found themselves settled in the same snug quarters of years ago. One day, not long after their arrival, Bushy decided to carry out a pet ambition, and that was to climb to the top of Bald Mountain. She got to the very summit and Rover managed to follow her, but it took them longer than Bushy had thought it would. Hence they were far from camp when black night came down upon them.

"Strange!" suddenly cried Bushy, "the light is quite to the left of us, Rover, old fellow. Our noses are pointed in the wrong direction. I didn't think I could get so badly twisted going such a short distance." Bushy and Rover made direct for the light on the left. All went well until, as they drew close to what they thought was the camp, Rover showed signs of great uneasiness. Bushy's attention was attracted to the dog's queer actions and she remarked to herself: "Something's wrong, sure!

"Rover, be careful! Let us go closer. I don't

know this place at all. This light doesn't belong to Great Pine Mine. I wonder where we are ! It makes me think of the goblins that Big Bill said walked about on Halloween. Softly, softly, Rover ! There is no animal that I ever heard of that has an eye like that. Maybe it is a ghost. I never saw one and don't know how they look."

Blinded by staring so fixedly at the light Bushy did not realize how close she was to it until she came bump against a wall of rock. The ray of light that had led her on shone through a crack between the stones. " Down, Rover, down ! I say," commanded Bushy, expecting every minute that some one would pounce upon them and perhaps kill them. Rover obeyed, stretching himself reluctantly on the ground, while Bushy crouched close within the black shadow of the wall.

" Hist ! What was that ? " said a gruff voice close to the opening.

" Confound it, Barkley, something is prowling around here, I feel sure ! "

" Bah ! always skittish—on the lookout for something to be afraid of," remarked a sneering voice farther away. " Let up with your fake ghosts and help us finish the plan of attack. The leader is old man Sukolt. I know him well." They were talking in a Mexican lingo, but Bushy understood them.

" Sukolt ! he means the Padre," she murmured, and her fist clenched tighter the revolver hanging in her belt.

" What have Mexicans like these to do with my Padre ? Still, Rover, don't move, there is work for us here, I'm afraid ! "

" There is no way he can be taken except to hit him in the back, for no one of us dare meet him face to face," grumbled an old man. Bushy was now clinging to the rocks outside like a bat, with both of her eyes peeping upon the scene in the cave.

The last speaker was the centre of the group of men, who were evidently brigands of the Rockies.

" How many are we ? " asked the leader of the gang. " Ten," was the reply.

" There are over thirty miners, but we must kill them or drive them away. We have too much valuable stuff here, and, besides that, too comfortable quarters to be driven out by a set of gold diggers," added the chief of the bandits. " They are getting too thick here, altogether."

" We will set fire to the camp first. Ten cabins must be fired at once, and as the miners come out to fight the flames they must be picked off one at a time. We can do it, because we will be in ambush and they in the bright light. Mind you don't leave the scene until you can each count your three dead men."

"What about the girl ?—must we kill her, too ?" asked a fine looking bandit, whose moustache would have been the pride of a story-book cavalier.

"No," said the chief, "take her captive. She will be useful to cook for us and keep the cave in order. She must be a good shot, so keep an eye on her, even after you catch her."

Bushy put her ear to the crack, and listened closely.

"Two o'clock, do you hear ?" the chief was saying. "Each of you must pick out a cabin and attend to its inmates himself without further instruction; I will look out for the girl."

"Oh, you will, will you ?" thought Bushy, as she slipped down softly, and again taking hold of Rover's collar, said: "To the Padre, Rover, for he is in danger."

Rover sniffed about for a few seconds and then started off so fast that Bushy had difficulty in keeping up with him without stumbling and falling every few yards.

When once so far away that there was no danger of the robbers hearing them, Bushy began to realize for the first time how serious the danger was.

"We are not one bit brave, are we Rover ?" she said, ready to cry with joy on seeing the lights of the camp once more.

It was not very late, yet Mr. Sukolt had grown uneasy and felt sure something had happened to keep his daughter away from home at that hour, so he had sent some men north, and he himself had just started out toward the mountain that she had climbed.

"Where is the Padre?" she cried, excitedly, as she rushed into the tent, where Shanks had gone to get lanterns for farther search.

"Gone to hunt you!"

"Call him back immediately, and send out the alarm for all the men, too, for there is to be an attack on the camp at two o'clock to-night," and Bushy threw herself excitedly on the robe at Shanks's feet.

The signal was sounded, and in less than twenty minutes every miner was in front of Mr. Sukolt's cabin.

Mr. Sukolt had Bushy tell her experience to them, and they doubted not one word. No man was to close his eyes that night. Bushy, Shanks, and Tom were to take the centre cabin, which had a cellar with portholes.

"All wounded must be taken immediately when hurt to the centre cabin. So, Tom, take there now, everything necessary for hospital purposes," said Mr. Sukolt. He then considered the problem how to save their property from fire. Every miner was to be his own watcher, and the instant a brigand appeared he was to be shot. If a cabin should be fired no one from outside was to go near it.

Bushy could not sleep, though she tried to obey Shanks and get a nap before the attack was to be made. Twelve, one, and half-past one o'clock came, and her eyes were still wide open and bright.

"Sh!" said Tom, who kept going from one porthole to another, trying in vain to see something through the darkness. "It is the gloomiest night I ever saw. No wonder those wicked devils selected this time to do their work! Hark, I hear a foot-fall!

Bushy, Shanks, and Tom held their breath and listened.

"What time is it?" asked Shanks, softly.

"I don't know," whispered Tom, "but it must be after two. It "——

"Tom," called Bushy at his elbow, "a man is on my side of the cabin. He is trying to strike a match. He "——

She hurried back just in time to see the flash of light, and recognized the chief of the bandits. Bang! went her rifle, and with a yell that brought every man in camp to his feet in alarm, he fell over in the shavings he had been trying to fire.

"Bang! bang! bang! bang! sounded from all sides. Screams of alarm and pain were heard so distinctly that Bushy threw herself on a buffalo-robe and covered her head and ears.

" Oh, Tom, I can't stand it ! " she cried. " Perhaps the Padre "——

Then came a loud pounding on the door and the cry: " Tom, open ! It is I ! " The Padre had a wounded man in his arms and his own face was covered with blood, but he called to Bushy: " I am not hurt, but Big Bill is, and this is the robber chief, he was the only one of the ten near enough to bring inside. Everything is peaceful now. Nine men, dead or wounded, are guarded by our miners, who were saying, when I left them, that our death would have been inevitable had the attack, so well planned, been carried out without a warning."

" And would you mind telling me how we were given away," asked the wounded chief.

Mr. Sukolt told how Bushy had heard and seen the bandits through a crack in the wall of their cave. The chief of the ruffians looked on her with wide eyes of astonishment.

" Defeated and my men killed, myself taken prisoner, and my cave and goods fallen into the hands of the very mining superintendent we started out to do up, and all this done by a girl ! " he muttered.

" By your new cook," said Bushy, who felt braver now that she held her father's hand.

Tom and Shanks were helping to place the chief in an easy position, but when he heard her words he raised himself up and, with a half laugh, said: " Well, you have done us up brown, my little maiden ! I must say every dish you served to-night was well done," and then he fainted.

CHAPTER XXXVI

When Bushy awoke the next morning, her father, Tom, and Shanks were busying themselves over the wounded brigand. " Do you know," said the chief, as he lay stretched out full length on the stone floor, " do you know, Mr. Sukolt, that you have a very fine girl ? "

" Well, we are all inclined to think so," replied her father. " Had it not been for her last night you would have soon wiped us out."

" I think that last bullet is going to end my career," murmured the wounded man.

" I have nobody to leave my money to," he added, turning seriously to Mr. Sukolt. · " I became an outlaw first because I had murdered a man I hated. I am rich and came by my wealth, honestly enough, from the sale of lands left me by my people. I would like to will it to your girl, for she is the bravest little creature I ever met. I don't suppose you are anxious to take things so ill-gotten as those we have in the cave, but Bushy knows the way, and you can do what you wish with everything there. My bank account goes to the little girl. Now give me paper, pen, and ink. Quick ! for I feel I am sinking ! "

Tom, thoroughly realizing the seriousness of the case, and filled with wild delight over the thought of Bushy coming in for perhaps a good round sum of money, made a dash over to the main cabin, snatched the required articles and hastened back again to lay them before the brigand, saying:

" There you are, sir; now is your chance to leave the child a mite of money, if you see fit."

Mr. Sukolt was not altogether satisfied with the idea of such a legacy, but both Tom and Shanks insisted that the man be allowed to do as he wished, and the Padre at length yielded. The outcome of it all was that the wounded chief turned over all his honestly acquired property to Bushy. Shanks understood the law well enough to see that everything was done correctly. The wounded man died within an hour.

A month afterward Mr. Sukolt explained to Bushy that he had written and ascertained that the bandit's real estate amounted to nearly $25,000, of which she thus became heiress in her own right.

" It is my duty to tell you," said her father, " and to add that you are old enough to realize in a measure what that amount of money means."

Bushy sat stunned, and was only aroused by

Rover's cold nose being poked into her closed hand.

Mr. Sukolt returned to his office near the mine. He was there confronted with a great surprise. A Mr. Richard Hamilton laid his card on the desk. He was the man whom Bushy had lariated when his frightened horse was rushing toward a precipice at Cross Roads. Mr. Sukolt hardly recognized him at first. When the visitor recalled the circumstances, the two men shook hands warmly. Mr. Hamilton had a proposition to make with reference to Bushy, and had come far out of his way to speak to Mr. Sukolt.

" I am going to New York," he said, " and she can go East with me, remain with my people and attend school. " I insist that you consider my suggestion."

" Bushy's action scarcely merits your exhibition of feeling; any one would have done the same in similar circumstances," said Mr. Sukolt.

" Must I be deprived of showing my gratitude for the care you took of me ? Can I forget how Bushy ran her horse to Cross Roads for Tom and the wagon, in order that I might be taken to your camp comfortably ? "

" Your offer alone amply repays me for the little trouble we may have taken," replied Mr. Sukolt. " Your proposition," he added, looking the young man gravely in the face, " is to take Bushy with you and have her educated as a young lady should be ? "

" Exactly; her talents might, perhaps, be cultivated in this solitude, where she never sees a child, seldom a woman, and rarely anybody outside the camp; but her character must be developed by coming in contact with the world itself. Let me take her. It's the best thing you can do for the child."

" She is the last link that binds me to life. You do not know what you ask of me; yet, I have been conscious lately of a guilty feeling in keeping her so long with me. The miners and myself have tried to think we could give her all the education necessary, but I find that while developing her rapidly in some ways, we are neglecting her in others, quite as essential, perhaps. I know she needs the companionship of her own sex." His broad frame shook with emotion as he concluded, " You can take her if she is willing."

" Thank you," replied Mr. Hamilton; " you will not regret placing her in the care of my mother."

" Your letters from home not only confirm that statement, but have revealed to me the fact that I have met your father. I remember your family well, and since I have decided to part with Bushy, I consider myself very fortunate in being able to place her in the home of Dick Hamilton, your father."

" Hallo ! Oh, Mr. Hamilton, is it really you ? " cried the cheery voice of Bushy as she burst into the office. " How do you do ? "

Something in her father's face told Bushy that Mr. Hamilton's visit had a serious meaning. She shook his hand, and then asked: " Any thing happened, Padre ? "

" No, dear, I have just begun to realize that you are almost a woman and quite old enough to go to school. So Mr. Hamilton and myself have been planning to send you away for four or five years. And "—trying in a sad way to make a joke—" he is doing all this because you lariated him, Bushy."

Bushy could not smile, but she listened bravely to the plans for her future. Then she found an excuse to get away, and as soon as she was by herself she broke into tears, but she was quieted down by the time the men came home. At night the tears began to flow again and she cried herself to sleep. It was decided that she was to start in two days for Denver with Mr. Hamilton in the buckboard that carried the mail.

CHAPTER XXXVII

Bushy's packing was the source of much hilarity. "You must not forget," said Tom, as he carefully rolled up her guitar, " that you are to spend Christmas in New York City. It is a big place, a lot of people in it, and oh, thousands of boys and girls ! How often are you going to write to us ? "

"Oh, don't put in my snow-shoes, Shanks !" cried Bushy, taking them from his hands. " I don't know much, but surely I know I won't want those things in New York. What was it you said, Tom ? Oh, yes, about writing ! Padre, how often will you folks write to me ? I promise you a letter for every one I get. How is that ? "

" We will send you one every day," exclaimed Tom.

" That won't do," interrupted Mr. Sukolt. " Bushy is going there to study, and if she spends every Saturday evening in writing a bouncing long letter home we will let her off with that. She can begin next Saturday, and no matter where she finds herself she must stop and send word how she is, and what she is doing."

After much trouble the great box was filled. Of course, there were many things that Bushy positively refused to go without. There was her rifle, for example. " I won't stir a step if you don't put it in," she said. And just so she acted about her revolver, her skates, her bow and arrows; and a small lariat was put in by Tom to use as a fire escape if she had to sleep in one of the top stories of those dreadful tall houses he had heard about.

That evening a grand ball was given in the Sukolt cabin. There were so many people who seemed sorry because she was going away that Bushy was constantly choking down the big lump that would rise in her throat. Every old miner said: " Oh, Bushy, it's so far and we will miss you so ! "

" Padre, if they would say nothing at all about it," said Bushy, " I could stand it, but when they talk so much, I—I get shaky and shivery, and if it keeps up this way much longer I'll go on a strike, so I will, and empty all my things out again and not go one step ! "

" Take care, take care, little woman ! I'm inclined to think it will be much harder for us old fellows left behind than for you who are going into a new and beautiful world. Then, dear," said Mr. Sukolt as he put his arm about her waist, " you need not feel so bad about it; you are going to have Jip and Rover. They will be sent after you, and

Mr. Hamilton says you will have a first-rate stable for them."

" Yes, Padre, I know." Then, much to the surprise of everybody she broke down and cried aloud. After the shower of tears she bravely pulled herself together and with the true Bushy grit, shook herself well and volunteered to dance a good-by jig.

" Bravo ! " shouted the men, and one by one they sat down close up against the wall that there might be a lot of room for the dancer. To the accompaniment of the banjo, guitar, and fiddle, Bushy not only gave them the negro jig, but the Mexican fandango, as well.

> " Tra, la, la, you and I,
> We'll be happy till we die ;
> Not a flaw if you try
> Can you find in my right eye."

So sang Bushy, and then came the chorus, which is quite as meaningless, its only merit being its happy tune, which the miners rang out so lustily that the mountains echoed and re-echoed with the glad sound :

> " Ha, ha, ha ! jig it out,
> We've no time to think or pout.
> Tra, la, la ! sauerkraut—
> What would you have us think about ? "

Next came the call for the " Bushy Whirl," a favorite dance with the miners. The men stood in a ring around the room, and while the girl was dancing and singing the song she would suddenly touch one of the men. If he did not swing her immediately he had to pay a penalty. Big Bill got enthusiastic. He cried:

"Go it, Bushy! Shove back, you fellows, and give her room! Whale away there! Don't drag your music like that; can't you fiddle and look on too? Ha, ha! you lost your swing; serves you right and you'll pay the fine! What! it's my turn now? Never thought you'd pick out an old fellow like me, Bushy. Ah! you are a heap better'n "——

Bill's sentence was left unfinished. He went whirling around and around and would have fallen full length on the cabin floor had not a good-natured miner stretched forth his knotty arm and saved him.

Shanks manipulated the banjo, and from his first position cross-legged on the floor, he had, with renewed exhilaration, worked his way to the top of a convenient pile of freight-boxes. From this high seat his eyes could follow every step of the fairy-footed Bushy.

> "Come, look out! your time is nearing,
> Don't stand napping like a deer.
> See; I'm pointing. Oh! you're out, sir,
> And you'll have to pay the beer."

So sang Bushy as she floated and spun about, swaying her body at times until the dusky cloud of tangled hair almost swept the floor. She wore only her flour-sack slip. On the front and back of the waist, in big blue letters, were the words " Extra fine XXX," and the same ornamentation appeared four times in the full skirt that was gathered with twine on to the waist-band. Black cotton stockings and white-beaded moccasins completed her travelling costume.

In the ten minutes' whirling, Bushy had touched six men, who were so engrossed with watching the vision gliding about in such mysterious and picturesque fashion, that they hesitated too long in answering the call to swing her, and were therefore marked down by Long Nosed Jim in his dirty note-book—of course, to the great delight of everybody —as the victims who were to stand treat for the evening.

At last her plump finger touched Mr. Hamilton. His merry blue eyes had not for a minute left off drinking in the—to him—remarkable scene.

Bushy was full of fun and especially desirous of giving him a tumble, but he firmly gripped her hands and held fast, and they spun around and around like a French top.

Mr. Sukolt suddenly called out: " Take your partners for a quadrille," and the whirl was ended.

A voice like a small hurricane took up the cry: " Choose your partners for a quadrille ! Clear away, there ! Get a move on yer ! Now—then ! Hands half round and back again ! Up—the middle and turn back home ! Swing—your corners ! (Spring yer heel.) Ladies back and gents to the front. Heigh—oh ! Tra, la, la, la, la, la ! Swing —your partners ! (Keep it up !) Ladies in the middle and ring 'round a rosy ! Shake—your soles ! All—hands around ! (Tum, tum, toodle doodle dum !) "

The voice that thus gradually grew from an occasional high wind into a continuous roar belonged to Tom, the master of ceremonies. His call " Balloon Sal ! " brought the gay crowd upon its feet with a vim that made every log in the cabin quake.

Mr. Hamilton and Bushy led the dance and six of the jolliest miners in the camp completed the set.

In order that he might be seen as well as heard Tom had mounted a big keg, the head of which, about twice every minute, found itself too small to accommodate the gyrations of his feet. He would at times put his fiddle behind him, over his shoulder, on his knees, and once in a great while it found its right position, yet Tom was never known to miss a note in any tune he played.

" Dos-a-dos and don't get lost; lose your lady at your cost ! "

Away they went, four couples at once, and as the

time increased, the bodies bent, the heads tossed, and the arms swayed in manner most alarming. When opportunity permitted, the boys got in the single and double shuffle; the backs of their legs were mysteriously brought in front, their knees turned in and their heels turned out, and not a little off-hand inspiration was gathered from the clicking of the home-made " bones " played most vigorously by some of the sympathetic lookers-on.

" Allaymantle-left ! " shouted Tom, and his fiddle gave out an extra squeak of delight as the hands of the dancers got wofully mixed up in the change.

The laughter, the " Hi-hi-yeps ! " and the wild swinging of the partners were at their height when everything was brought to an unexpected halt by the violin suddenly shifting from the intoxicating tune of the " Arkansaw Traveller " to the doleful, discordant braying of a burro: " A-a-ah !—Uh ! —A-a-ah ! "

The burst of good-natured shrieks that followed was cut short by Tom's voice again, as he yelled: " Prom-Nah-Dall ! Yank yer partner to the lemonade stall ! " winding up with three of the most dreadful donkey-brays ever uttered.

The morning after the dance dawned clear and bright, the sun rising with that peculiar splendor never seen outside of Colorado, but no one in Great

Pine Mine made one word of comment on its glory. Indeed it is doubtful whether any one even noticed it, for it was the day when Bushy was to bid good-by to the camp.

"God b-b-bless you!" stammered old miner Walt, who had come, like a dozen others, from far back in the mountains to bid Bushy adieu. The words got all tangled up in his throat as if they had a hard time to find their way out. Both of his big hands clasped Bushy's small fist, and with a silent squeeze he turned and walked away, giving a savage kick to a clod in the road, as if blaming it in some way for the queer feeling in his throat.

"Well, good-by Bushy," said another one. "We'll "——

The trembling lip frightened the rest of the sentence away, and, grasping the outstretched hand, Bushy dropped a tear or two on the knotty knuckles of one of her most faithful admirers.

One by one the gold-diggers pressed forward to give their farewells and their blessings. Then came Shanks, Tom, and the Padre. Mr. Hamilton had been waiting some time on the buckboard, all ready to start.

Shanks, the big-hearted Englishman, who had grown to love Bushy as he might have loved a daughter, took her into his arms and murmured: "God help me, child! for the first time in my life,

Bushy, I'm no good as a doctor. The whole kit of bottles in my medicine-chest can't cure one of the aching hearts you leave behind."

Bushy smiled through her tears and turned to Tom.

"Dear old Tom," she murmured, and as her arms clung about his neck, she patted his poor scalped head and gave way for the first time that morning to uncontrolled weeping.

Sob after sob shook her whole frame, and a second later she was pressed close to her father's heart.

Mr. Sukolt was the last to bid the little Rocky Mountain girl good-by.

He held her clasped in his arms so long, and was so silent that the miners gradually drifted away to one side in little whispering groups, leaving only Tom near by—faithful old Tom, who, as he gazed on Mr. Sukolt's white face, recalled the scene, twelve years before, when the Padre had held his little girl just so, trying to decide whether it was wise to do as her baby head had planned, and let her go " wiv her papa's tachel."

Now he was sending her back to the " States " for the same reason that he had taken her away— because she was the one thing in the world left to him and he loved her better than life.

The buckboard that waited would convey the two travellers to the stage line, and once in the stage they would soon reach Denver; from Denver they would take the cars straight across the plains.

Mr. Sukolt kissed his daughter's lips and then, without a word, handed her over to Mr. Hamilton who lifted her up beside him.

"Good-by!" she called as the driver whipped up his horse—her face was turned wistfully toward the Padre.

"Good-by!" came from the throat of every man in camp. Not a miner moved till the odd vehicle with its precious burden passed out of sight.

It was thus that the pet of the Rocky Mountain gold-diggers left them. She was seated on a wooden box that was marked in big charcoal letters:

BUSHY SUKOLT,
New York City.

THE END.

"GOOD-BY!"

Bushy Poster——

UNIQUE

ARTISTIC

ATTRACTIVE

FULL OF LIFE

PRINTED IN FIVE COLORS

Will be sent, post-paid, on
receipt of price, 25 cents

THE MORSE COMPANY

PUBLISHERS..   96 FIFTH AVENUE
NEW YORK

www.ingramcontent.com/pod-product-compliance
Lightning Source LLC
Chambersburg PA
CBHW032014120726
47902CB00013B/775